Len

The
Electric Sewer

War Stories of the New York City Transit Police

Just remember where you came from!

All the best,

BB

The
Electric Sewer

War Stories of the
New York City Transit Police

Trebor Nehoc

Oak Tree Press
Springfield Il

Oak Tree Press

THE ELECTRIC SEWER: War Stories of the New York City Transit Police, Copyright 2004 by Robert Cohen, All Rights Reserved. Printed in the United States of America. No part of this book may be used or reproduced in any manner whatsoever without written permission except in the case of brief quotations embodied in critical articles and reviews. For information, address Oak Tree Press, 2743 S. Veterans Parkway #135. Springfield, IL 62704-6402.

Oak Tree Books may be purchased for educational, business, or sales promotional use. Contact Publisher for quantity discounts.

First Edition, October 2004

10 9 8 7 6 5 4 3 2 1

Cover Design by Mick Andreano

Library of Congress Cataloging-in-Publication Data

Nehoc, Trebor, 1959-
Electric sewer / by Trebor Nehoc.
p. cm.
ISBN 1-892343-37-1 (alk. paper)
1. Nehoc, Trebor, 1959- 2. Traffic police--New York (State)--New York. 3. Crime--New York (State)--New York. 4. New York (N.Y.). Police Dept. I. Title.
HV7914.N45 2004
363.28'7--dc22

2004019155

For my wife

Acknowledgements

"When You're Hot, You're Hot"   renewal 1999 on behalf of SIXTEEN STARS MUSIC / VECTOR MUSIC, used by permission, all rights reserved.

Special thanks to Teresa Cohen, Steve Douenias, Joe Leib ("The Jack Files"), Liz Martinez, Lorrie McCarthy, Arthur Olivella, Pete Scheinflug and Bob Valentino.

Ed. Note: Glossary begins on P 211

Foreword

I will never forget the date, July 15th, 1986. It was on that day I was sworn into the New York City Transit Police. And it was there that I remained for the next eleven years, eight months and twelve days, but who's counting? I thank God every day that I was lucky enough to have busted out of the MTA-prison in such a short time. I used stand-up comedy as my escape route.

I don't think I could have taken one more day. It was like working in a coal mine. Actually, working in a coal mine would be better, it doesn't smell like a public bathroom. Whenever anyone asks me what it was like to work in the subways of New York, I reply, "You really want to know what it's like to be a transit cop for twelve years? Go out in your garage, on the hottest day in August, urinate in the corner, and stand there."

Not many people can identify with me, not many people can feel my pain. And even though Trebor Nehoc and I have never actually patrolled together, he feels my pain. He has worked all over the New York City subway. And not just as a cop, but also as a sergeant and lieutenant. He has been assigned to everything from late night solo train patrol to an academy instructor and finally as an anti-crime supervisor. As they say here in New York, he has been around the block, twice.

Trebor has taken his years on the job and transcribed them into some very funny, very touching stories. With great wit, sharp details and some brisk writing, his War Stories describe what life was like down there in the Electric Sewer.

Covering south Brooklyn to north Harlem, Trebor has worked in almost every subway station in the system. His stories brought back tons of memories for me, from what us cops were forced to eat while on duty to how we had to deal with members of the public. Or as they used to say in District 34, members of the pubic.

Trebor has great anecdotes on DOA's, arrests, drunks and wolfpacks. When was the last time you heard that word in a sentence, wolfpack? He also uses more police jargon than I have ever seen in any police-related book. I even learned a few new terms, i.e., "Piss Ranch."

It's always nice to see a brother officer putting his inner thoughts down on paper for the rest of us to enjoy. I congratulate Trebor on two things: I congratulate him on his promotions. And I congratulate him on the completion of his first book, may there be many more. And maybe a few screenplays?

Transit Forever

John DiResta

Prologue

It was a pretty miserable December day in 1983 and I was having coffee with my friend, Chief Petty Officer Jim Shea. Looking out his office window, we noticed that a flock of secretaries from the office-temp agency on the floor beneath us were standing around in the parking lot behind our building on Hempstead Turnpike. "Must be an Atlantic City trip or something." Petty Officer Fischer, one half of a husband/wife team who worked with us, was out the door on the way to lunch and also couldn't help but notice everyone in the parking lot. "Hey, you guys going somewhere?" One of the temp-girls replied, "No, we just figured it'd be better to be out here, than inside the building where the bombs are." Nodding in agreement, Fischer said, "Yeah, I know what you—*What?*" Snow and slush flew as the petty officer ran back inside, shot up three flights of stairs, burst into the Navy office and sounded the alarm. Jim and I put down our coffee and immediately began to clear the building with extreme professionalism. Yawn. We went up to the top floor and systematically banged on office doors, rang bells and passed the word until the entire building had been evacuated from top to bottom. I'm not patting myself on the back, but I might add we got it done just in time for our local neighborhood watering hole to open. Imagine the looks on our faces several minutes later when the twenty sticks of dynamite planted on our floor detonated, destroying the New York headquarters of the United States Navy's recruiting command. Mrs. Petty Officer Fischer got a medal, and rightfully so. Jim and I got hammered.

As the investigation unfolded, the terrorists who planted the bombs claimed credit and voiced their political grievances. It seems they were not pleased with the United States' foreign policy concerning Central America. There was more: Their communiqué stated that they also wanted "...to avenge the death of brother Michael Stewart at the hands of the New York City pigs." Well, the foreign policy gripe was one thing, but this Michael Stewart guy died in custody after he was arrested by transit cops for doing graffiti in a subway station. What the hell did that have to do with the U.S. Navy? I almost got blown to smithereens, and I never took a subway ride in my life!

About a year after the bombing I left the Navy. Just before getting out, I filed for the Civil Service exam to become a New York City Police Officer. That was my father's idea, not mine—he did twenty years in the NYPD like his father before him. I had no birthrights in the Navy so there was nothing keeping me there, but I knew what I wanted to do with my life and it *wasn't* joining the police department. Although I took the test and then proceeded with the application process to become a cop, I was only going through the motions.

Under a misguided hiring policy known as "Tri-Agency," all NYC police department applicants in the 1980's were arbitrarily assigned to either the NYPD, the Transit Police or the Housing Police on a strict 7:2:1 ratio, with the applicant having no choice whatsoever other than to turn down the job and continue flipping burgers. When my name was called off the list I was directed to a room with about a dozen other applicants. A police sergeant introduced himself to us and said, "You people got Transit... Uh, sorry." Wow. Good thing I didn't need *this* job.

As things turned out, my career plans fell through. So, on July 8th, 1985, I was sworn in as a Probationary Police Officer in the New York City Transit Police Department. For the next six months as a recruit in the NYPD Police Academy, I learned all about being an NYPD cop. For the next ten years after that I learned all about subway trains, graffiti and other things they don't teach in the Academy.

Don't think for a minute that I'm passing myself off as some kind of expert on the Transit Police. I'm not. My own experiences as a transit cop weren't exactly typical. The chance to advance in rank presented itself early and I took advantage of it. Plus, I never stayed too long in any one command—rumor had it I'd leave just before they figured out how incompetent I really was. All in all, it's been an interesting and unusual ride, and along the way, I've worked with what is without a doubt the best bunch of cops anywhere.

About a decade after I joined the Transit Police we were absorbed by our Big Brother, the NYPD. Talk about an identity crisis! First, they trained us as street cops but then stuck us down in the subway. Now, we are NYPD, but we'll *always* be Transit. Like the expatriate Polish airmen flying with Britain's Royal Air Force after the fall of their country, we don't always speak the same language or fight the same way as our comrades in arms, but we do fight on.

The stories you're about to read are presented in roughly chronological order. They're all absolutely 100% true, unless somebody wants to sue me or something like that. Then I made them up. I hope you enjoy reading them as much as I enjoyed writing them.

Trebor Nehoc

Act I

'There has to be a beginning
to every great undertaking.'

Sir Francis Drake

A Hat In The Ring

As a recruit in the NYPD Academy, you're told over and over not to lose 'your gun, your shield, or your ID card'. They drill this into your head for six months. After graduating the academy, during your three additional weeks of Transit training, they quietly add 'your cap device' to the list of things not to lose. The cap device is the small metal emblem worn on the uniform hat. Why this particular item was important to the Transit Police, we may never know—but it was.

Once you finally finished training and were assigned to the late-night train patrol unit you were told over and over not to lose your trains. Pretty hard to lose a train, unless of course you get off it. Then they were real easy to lose. Make no mistake, they wanted you riding the trains. Not just any train, but the *exact* train they'd assign to you. If you got off your train, you were in effect 'off-post' and unless you had a good reason, you stood to get in trouble.

My first week of solo train patrol, I'm on a '7' train which runs from Main Street in Flushing, Queens to Times Square in Manhattan. For the majority of this train's route it runs above ground on elevated tracks. Here I am, diligently patrolling, going from car to car. The train was headed toward the city and had just left the

Willets Point station by Shea Stadium when a gust of wind blew my hat off my head as I changed cars. I looked down real quick from between the cars and saw we were over water. Yikes! Oh, well, looks like I gotta go buy myself another hat.

I made it to Times Square in just enough time to catch my scheduled train back to Main Street. Since this train was also running late, I jumped off at Willets Point again to catch my next scheduled Manhattan-bound train. I'm starting to feel like a real loser, trying to adhere to this train schedule that even the Transit Authority couldn't keep up with. While waiting I figured I'd make my 'ring', a phone call to headquarters to let them know where I was. What with the impossible train runs, it was pretty hard to call when they had scheduled you to. I make the call anyway, leading off with an apology for not calling when I was supposed to. The cop on the other end of the phone knew I was brand-new so he asked how everything was going. I rattled off the list: my train was late, I lost my hat, I didn't know the code for a summons, my other train was late—he interrupts with, "Wait a minute, go back to the hat, okay?" I told him I lost it over Flushing Bay while changing cars about forty-five minutes ago. He asked me if I had notified anybody. I said I hadn't, but I *was* on my trains. "Uh-oh, that cap device is department-issued equipment..." He gently explained that I had screwed up a little and told me what the official procedure was. "Oh yeah, they did mention not to lose that cap device, didn't they?" I asked if I was going to get in more trouble because I didn't call my boss right away. He said, "Hey, you never spoke to me, you know what I mean?"

I phoned the sergeant at the district and he's happy to hear from me. I'm surprised, since I didn't even think he knew who I was. He certainly seems to. I tell him I've lost my hat. "Really?" he says, "About how long ago did this happen?" As he asks this, I hear a popping sound. Over my left shoulder is a tiny little red devil whispering in my ear, "Tell him you lost it five minutes ago!" After all, I was back at the same station, Willets Point. Before I could say anything I hear another little pop. Over my right shoulder, there's a little white angel (no shit) saying, "Tell him the truth!" Hmmm... "Actually Sarge, I lost it almost an hour ago." Silence. Then he says, "Yeah, I know. We've had your hat in the district for twenty minutes, we were waiting for you to call." Turns out my hat had landed on a police car driving down the Grand Central Parkway, not in the water like I thought. Fortunately for me, the sergeant understood that I had tried to do the right thing. He explained to me what I should've done when I first lost the hat, but since it was recovered, there was no harm done. I was very happy I wasn't getting into trouble, although I never did understand why they weren't more concerned about my whereabouts during the time they had my headless hat.

Unfortunately for me, this incident occurred while a political pissing contest was going on between the district command and the train patrol unit. It had nothing to do with me personally, but the district desk lieutenant decided to initiate disciplinary proceedings against me despite the fact that my sergeant had already straightened the matter out. It struck me as a little bit vindictive, and his actions became incorporated into the ongoing dispute between the two commands. It must've struck somebody else as vindictive also, because within a few days, the lieutenant was told to sit down and shut up.

About a week later, Stanley, my sergeant, calls me into the command for a talk. He invites me into the captain's vacant office and offers me a chair. "Coffee?" We sit, he gives me this conspiratorial grin, and asks, "Who's your hook?" A hook, in Transit Police jargon, was a connection to someone higher up, someone with power. With a blank look on my face I tell him I have no idea what he's talking about. Stan isn't buying it. He brought up the thing about the lost hat and the lieutenant and how anybody else would've gotten into trouble. He *knew* I had a hook, and he wanted very badly to know who it was. I told him, "I dunno, Sarge, maybe they gave me a break 'cause I'm a veteran..."

Stan was a good guy but a little bit of a nudge. Of course I had a hook; I just wasn't about to share that information with him. Stay tuned, though, because he wasn't at all satisfied with my patriotic explanation.

A Shaggy Dog Story

When I was a train-patrol cop, I sometimes rode the 'E' train from Queens to Manhattan. The 'E' train was an express train, meaning it skipped many stops on the route. It was a long and tedious run... then again, most of them were. Maybe that's why train patrol was an involuntary assignment in the Transit Police.

I'm on a Manhattan-bound 'E' train one night. I'm in the last car of the train. As the train stops at the 75th Avenue station, I notice a guy get on the train several cars up from me with a small dog. It's against the rules to have a dog on the subway other than a seeing-eye dog and this guy didn't look blind to me. At the next stop I started to move up. The design of these particular trains affected the way we would patrol—the doors between the cars had to be keyed open, so for safety's sake we avoided going between the cars while the train was moving unless it was an emergency. Normally we would change cars by walking on the platform while the train was stopped in a station. You had to be quick doing this since some conductors, because they couldn't see you (or because they just didn't like cops) would close the doors while you were out on the platform, and your assigned post would pull away and leave you in the dust. Anyway, the train stops at the 71st/Continental Avenue station and I move up one car. Now the train runs express for five stops. The next time the doors open up are at the Roosevelt Avenue station, and I move up another car. The doors close again and the train runs express for five more stops. Next stop is the Queens Plaza station, and I move up into the car behind the guy with the dog. At the 23rd/Ely station, the last stop in Queens, I finally stroll into the car he's riding in. It's only taken me twenty-five minutes.

"Excuse me, sir, but it's against the law to have a dog in the subway system." He gives me an innocent look and says, "But I'm only going one stop." *Wrong* answer. By my count he had already ridden fifteen stops, which is easily long enough for even the brightest pooch to mistake a train for a fire hydrant. "May I see some identification, please?" He gives me his driver's license, exactly what I need to write his summons without any further conversation.

I'm writing, and he's talking. Nothing he's got to say interests me, so he's doing a monologue. I'm enjoying it. Like most people, he didn't realize that once I started writing the ticket, he didn't really have a chance of talking his way out of it. He's babbling on about how good it is to see police in the subways, how he didn't know it was against the rules to have his dog in the subway, how his dog is such a nice dog, well trained, blah, blah, blah...

The train pulls into the Lexington Avenue station in Manhattan. He says to me—like we're just old friends chatting—"Well, this is my stop. By the way, do you have a dog at home?" As he stands up to get off the train I pull the ticket out of my book, hand it to him and say with a smile, "No, sir, I hate dogs." He grabs the ticket and says, "Oh, yeah? I bet they hate you, too!"

Thanks For Keeping An Eye Out

As I walk into the subway station at Woodhaven Boulevard to catch the train to work, I see Timmy has got somebody stopped and is giving him a summons for something. I don't need to know anything else about the situation and I don't need to discuss it with Timmy. It can be a pretty touchy thing giving someone a ticket when you're all alone since you can't write the ticket and watch the person at the same time. Maybe that's why the New York City Transit Police had one of the highest injury rates of all the police departments in the country—we did this *all* the time. Even though I'm off-duty and on my way to work (I'll actually be late because of this), I walk over and casually take up a defensive position by Timmy. He nods and now devotes his full attention to writing the ticket. It's a little easier with someone watching your back.

It's pretty obvious from the non-verbal communication between Timmy and me that I'm a cop, and the violator knows it. He just kinda sighed and stood there, resigned to that fact that he's getting a ticket for whatever it is that Timmy caught him doing. There's nothing to talk about.

Timmy's scribbling away, and this guy starts rubbing his eye. Don't tell me he's gonna start crying? Oh, what a sissy. I ask, "What's the matter with you?" Still rubbing, he says, "I got something in my eye." Without looking up from the summons, Timmy says, "Then take it out." *Pop.* The guy's got his eyeball in his hand. I'm looking into this black hole in his face. "Uh, Tim..." He looks up from his summons for a second and barks, "Put that back and quit screwing around!" *Pop.* The eyeball's back in and the three of us continue to stand there silently while Timmy writes, as if nothing's happened.

Music Under New York

The Transit Authority had a habit of permitting certain activities to go on in the subways, provided that dizzying sets of rules were adhered to. For instance, some musicians were allowed to play at times, but only if they were so many feet away from this, and no closer than so many feet to that, and if their permits were issued on even days of the month, et cetera. Luckily for the musicians, most of the cops were thoroughly baffled by the procedural maze. Besides, even listening to a lousy band was better than counting tiles.

One night, I was standing around with the gathering crowd listening to an impromptu underground concert. People are tossing coins and bills into the open guitar cases lying on the subway platform, and some even forego their trains. I'm applauding along with everyone else after one set, when a concerned citizen tugs on my sleeve: "Officer, they're not supposed to be playing down here. It's illegal." Hmmm... He's right. "Hey fellas, sorry, but it *is* against the law for you to be playing here." The entire crowd turns silently and gives me a collective dirty look. "So, uh, as soon as you're finished playing, you're gonna have to stop..."

Tough Guys Finish Last

Garry and I are having coffee in the diner upstairs from the West Fourth Street subway station located on Manhattan's lower east side.

We're between train runs, and like most train-patrol cops we're trying to see just how many cigarettes we can smoke on our break since who knows how long we'll be stuck on our trains after this? We never did get the final count, because as we're puffing away there's a radio distress call from a cop at the Christopher Street station. I'm from 169th and Hillside in Queens and haven't got a clue, but Garry's from Manhattan: "I know where that is, let's go!" Two quick last drags and we're off and running.

Two cops in full uniform running down the block is not that uncommon a sight in New York City, since it was a standard Transit Police mode of emergency transportation. It certainly doesn't seem to alarm passersby, because *nobody* gets out of your way. I'm wondering if it would be possible to mount a flashing red light on my hat. We're chugging along, snaking around all the strollers and window-shoppers who refuse to yield. "How much further?" Garry says, "It's right down the block!"

I'm not one to complain, but we're running an awfully long time. It's the end of the winter season and we're not in the summer short-sleeve uniform yet. Plus we're both schlepping about twenty pounds of gear and we're wearing leather shoes. "Almost there!" We nearly get hit by a car running across the street. *"Garry—how—much—further?"* Almost there my ass.

We come up to this big intersection and he yells, "Here!" We run down the stairs into the subway station and we see the cop who called for help—on the other side. *"Shit!"* Now we have to run back up the stairs so that we can cross the street and come down on the side that he's on. At this point, we've been running for about, I don't know, two, maybe three hours. We've gone at least ten miles. And I'll tell you, not to complain, but they added a dozen more stairs going up, the bastards.

So we're running across the street again and my legs turned to rubber. I'm trying to figure what would be worse—to get hit by a car, or to fall down and get run over. We make it across the intersection and run back down the stairs into the subway. The cop who called for help is trying to lock up these three guys and they're not having it. We run up to him and we're in such respiratory distress we can't speak; we're both foaming at the mouth and there's snot flying out of our noses. The three guys took one look at us, figured we had rabies or something, and just turned around and put their hands behind their backs in the surrender position. The cop asked me for my cuffs but I couldn't even lift my arms. He had to take them from my belt. Click, click, three under arrest.

Reader's note: In 1986 I quit smoking after thirteen years and haven't smoked since. I spoke to Garry a year or so later and found out he quit too. Sometimes, you just gotta get the right motivation.

First Impressions

They say that the first impression you make is important. I'd have to agree. When I was a recruit in the Police Academy, one of the other guys in my company made a distinct and lasting first impression on me: Brad struck me as a real mutt. I had joined the Transit Police after seven years in the military, so I was a little older and hopefully not as naive as some of my fellow police recruits.

It didn't take long for Brad to rub just about everybody the wrong way. For instance, one of the first things they taught us was that while we were legally police officers, until we finished our six-month training course, it would behoove us not to take any police actions. We're not in the academy two weeks and he makes an off-duty arrest, the first of several he'd make. Speculation was that he was screwing his neighborhood friends. By the end of our training, he was almost totally ostracized. He had a really annoying way of talking to his peers as if he was a real cop and the rest of us were just recruits. He was big on trying to impress everybody with how streetwise he was and how much he knew. It didn't work. Everyone just thought he was a dick.

Brad's mouth almost got the best of him during a classroom discussion one day—we were talking about police fraternal associations and off-duty conduct. As usual, he's the class expert. He starts spouting off about a fraternal function he had been to, describing some of the off-duty conduct he'd observed. The instructor cautioned him several times to consider the appropriateness of his story, but he just kept going, and described witnessing his 'fellow'officers getting high. When he finished, he sat there with this self-satisfied look on his face. It was real quiet in the room. The instructor said, "Brad, come with me." They took him away to the disciplinary office, where an official investigation was initiated. He didn't graduate with us.

It was a real unpleasant surprise when, several weeks later, Brad is with us again. It didn't take too long for him to have the same effect on everybody at his first patrol command in Brooklyn that he'd had on us at the academy. Nobody knew what was wrong with him, but after a while everybody just stayed away from him. I'm almost sorry to say, but the feelings against him were so strong that many of his fellow cops would refuse to respond to assist him.

Nobody was really shocked when Brad was suddenly suspended from duty. After a fairly lengthy and secretive Internal Affairs investigation, he was arrested and fired. No tears were shed. The rumor was that he was implicated in a string of armed robberies which were committed with the protection of police radios he had signed out.

Months later, Max and his partner were on patrol, in plainclothes, in a subway station at the same Brooklyn command. Who beats the fare by walking in through the exit gate, but Brad. The officers approach him. "Hey guys, what's up?" Max notices the bulge underneath Brad's shirt, but says nothing about it. They make conversation with him for a couple of minutes like they were old buddies, then Max says, "By the way, how come you're carrying a gun?" Brad tries to doubletalk, "Oh yeah, no, I got reinstated a while ago, maybe the orders didn't come out yet..." Click, click, Brad's locked up again. He was carrying a fake shield in addition to the handgun with no serial numbers.

Good collar, Max. Good riddance, asshole.

A Matter of Trust

If you were into playing cops and robbers, late-night train patrol was not the best place to be. We had our moments, but for the most part it was pretty dull. The subways weren't exactly crowded after hours, and at three in the morning it was like the night of the living dead. Of the few passengers on the trains, most were asleep or unconscious. Nobody will ever know how many summonses were written out of sheer boredom—or for that matter, how many weren't written at all.

I'm on some endless train run one night. Other than the conductor, I'm starting to think I'm the only living soul aboard. I'm busy patrolling my post anyway because that's the kind of guy I am. Besides, if I stopped moving, I'd start snoozing. Even diligent patrol could become boring, though, since there aren't too many ways to patrol a moving subway train. You either walk from the front to the back, or—you got it—from the back to the front.

I'm about to change cars, and as always, I take a peek through the windows into the next car. This way, in case something's going on, I don't just stumble into it. Like I should be so lucky. Anyway, as I look through the two dirty, scratched-up windows separating the two subway cars, my heart skips a beat—at the far end of the next car I can see the small, bundled-up seated figure, and... wait, wait... There it is! Years of training and experience pay off as I just barely make out the telltale orange pinpoint of light. Yes indeed, it looks like I've got me a *smoker!*

I wait for the train to pull into the next station, and when the doors open I swagger into the next car like Wyatt Earp. I walk right up to the man who's now sitting with his head down, hands in pockets, feigning sleep. Evidently he doesn't know who he's dealing with. "How're you doing, sir?" He looks up and says, "Well, hello officer! Very nice to see you." This guy's about seventy years old and he looks just like the actor Burgess Meredith as 'Mick' the boxing trainer. "Sir, were you smoking?" He smiles and says, "Why, no, everybody knows you can't smoke in the subway." There are still clouds of smoke hanging in the air, and I say, "That's right, sir, you can't." We're just smiling away at each other as I look down: "You mind lifting your feet up for me?" He laughs, "Hey, I told you I wasn't smoking." But I insist—"Your feet?" He lifts one, then the other. Nothing. "See? I wouldn't lie to you, officer." I'm standing there like a big dummy but there's still smoke coming from somewhere. "Do me a favor, sir, you wanna take your hands out of your pockets for a minute?" He pulls the still-smoldering butt out of his coat pocket. "Well, maybe I would bullshit you a *little...*"

The Pot And The Kettle

One of the things transit cops hated the most was when our brother officers in the NYPD would look down their noses at us as if we were second-class cops. Funny, though, within the Transit Police Department some transit cops would look down their noses at transit cops in other units. The most frequent offenders here were district cops treating the late-night train patrol cops with disdain. Must be human nature.

I ran into a cop from District Two one night at the 34th Street & Sixth Avenue subway station. We didn't know each other but I said hello anyway. He looked at my 'TPF' collar brass and just walked away. Rather than talk to me he goes to a different part of the station by himself. Then the radio goes off: a cop needs help at the 34th Street & Seventh Avenue station. I wasn't too sure how to get there so I ran after my buddy. Up in the street, we commandeered a taxi together. On the ride over he doesn't say two words to me. It was like I was all alone, by myself—but not for long.

There's a big commotion going on outside Madison Square Garden. There's gotta be eight police cars and maybe twenty or thirty cops. There's a guy laying face-down in the street with his head cracked open. There's an ambulance pulling up, lights and sirens. There's another guy yelling and screaming; he's being arrested. This whole thing is going on in the street, taking up several lanes of Seventh Avenue right in front of the Garden. Most of the cops, as far as I could tell, were just standing around gawking. I asked a couple of them what was going on and I got a couple of shoulder shrugs. For lack of anything better to do, I figured I'd try to move the crowd back onto the sidewalk so the medics could work on the guy laying in the street. Of course, being New Yorkers, nobody moves back when you address them as a group. Everybody thinks you mean someone else, not *them*. So, I get right in one guy's face, put my hand on his chest and order him to "Move back!" He looks at me and says, "No, officer, I'm part of this!" Bingo. Forget the crowd control; I ask him what happened. He says these two guys were having some kind of an argument and one guy hit the other in the head with a jack. "You mean like a blackjack?" He says, "No, like a *car* jack!" I figure he means, "Like a lug-wrench?" Waving his arms, he says, "No, no, no! Like a jack! A jack! The whole fucking jack!" The guy jumped in a taxi to escape, he says, but three or four other people who saw the whole thing stood in front of the cab to prevent him from getting away. *"Which* people?" He starts pointing out people in the otherwise anonymous crowd. I told him to stay with me as we waded through the sea of cops to get to a sergeant who was pulling up. Next thing you know, this sergeant is ordering several police cars to take me (and the witnesses they're about to help me gather up) back to the precinct.

So, I'm at the Midtown South precinct with this mess and it's starting to get a lot of attention since it looks like the victim of the assault is likely to die. Turns out, the arrest was made by the transit cop who had the post at the 34th Street & Seventh Avenue station. He had stepped into the middle of the melee when he came upstairs for a cup of coffee. My witnesses were shedding light on the incident, helping to make the arrest a solid piece of police work. There was a third transit cop in the precinct who had recovered a big, bloody automobile jack as arrest evidence. Thirty cops on the scene, and three transit cops ended up handling everything. As I was leaving to go back to riding my trains, the cop vouchering the jack said to me, "Hey, that was some caper, huh?" It was my carpool buddy from 34th & Sixth. I said, "Yeah," and left without any further comment.

Knowledge Is Power

There is an axiom in police work about giving people tickets: Give the summons, or give the lecture—but not both. It would seem to be a simple and fair rule. However, unlike other cops in the city who wrote most of their tickets to cars or drivers, transit cops were stuck giving the vast majority of their tickets to people who were misbehaving on a very personal level, and this rule sometimes became difficult to follow. Okay, sometimes it was just impossible to follow. If you're a robot it's easy to just bang out tickets and not engage the person in conversation. The problem for transit cops was that due to the up close and personal nature of the encounters, you were almost always forced to have some back-and-forth with the person—now, does that mean you can't give the ticket?

It's possible that one of our favorite games came from the constant close contact with the violators and the resulting conversation. It's also possible that the game was a natural outgrowth of the investigative process involved in giving a ticket. You had to ask a lot of questions to make sure you knew who you were dealing with in order to write a summons. Then again, it's also possible that since we went on duty every night at 7:30, that we were just conditioned by watching 'Jeopardy' on the TV in our lunchroom.

It was called 'The Five States' game. Every so often, you'd have somebody who really didn't want to get a summons but wasn't quite smooth enough (or hopefully, not smart enough) to talk their way out of one. Now, most cops aren't crazy about giving out tickets, but mercy wouldn't really be appropriate for a lot of the people we have to deal with. Not at first, anyway.

It went like this: "I'll make you a deal, okay? Name five states, and I won't give you this ticket." The answers were sometimes amazing and almost always entertaining. "Five states? Uh, New York... New Jersey... Florida? Uh, Brooklyn..." Sounding the buzzer was optional. A variation of this game was known as 'Five Presidents'.

While this may sound cruel and abusive, you've got to remember that in a way, it was only fair. Any cop who's ever tried writing tickets to people has sooner or later run into the situation where the violator plays the cop like a violin, and the cop ends up red in the face. Besides, if you played the 'Five States' game, it was an unwritten rule that the contestant didn't get a ticket. Plus it was really funny.

I will admit that some cops may have taken the games a bit too far. My wife, also a train patrol cop, told me this story: One night while on patrol in Brooklyn, she stops this guy for some summonsable violation. As she asks for his identification, he drops to the floor and starts banging out push-ups like he's on Parris Island. "Hey, hey, what are you doing?" Without missing his count, the guy says, "The *last* cop made me give him twenty..."

Yo, Adrian!

Some of the best war stories come from incidents where the cop was exposed to danger. Getting hurt usually adds to the drama, provided that the injuries aren't too severe—just enough to qualify for the Purple Heart. Nobody *really* wants to win the Medal of Honor, since that one's almost always given posthumously.

Tony came in to work with a soft cast on his hand. We're sitting around in a circle as he regales us with his tale:

"So I'm standin' there, right, and this big motherfucker with a shaved head just walks in through the gate without paying, right, and he looks me square in the eye and says, 'Fuck you!' I'm in full uniform and this guy says fuck *me*? Nah—fuck *you*! So I grab him, but he shoves off on me and says, 'You ain't takin' me!' So, I call an 85 [radio distress call] and I go to grab him again. He comes at me, right, now we're rollin' around on the ground. This guy's a fuckin' monster, too, he's like six-two, two-fifty. I know he gets my gun, I'm dead, right, so I break away, and—*crack*—in the head, but he don't go down! He's still comin'! *Crack!* I hit him again, and my fuckin' stick breaks! Bam, bam, now I'm punchin' this guy, hittin' him right in that bald fuckin' head, and—" One of the guys interrupts—"Hey, Tony, if you just busted your *stick* over this guy's head, what was the point of *punching* him in the head?" Tony looks down at the cast on his hand and says, "Yeah, well—uh, I don't know..."

The Booth Robber

"All units, booth robbery in progress, Court Square on the George! Perp is a male wearing a checkered coat. Units to respond?"

Like an actor in the wings waiting for the cue to go onstage, I'm riding the 'G' train towards Court Square. Unlike a police car, the train couldn't care less what type of job I'm going to and it routinely rolls into the station. I radioed, "Twenty TP Twenty, central, detraining at Court Square," as I cautiously stepped off the train. I peeked up onto the mezzanine and I could see a guy with a checkered coat just sitting on a bench. I slowly come up the stairs. When the token booth clerk saw me, he started frantically gesturing toward the guy on the bench. Hmmm...

Since he wasn't going anywhere, I walked over to the token booth. The clerk opened the door and babbled that the guy had entered through the exit gate, and when the clerk told him to pay his fare, he came over to the token booth and slapped the glass. Then he went back in through the exit gate, took a leak in the corner, and sat down on the bench to wait for his train. I walked over to him. "You got ID?" He sucked his teeth. "Nope." Click, click.

I called the district from the telephone inside the token booth. "Yeah, it's Nehoc at Court Square. It's just a farebeat who scared the shit out of the clerk, that's all. I'm bringing him in, okay?"

When I stood him in front of the desk, the desk officer simply gave me the penal law sections for what I had described on the phone: "One-sixty-five fifteen, sub three; two-forty twenty and twenty-five. You can go ahead and put him in the back and start processing." My prisoner seemed bored by the whole affair. So bored, in fact, that when I put him in the cell, he laid down for a nap.

As the other cops started coming by, though, he gradually began to develop in interest in the proceedings. "Hey Tre, is that the guy from Court Square?" I nodded. "Hey, Nehoc caught the booth robber!" Hearing this, the prisoner sat up. One cop came over to the cell and looked at him through the bars. As he walked away, he said, "Alright! You got him!" The farebeat says quietly, "What are they talking about?" Without looking up from the typewriter, I said, "Ah, nothing. Just ignore them." Now he's starting to get a little uncomfortable. "I didn't rob no booth." I'm typing away, "Yeah, yeah, I know. I told you, don't pay any attention to them." The cops are still carrying on out by the desk. "Nehoc caught the booth robber!" Now he's standing at the cell door: "Hey man, I didn't rob that booth. Okay, I hopped, but I didn't rob *nobody!*" I stopped typing. "Look, try to understand, it's the end of the month, I need a number. I'm sorry." He sat down in a state of shock and I continued typing. "Nehoc caught the booth robber! Nehoc caught the booth robber!"

Subway Gator

There's an old myth about New Yorkers vacationing in Florida, bringing back cute little baby alligators as pets and flushing them down the toilet as they become unmanageable, only to have them survive (and grow to huge proportions) in the New York City sewer system. It's only a myth—there really aren't any sewer alligators. Other transplants *have* been known to occur, however.

My buddy Jeff joined the Florida Highway Patrol after he got out of the Marines. I paid him a visit on my own Florida vacation. He and his fellow troopers were awestruck as I filled their heads with images of roving street gangs, rats and psychotic homeless people terrorizing innocent New Yorkers beneath the graffiti-covered urban landscape—and one courageous transit cop facing it all with grim, steely-eyed determination: me. I didn't lay it on too thick, I don't think, since only two or three of his friends actually asked me for my autograph.

Jeff's 'post' was a lonely stretch of highway somewhere in central Florida. We went out on patrol together one night. We're driving and talking, just like old times, when he interrupts—"Now, that boy's speedin'." He taps on the readout of his radar thing. I turn in my seat, and all I can see are the taillights disappearing behind us. "Yeah, so anyway, like I was saying—" He starts to slow down. I ask, "Uh, what are we doing?" He pulls onto the median and begins a U-turn. "I *said* that boy's speedin'." Oh, no. "C'mon, Jethro, he's in Georgia already!" Robohick says nothing as he stomps on the gas. "*Heyheyheyheyhey!*" The nitro boosters cut in, and the acceleration pins me back in my seat. Our speed tops three digits as I start to black out.

In amazingly short order, we catch up to the speeding fugitive and pull him off on the side of the road. Jeff says, "Wait here." As he gets out of the car, he unlocks the shotgun pinned to the dash. Good, I'm thinking, as I watch him put on his Stetson and slowly walk over to the car in front of us. Now I've got something to kill him with...

He's preparing a citation for the motorist, and as I pull my fingernails out of the upholstery, I notice that he left his portable radio in the battery-charger. Well, I've got his back *this* time, so it's really no big deal. However, I've got to point this tactical error out to him when he's done. Diplomatically, of course.

"Hey, stupid, you think it might be a good idea to take your radio with you when you get out of the car?" Puzzled, he says, "Why? If I need it, I'll come back to the car for it." I'm shaking my head. "What if you have some kinda problem out there—or do you country boys just know how to write tickets?" He laughs at me: "If I got some kinda problem, I gotta take care of it, and that radio ain't gonna help me none. My closest back-up's twenty minutes away. Shit, we out in the swamp, son!"

I guess ceramic tile and steel dust isn't so bad after all.

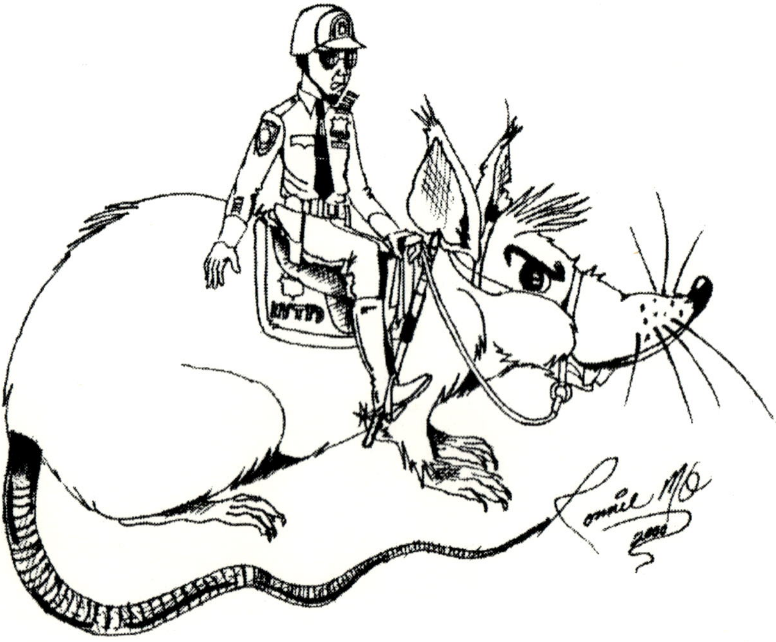

The Second Front

Although police paychecks are pretty good in New York City, many cops find it necessary to take a second job of some sort to make ends meet. Most people have heard of this referred to as 'moonlighting'. We never used that expression. In Transit Police slang, we called these jobs 'the second front'. I don't really know the origin of the term but I suspect it has something to do with being at war, with fighting for survival.

Sal had a pretty good second front, and an unusual one at that. He sold police equipment but was best known for selling police trinkets and other junk. Sal was a regular visitor to all the police commands. He had some really neat stuff. My personal favorite was this tee-shirt with big, bold lettering that said, 'Transit Police' across the top and 'Mounted Unit' across the bottom. In the middle, there was a dramatic design of a cop in full battle regalia riding a giant rat.

Sal got into trouble once. At the time we were both in the same command, the Tactical Patrol Force. That was the glorified name of our late-night train patrol unit. Our commanding officer was this old inspector who came on the job with Jesus. His policy was that any time one of his officers got into trouble he would personally interview him before writing him up on charges. Going to see the inspector was not considered to be a good thing. With most of the cops in our unit being very young, it was reminiscent of being sent to the principal's office.

When a cop would get into trouble for breaking departmental rules (like the rules against peddling merchandise on department property, for instance), the process of getting written up or otherwise being brought up on departmental charges was known as getting a 'complaint'. Getting a complaint from the inspector was nothing to smile about—if found guilty, and you *would* be found guilty, it generally resulted in the forfeiture of paid vacation days as punishment—in effect, you'd be monetarily fined. This would not help your personal war effort at all.

Sal came up to the office to see the inspector. We all said goodbye to him like it was the last time we'd see him, and he knocked on the door. He disappeared into the inspector's office and the door closed behind him.

About twenty minutes later the door opens up. Sal walks out with his head down, says nothing to anyone, and leaves. Poor guy. A few minutes later, the inspector comes out of his office. None of us say anything to him; we all make like nothing's happened. He walks over to the window and looks out over the Brooklyn skyline. "Y'know, I was gonna give that kid a complaint," he says to no one in particular, "but I ended up buying this tie-clip..."

Reader's note: Writing is not my second front, in case you were wondering. I write simply for the pleasure of it. Good thing, too.

Me and Casey Jones

I was riding the 'F' train when there was a report of a man with a gun at the 71st/Continental subway station. Luckily for me, I was pulling into the 75th Avenue station, one stop away. Then the radio dispatcher said, "All units, be advised, the perp fled into the tunnel towards 75th Avenue..."

I signaled the conductor to hold the train as I went to the motorman's position. "Twenty TP Seven, central, I just pulled into 75th Avenue. Send me some back-up." Walking into the lead car of the train, I knocked on the motorman's door. From inside his cab there was a clear and ominous view into the tunnel. He asked what was going on, and I told him. "We're just gonna stay here until the other cops get here." He didn't seem impressed. We're just sitting there in silence, watching the tunnel.

Then the motorman's radio started blaring: "TWO-OH-FIVE 'F' OUTTA STILLWELL, COME IN TO COMMMAAAAND CENTER!!" It was so loud it hurt my ears. "GO 'HEAD, COMMAND CENTER!" Now I know why these guys are all going deaf—they're always yowling at each other. "WHY YOU STOPPED??" The motorman yowls back, "THERE'S A PO-LICEMAN HERE, HE SAY I CAIN'T MOVE THE TRAIN!!" I'm covering my ears. "YOU GOTTA MOVE THE TRAIN, TWO-OH-FIVE!!" He looks at me, and I say, "Don't move the train, stay right here." He yowls away, "HE SAY I CAIN'T MOVE THE TRAIN!!" My hat is vibrating. "YOU GOTTA MOVE THE TRAIN, TWO-OH-FIVE!!" I tell him, "You move the train, I'll lock you up, understand?" The yowling stopped when he yowled that one at the command center.

About a minute later, the police dispatcher calls me, "Twenty TP Seven, you holding the train at 75th Avenue?" I answer, "Ten-four, central. You got back-up coming?" The dispatcher calmly says, "Release the train, Twenty TP Seven." Now *I'm* yowling: "Central, there's nobody here but me! Where's my back-up?" The plan was that at least two cops would secure the tunnel entrance from the platform, while two of us would do a 'ride-through' to 71st Avenue—as soon as there were enough cops to do it. After all, this was a man with a gun we were looking for. "Release the train, Twenty TP Seven."

Well, if this job wasn't important enough for the Transit Police to stand up to the Transit Authority, then it wasn't important enough for me, either. "Ten-four, central, I'm outta here." In disgust, I said to the motorman, "Okay, let's go." He yowled at the conductor to close up. He smiled and said, "Maybe they caught him." He was enjoying the moment. As we rolled into the darkness of the tunnel I said, "I doubt it." Out of the corner of my eye, I could see he was trying not to laugh. I asked, "Hey, can you turn off these interior lights?" He looked puzzled and said, "No, why?" I just shook my head. "Nah, nothing, never mind. Listen, there's another gun on my left ankle. If anything happens to me, take care of yourself..."

Mi Casa Es Su Casa

In the Police Academy they told us horror stories about the facilities used for district offices by the Transit Police Department. They were all actually underground and in the subways, and were cramped, dirty, and generally unsuitable as police stations. They even told us that in one district, the cops had to go out on a *catwalk* into the tunnel to get to their locker room. Naturally, we thought they were kidding. Well, they weren't.

When I got to my first command at 169th Street and Hillside Avenue in Queens, I couldn't believe it. What a dump! The place was so small that we used to have to push the table in the 'lunchroom' up against the wall to hold roll-call. It was so small we didn't even have standard subway rats, we had mice instead. All over. I think they chewed the phone lines, because none of them worked. The very walls of the command were crumbling into sand from the constant vibrations. Everybody said not to worry, we were moving the district to a new location in Jackson Heights soon, and the 169th Street office would be condemned. We did, and it was.

Several years later, when I was in the Tactical Patrol Force, we lost our office space in the headquarters building over some political turf battle. Not to worry, they said, there's another facility just waiting for us... Welcome back to 169 and Hill.

Since we weren't using it as a full-fledged police station, it wasn't that bad. It's not like we were operating out of a cardboard box on top of a subway grate—but at least then we would've had heat in the winter and air-conditioning in the summer! Still, we tried to make the best of it. Like all offices, we set up a coffee pot.

John Z. was in charge of the house fund, but nobody would pay him coffee dues because the coffee always sucked. This pissed him off. So, one day he took a sample of the water we used to make coffee and brought it to a swimming-pool company for a test. The test was free, and John always could spot a bargain. He came back to the office with the results: "They said to get everyone out of the pool."

Aim to Please

This guy was giving me a problem, so I made it clear to him that there wasn't enough room in the subway station for both of us—and I wasn't leaving. I'm walking him toward the exit stairs and he's spewing a non-stop stream of verbal abuse. Very loudly, I might add.

We get to the stairs and he decides to draw the line in the sand: "Fuck you, I ain't leaving!" As I'm considering my options, two scruffy-looking guys walk over to us. One of them discreetly 'tins' me with a shield in the palm of his hand. He says, "It's okay, we got it," as they quickly grab an arm apiece. "Hey! Get the fuck off me!" Now he's going up the stairs whether he likes it or not, and I'm following along behind. One of the plainclothes cops, a grizzled veteran, says over his shoulder, "It's okay, officer, we got it." I continue to follow, and he repeats with exaggerated politeness, "Really—we got it." Hmmm... I do have a train to catch, so I said, "Thanks, fellas," and I turned to leave. The guy is still carrying on but they're all going up the stairs. I can hear the racket echoing down into the subway while they're up in the street. "Get your fucking hands off me! I want your badge number, you fucking asshole!" Then I heard a different voice: "You want a badge number?" *Whap!!* "Owwww!" I went back upstairs to see if they needed a hand, but by the time I got up there the two plainclothes cops were gone. My very subdued friend was standing there quietly, holding his forehead.

Reader's note: They gave him a badge number like he asked. Too bad they didn't give him a mirror to read it with.

My Hero

Like any police department, the Transit Police had a system of recognizing our members' deeds with departmental awards. Whether or not we had a fair system is debatable. It was usually a hot topic for conversation, especially amongst the dissatisfied members. Other cops that is, not *me*...

The general beef was that it seemed some people got recognized while others didn't. One problem was, for starters, you had to 'write yourself up'. Then, after a very lengthy paperwork process, the final decision was made downtown from behind closed doors. Also, the criteria for each award was almost deliberately vague and ambiguous. And so on. Anyway, during one of these discussions about the fairness of our system I asked a co-worker to tell me the story behind his 'Exceptional Duty' medal. He told me that some woman had gotten run over by a bus and was pinned beneath the rear wheels. He called for an ambulance. "That's it?" He nodded. I had to ask, "No offense, but why did they give you an *exceptional?*" He shrugs, "I dunno, my partner wrote it up." The 'Exceptional Duty' award was exceeded only by the 'Combat Cross' and the 'Medal of Honor'.

One afternoon in 1987, I was coming out of a restaurant on Lawrence Street in Brooklyn. I've got my take-out dinner in one hand and flowers for my wife in the other. I'm in the vestibule at the front door when gunfire erupts in the street outside. I immediately flattened out as the bullets were whizzing by, but now it's decision time: I go out instead of retreating inside. There's a plainclothes cop on the sidewalk screaming for help on his radio. I come up behind him with my gun out (not my smartest move) and shout, "I'm on the job, what do you got?" Before he could answer me we're both diving out of the way of the van coming up on the sidewalk. It missed us, but slammed into the side of the building. The driver throws it into reverse, spins his tires, and as soon as he was clear of the wreck, puts it in drive and floors it. He didn't get too far before he slammed into a row of parked cars. He didn't take his foot off the gas except to shift back and forth from forward to reverse. My keen police mind told me that there was a problem with this van. As I came up behind it, it came back at me and I dived again. Okay, okay, I'm starting to get the hang of this. So, we're chasing this van down Lawrence Street, back and forth anyway, and I've got my father's dinky little five-shot Smith sighted in on the driver's head. I'm just waiting to see some kind of gun in the van since our shooting guidelines prohibited shooting at a moving vehicle unless it was shooting, or about to shoot, at you. If they're just trying to run you over, you're supposed to just get out of the way—which I became very adept at over the next two blocks running alongside this van as it wrecked at least a dozen more parked cars. Throughout this pandemonium, I managed to stay so close that it didn't matter all I had was an off-duty gun. When it finally got pinned in a crash on Fulton Street, I ran up to the rear of the van with some other officers, pulled the occupants out and cuffed them up, including the gunshot driver. The van was stolen. Although I didn't know it when I was in the restaurant, the gunfire was from the *cops* across the street. The driver had dragged one of them as they tried to stop him and they fired at him—and at me, since I was on the opposite side of the van. No wonder this guy was driving like a maniac to escape; he had a bunch of holes in him. Turned out it was a good thing I held my fire too, since it would've been in violation of the shooting guidelines.

When this incident happened, I was pretty well shaken up. I went back to the restaurant, got my food and squashed flowers, and left. It was about a year later when I was telling the war story when a friend asked, "Did you write it up?" Hmmm... "I guess I should, huh?" So I did.

According to our cumbersome rules, since I didn't write it up when it first happened I had to wait for a scheduled 'appeal' period to be announced, at which time I could submit the late paperwork. The appeal period was a thirty-day window—after that, it was forever hold your peace. It had to be submitted to the command I worked in at the time of the incident even though I no longer worked there, so I sent it to the Tactical Patrol Force.

About a week before the end of the thirty-day period I called TPF to see what was going on with this thing. I was getting a little excited because it *was* a pretty heavy incident. Even though I didn't shoot, there was a lot of gunfire, and we had given guys the 'Combat Cross' before for shooting incidents where the cop held fire. In any case, I figure I gotta get something good. So, I get this lieutenant on the phone and ask him what's happening with it. He gets the file in front of him and says, "Uh, what are you looking for here, anyway?" He didn't mean what *award* did I want, he meant why was I bothering him *at all*. I'm flabbergasted: "Gee, I dunno Lou, I almost got shot, I almost got run over a couple times, I chased a stolen van on foot a couple blocks—why?" He says, "Well, you weren't even the arresting officer." Couldn't argue with that. Anyway, my paperwork never even made it downtown. It went right in his garbage can as the window closed.

Maybe I should've called for an ambulance...

A Snake With Arms

The Transit Police, for the most part, followed in lock-step with the NYPD as far as equipment and uniforms. Other than the shoulder patch (and the attitude) our officers appeared to be the same as theirs.

The police revolver we carried dates from the turn of the century. There's very little about the gun to be improved on, and that was it. The only really new innovation in police firepower was the advent of the 'speed loader'. For whatever reason, the police hierarchy steadfastly resisted this new device until when, in 1986, an NYPD officer was tragically killed in a Far Rockaway gunfight while desperately trying to reload his empty six-shooter.

Suddenly, speed loaders seemed like a good idea, and they were authorized in quick succession by the NYPD, Housing and Transit. The new equipment presented a minor problem, at least to me: my service revolver was a six-shooter, but my backup gun was a *five-*shot. Do I carry two different types of speed loaders? What if I mix them up? How about if I carry one type, but I mix the *guns* up?

I started to look around to see if I could buy a six-shot backup gun from somebody secondhand since that's usually more economical, but they weren't too commonly carried. Ronnie was a gun buff; I asked him if he had a six-shot snub-nosed Smith. He said no problem, he'd get me one. "Yeah, but how much?" He said a hundred bucks, which didn't seem too bad.

A couple of days later, while I was talking to John, I noticed that he had a six-shot snub-nosed Smith in his waistband. I asked him if he liked the gun. He said it was okay, but just a little bit heavy. I asked if he was interested in maybe selling it, and he said, "You know, you're the second person this week to ask me that." He takes it out of the holster and we're examining it. "Funny, it's not a popular gun." I asked who else wanted one. He said, "Ronnie offered me fifty bucks for it yesterday."

...Or Are You Just Happy To See Me?

Sometimes, I'd take the train to and from work. One of the subway stations I would use was the Aqueduct/North Conduit station in Queens. As it's name would imply, the station was near the Aqueduct Racetrack on North Conduit Avenue. The area is pretty desolate. It's what's known as an 'open-cut' station—the train tracks are neither above nor below ground, they're right at ground level. Originally it used to belong to the Long Island Railroad but now it's part of the NYC subway system. The station itself is quite beautiful, architecturally speaking. The exterior design of the station is really cool Art Deco. Of course, everything's covered with graffiti and the whole place stinks like a urinal, but you have to look past that.

One winter night I get off the train at Aqueduct. There's a precinct cop standing in front of the token booth, and boy, does he look thrilled. Not only is he freezing his ass off, but he's stuck in this godforsaken subway station. Since I was off-duty and didn't know him plus he didn't look too friendly, I didn't say hello. I walked past him and out the front doors of the station, and then turned right onto North Conduit Avenue.

The first thing I notice is all the snow; the place looks like Antarctica. The second thing I notice is the teenaged girl dressed in nothing but jeans and an unbuttoned blouse running down the Conduit screaming, "Oh God, help me, somebody help me!" The third thing I notice is the car backing down the Conduit after her, wrong-way, with the passenger door open. I sensed that the second and third thing were somehow related.

I backpedaled to the subway station and stuck my head in the door: "There's a kidnapping in progress out here!" In a very official tone, the frozen cop says, "Huh?" Fumbling for my shield, I yell, "You wanna give me a hand here, or what?" Now he comes running. Bear in mind this is all happening very quickly. As we both exit the subway station the girl is running past. The driver has ditched the car in the middle of the Conduit and is now chasing her on foot. He runs right into two Smith & Wessons, so close in fact we almost poke his eyes out. In a scene right out of *Starsky and Hutch*, we throw him against one of the big Art Deco pillars. "Get your feet back! Spread 'em!" I start to frisk him and I feel this hard object in his pants. With reflexes honed by years of street encounters, I yell, "Gun!" and slam him face-down into the ground.

So far, this is looking like a really great collar. I think kidnapping is an 'A' felony. The precinct cop is even starting to smile, but I think that was because of the snow-angels the guy was making. Hey, I'm a happy transit cop. Then the girl starts screaming, "What are you doing? Are you fucking crazy?" At first I thought she was yelling at the guy, but then I realize she means *us*. This guy's her boyfriend. We get him up off the ground, she kisses him, brushes the snow off him, then they start going at it again right in front of us. While they're busy arguing, I ask the cop, "Uh, what do you want to do with this?" He's got that thrilled look on his face again—"What am *I* gonna do with it?"—and he walks back to the subway.

As far as the gun, well, it wasn't.

Hard Living

When I first started dating my wife we frequently hung out in local neighborhood bars. I'm sure that hardly any cops *ever* did that, but I know how to show a girl a good time.

One night we were out in a bar in Rockaway, the place where we went on our first date. It was a cozy little place and it also held some other memories for me—when I was stationed in Newport, Rhode Island, I used to hang out there on weekends. Anyway, in some New York taverns, talking to strangers is a dicey proposition at best. Not this place. It had a circular bar, and on good nights with a friendly crowd, people would chat it up with each other. Very pleasant. On this particular night, everyone was friendly.

Coincidentally, one of the other patrons sitting at the bar was a young naval officer apparently home on leave. He was with a few friends, and what with buying rounds of drinks back and forth, everybody was pretty sociable. After overhearing a bit of their conversation I had a fair idea of who and what he was. Out of politeness, though, when we started talking I asked, "So, what do you do in the Navy?" Understandably proud of himself, he said, "I'm an officer." I smile. "Yeah, I figured that, but aviation, surface or what?" He says, "I'm a surface warfare officer." Hmmm... I've spent a day or two at sea on a destroyer myself. "What ship?" He says, "I'll be going to the USS Smith in a few days." Just as I thought, a little wet behind the ears. When I ask if he was recently commissioned, he tries to sound real salty: "Nah, I just finished Surface Warfare School in Newport." The Navy had two surface warfare schools—one in Newport, and another in Coronado, California. "Oh, I guess you're going into the Atlantic Fleet. I was Pacific; I went through Coronado." Now he looks at me suspiciously: "You were an officer?" I nod, and his eyebrow goes up. Okay, so I'm dressed in jeans and a tee-shirt, I haven't shaved for a few days and my eyes are a little red, but that's what most off-duty cops hanging out in neighborhood bars look like. I'm not sure he believes me since he's not asking any questions about my Navy background. In an effort to continue the conversation I volunteer, "I did go to MPA school in Newport, though." The young ensign almost chokes on his beer. "You went to *MPA school?*" That was the U.S. Navy's most prestigious engineering school short of the nuclear power program. He stares at me for a few seconds with his mouth agape, then asks, "What happened to you?"

Defensive Driving

I had to drop something off at the Transit Police headquarters building, an old converted factory at 300 Gold Street. As usual, there was nowhere to park anywhere around the place, so I figured I'd try the headquarters lot. All the spaces were reserved but I was just dropping something off.

The lot was full, too, except for a spot between the front steps and that part of the building which was a loading dock in another lifetime. The area was reserved for the big bosses, but again, I was only going to be a minute. All I had to do was snake my car between the steps and the side of the building that enclosed the dock area. It was tight, so I was backing in nice... and... easy... *tap*... CRRASHHH!! "Shit."

I got out of my car to see that the entire wrought-iron banister and front porch railing was completely knocked out of the concrete steps, and was lying in a crumpled heap behind my car. No way! I just tapped it! Upon close inspection, I could see what happened—there was fresh concrete work holding the sides of the steps together, and more fresh work everywhere the banister and railing was attached. Well, where it used to be attached, anyway. Apparently someone else had already destroyed it and I just ruined a patch job. It wasn't like *I* did it.

I went inside to report it at the front desk, and the old timer said, "Oh-oh. You gotta tell Chief Smith." I asked why I had to tell the chief, and he threw up his hands: "Can't help you kid, you gotta tell the chief." Looks like now I'm really in trouble.

So, I surrendered myself at his office door. "Uh, good morning, Chief, Officer Nehoc from TPF. They sent me up to talk to you." He looked up from his desk and said gruffly, "Come in. What do you need, Officer?" I walked in and stood at attention. "Well, I was just dropping something off, so I had to park for a minute, and, uh, right by the front steps, I tapped the banister while I was backing up, and uh, well the whole railing came off. They told me I had to report it to you personally." He didn't look pleased. "You knocked the railing off the front steps, huh? They told you to come tell me?" He's just looking at me. "Yes, sir." Long pause. Then he laughed, "Okay, you told me." Whew! He didn't seem pissed at all. Relieved, I said, "Yeah, Chief, it's funny, 'cause I only tapped it. I took a look at it and you can see where they just repaired it; there was fresh concrete all over. Some jackass musta really nailed it."

As I was being ejected from his office, it dawned on me just who musta really nailed it.

Nuts

I had just arrived at the 179th Street subway station in Jamaica and had crossed over to the other side to catch the 'E' back to the

World Trade Center in Manhattan, looking forward to yet another exciting train run. While standing glumly on the platform waiting for my next train to leave, I do a double-take—about twenty feet away, this guy does the 'dip'. In other words, he picked someone's pocket. They say that some pickpockets deliberately operate right next to uniformed cops; supposedly, the presence of the unwitting cop causes the unsuspecting victims to let their guard down. Who would expect somebody to commit a crime right under the nose of a cop? Not me, that's for sure.

I walk up to the thief and the victim with a shit-eating grin on my face. The victim is now frantically checking his pockets. "Excuse me, sir, did you feel that?" He's getting red in the face, "I sure as hell did!" Our apparently unskilled pickpocket is just standing there innocently. He's about thirty years old, five-foot five, maybe a hundred and forty pounds soaking wet. He doesn't look like much of anything. I'm obviously pleased with myself as I announce, "You're under arrest!"

He just stood there submissively as I smoothly placed a handcuff on his left wrist. Without any particular speed or abrupt movement, he just pulled his left arm out from behind his back before I could get the other cuff on, and he looks at it, kinda puzzled. "What are you, a wise guy?" Now I torque the cuff with the full strength of both my arms and wrench his left arm behind his back again (well, actually, somewhere between his shoulder blades). "Give me your other hand, right now!" That's when I heard the growling. In horrible slow motion, he simply powered out of my hammerlock with just one skinny little arm. As he gets his left arm fully extended out from his side, he shifts his maniacal gaze from the handcuffs—to me holding desperately on to them. Uh-oh...

I never even got my radio out of the holder. He charges at me, and while I'm sidestepping him, I key the mike and yell, *"Ten-thirteen, 179!"* I don't know if anyone's heard me, but there's no time to worry about it. He's charging again, and this time he managed to grab a piece of me. My shield is ripped from my duty jacket and goes sailing through the air. Holy shit! He's coming at me like a madman intent on ripping my eyeballs out—and eating them—while yelling something about "Electricity!" You know that nightmare where the monsters are chasing you and you're running through quicksand?

Timmy and Sam were upstairs in the Greek diner when they heard my distress call on the radio: "Who the fuck is *that?*" They had the post and didn't even know I was in the station. Down on the platform, I was quickly running out of options when I see Sam come running down the stairs with Timmy a few paces behind. Distracted, my monster turns from me and begins to charge at them. Seizing this brief instant of opportunity I run after him and grab his left arm. As he turns back on me, Sam grabs him by his right arm. Still on the stairs, Timmy sees that Sam and I have each got a hold of this guy, so he radioes, "Central, slow it down to 179, everything's under control!" Sam had a real funny look on his face as he starts to wail, "Oh, Timmy, Timmy, no it ain't!"

With the two of us helpless to stop him, this little bastard begins to spin like a top, swinging Sam and me around like two rag dolls. As if this isn't bad enough, now Babe Ruth takes out his nightstick and he's squaring off, hoping to get a shot in as we go whizzing by. *"Timmmmy!!"*

Thankfully, before he starts batting practice, two plainclothes cops dive on top of us, and we all go crashing to the platform. Timmy dives in, too. The passengers watching this show certainly got their money's worth as the squirming human pile now starts to move. Oh, no. He's dragging *all five of us* toward the edge of the platform, yelling some crazy shit about "Snakes! Snakes!"

It took two emergency service trucks, a whole bunch more cops, and about twenty minutes before we finally got him tied up. I extricated myself from the tangle, staggered up to a precinct sergeant and said, "He's under arrest; he's my prisoner." He took a look at me, all lumped up and bloody: "Oh yeah? Good for you!"

Sam and I were both hurt, so Timmy ended up getting stuck with the arrest. He was mad at me for a long time afterwards, so I can only assume it must've been a long night. Timmy later said that during one particularly memorable outburst, in a fit of rage the guy actually managed to tip over a gurney that he was chained and strapped to. The medical diagnosis? "Atypical schizophrenia with homicidal tendencies." Shit. I could told you *that*.

Several months later I get a call from the district attorney's office about some guy whose name I don't recognize. "You arrested him in the subway at 179th Street in December, 1987." Oh yeah, him... The ADA tells me that he's been confined to the psychiatric facility at Kings County Hospital since the arrest, and that he was recently found to be 'fit to proceed' with his trial. Then she asks, "How would you feel about a plea to a violation?" I thought she was kidding. She wasn't. "I got him for three felony counts and you wanna let him cop to a *violation?* What happened to misdemeanors? Aren't they in the middle there somewhere?" She says, "Well, they're not sure how long he'll be fit to proceed." Now I'm getting pissed: "What are you talking about? Either he's fit to proceed, or he *ain't*. Don't bullshit me, okay?" A defendant's sanity isn't measured by the seriousness of the charges he's facing. "No, no, you're right—that's not what I meant. Look, you seem to be very angry over this; is there some problem I should know about?" Very sharp, this lawyer. "Hey, this guy hurt me, and he hurt another cop, okay? If he's sick, fine, then keep him in the nuthouse, but don't tell me you just wanna let him go without upsetting him. If he ain't locked up in a psych ward, then fuck him, lock him up in jail! He's a bad guy!" She says, "Well, I don't know that he's that bad—I've got his rap sheet here, let's see... he's been arrested fourteen... no, fifteen... He's been arrested fifteen times since 1978. But there's only two or three 'A' misdemeanor convictions." I wanted to go through the phone wire and choke this ditz. "Let me get this straight—you say he's not such a bad guy 'cause he's only got a couple of 'A-mis' convictions? *You* wanna let him plea down to violations from *felonies*. You mind telling me what the fuck he had to do to get convicted on those misdemeanors? Kill somebody?"

A few weeks later, Sam and I showed up at the arraignment, but our defendant apparently forgot. It seems that when they released him from the hospital, they just took his word that he'd show up for court. That was the last we ever heard from him.

Many months later, I received a letter from the Queens DA's office. It was just a standard form letter, but I found it somehow deeply moving:

Dear Officer Nehoc,

As District Attorney of Queens County, I want to express my appreciation for your efforts in the prosecution of the case of

People vs. John Doe: This case has been concluded as follows:

Judge:	Honorable William Smith
A.D.A.:	Jane Jones
Charge:	Assault in the Second Degree, Grand Larceny in the Fourth Degree
Disposition:	Pled Guilty to Harassment
Sentence:	Time Served

The successful operation of our criminal justice system depends on your continued commitment to professionalism to help make our County a better place to live and work.

Yours very truly,
/signature/
Joseph Blow
District Attorney

Reader's note: My left shoulder still occasionally dislocates with quite a bit of discomfort, but hey, at least I got a conviction.

Practice Makes Perfect

When I joined the Transit Police one of my first questions was, "How do you get ahead?" The answer was to study the 'Patrol Guide' and take a test. The patrol guide was about as thick as a good-sized telephone book. Well, in my previous occupation I had to study a lot of books just to get through the day, and it didn't get me anywhere, as evidenced by the fact that I was now a transit cop. In 1988, the promotional list from the sergeant's exam was published and I was near the top. So near that they actually had to pass me over for promotion at first, since according to the Civil Service rules I didn't have the minimum legal amount of time on the job to make sergeant. I used to tell people I got lucky, but the truth is luck had very little to do with it. After my wonderful experiences in the Navy I would've *memorized* a phone book if that's what it took.

Evidently I wasn't alone in my motivational bent as there were a few of us who were looking at early promotions. They called us the 'Magnificent Seven'. Our chief had a great idea to give us a leg up in experience: the bunch of us were sent on a whirlwind tour of our department's specialized units. For two months at a pop, I was in the Communications Division, the Special Operations Division, the Detective Division and the Criminal Intelligence Section. I had a great time and learned a lot. I learned all about the units I'd never be able to get into later... The bright side is that (you guessed it) I got a few more war stories out of the deal.

I was assigned to the District Two Detective Squad for a month. These guys were making about five collars a week and I was doing a lot of the arrest paperwork as part of my 'training'. This worked out well for all of us, since I really hadn't made that many arrests in my brief time as a cop, and since they had better things to do—like make more collars.

We went down to court one day to grab a prisoner who was there for a trial and put him in a 'line-up' on an unrelated charge. The victim picked him out, so he's arrested again on the new charge. No big deal for the prisoner since he's already locked up. It's just a paperwork drop, and I'm the paperboy. To my surprise, the guy's got to be fingerprinted again. This is not good, since I'm not too proficient at printing. I told the boss, and he said, "Oh yeah? There's one way to fix that..."

So I'm trying to print this knucklehead, and it's not going well at all. I'm starting to wonder what's going to run out first—the supply of print cards, the ink or his jail sentence. I'm making all kinds of excuses about the equipment, the weather, anything I can think of. The prisoner is patiently suffering through my incompetence for maybe fifteen or twenty minutes, and I'm sweating like a pig (pardon the pun). Finally, he says, "Yo, 'bee', I'm gonna miss the bus back to Riker's. Allow me." I surrender and step away. This guy prints himself—city, state and federal—perfectly. All clear, no smudges. He smiled and gave me a shrug of the shoulders. I gave him a bag of potato chips not to say anything to anyone.

Reader's note: Many years and hundreds of arrests later, I *still* can't print, but now I can tell people I used to know how.

Have a Nice Day

Most people picture traffic enforcement as the stone-faced state trooper in the military uniform with the mountie hat, boots and mirrored sunglasses. The average motorist just hopes so badly that all he gets is a ticket that when he finally gets it, he thanks the trooper. That's not always how it happens in New York City.

Dorsey and I are driving down Eastern Parkway through Crown Heights in an unmarked police car. Eastern Parkway is a multi-laned main road, very heavily trafficked. We're minding our own business when a car in the next lane decides to abruptly change lanes, cutting us off and forcing Dorsey to slam on the brakes. We couldn't have come any closer to having an accident without actually having one.

Although we're not out there for traffic enforcement, this guy really needs some. We throw the fireball up on the roof, whoop the siren a few times and pull him off the road. We walk up on the car. Dorsey asks if we know why we've stopped him. Not only does he not know why, but he's annoyed that we have. Dorsey tells him that his earlier lane change almost caused an accident, and the guy says, "What? Dere's nut'ting wrong wit my drivin' mon!" Granted, we're in plainclothes, but there's no question that we're the police. Dorsey asks for his license and registration and the guy thinks it's a debate. What balls. Dorsey explains to him that we don't really give a shit about his opinion right now, but that if he doesn't give up some paperwork, that we'd be happy to give him a chance to talk to someone who does—like a judge. Luckily for him, his license comes out before our handcuffs did. His name? "Pierre St. Michel Souvenir."

Now, if you can't see this one coming, you really shouldn't be reading these stories. Our expert motorist is still arguing his case. The temperature is rising. Dorsey says, "I don't know where you learned to drive, but you better go take the class again." He's from some Caribbean island, and not only does he *know* how to drive, but 'down dere' the police know how to do *their* jobs. Oh yeah? "Hey, if you don't like it here, why don't you just go home?" The guy says, "Hey, mon, maybe I just do that!" Dorsey hands him a ticket: "Well, here's a fucking souvenir!"

Happy To Be Alive

They say cops develop 'gallows humor' as a defense mechanism against the horrors that we're exposed to on a far too frequent basis. Personally, I think that's bullshit. Most of us are just a bunch of sick bastards with really twisted senses of humor. When we're out on jobs involving dead people, the gags can get even more depraved because we've got more time to think stuff up. They're dead, what's the rush?

Ask a stupid question
An old derelict (a 'skell' in transit police jargon) was discovered, dead, on a train in Jamaica. A pretty routine job, as there's no evidence of foul play. We're all just hanging around the scene waiting for the medical examiner when the radio dispatcher called us and asked for "...an update on the DOA." We all just looked at each other. The reply was inevitable; it was merely a question of who would say it. "Still dead, central."

Get a stupid answer
The transit police radio dispatchers had a well-deserved reputation of being dopes, for the most part. I heard of another incident, same scenario as above with a different response to the same silly inquiry: "Well, he ain't getting any worse, central..."

Hooray for Medical Science
Cops are justifiably concerned about civil liability these days since just about any asshole can sue you for just about anything. This is evident when cops are dealing with what would seem to be a dead person. Technically, only a doctor or a certified emergency medical technician is supposed to pronounce someone 'dead'. It's a little far-fetched, but the worst-case scenario would entail an unqualified person making a death pronouncement on somebody who isn't really dead. Anyway, in this regard, we generally refrain from declaring someone dead until a medic has made the official pronouncement. This results in a lot of legalistic euphemisms, such as 'apparent DOA' and 'possibly deceased'. In one incident, a person was run over by a train. The Emergency Medical Service had yet to arrive on the scene. A cop said on the radio, "Central, be advised, I'm not a doctor, but I think this is definitely a possible DOA." The hapless victim's head had been severed and was about ten feet away from the body when the cop made his bold statement.

Good Luck

This guy is coming home from work one day, and he had a pretty lousy day, so he took the common-sense approach to his problems and jumped in front of a train. I'm down on the tracks with all the cops and EMTs and firemen. The guy is very much alive, with just a severed foot and a nasty gash on his head. The only fly in the ointment is that he's laying up against the third rail, and even though the power was supposedly off, nobody's in a real big hurry to touch him and risk getting electrocuted, especially since he had put himself in this predicament. So, we're all hanging out in the dark next to the guy waiting for Emergency Service to show up with these big rubber gloves, when one of the cops says, "Hey, look—a penny!" He bends over, picks it up and says, "And it's heads-up, too!" And after he was rescued, the guy filed a lawsuit against the Transit Authority.

The Truth, The Whole Truth...

Timmy was in traffic court. He had written a guy three summonses for blowing three stop-signs. The guy shows up with his brother-in-law who happens to be an attorney. Remember, this is only traffic court—the judge isn't even wearing robes, but they want their day in court. Well, they got it. Everyone is sworn in and the 'trial' begins.

The lawyer doesn't exactly plead his client's innocence, though. His ingenious defense strategy: Entrapment. With reckless disregard for public safety, he says, Timmy followed his client through all the stop-signs without even attempting to pull him over, so that he could write more tickets and thereby make his quota. The judge mulls it over, and asks, "But he *did* run all the stop-signs, correct?" The lawyer starts to embellish, but the magistrate's hand goes up, and he says, "Officer, what do you have to say about this?" Timmy says, "Judge, I would've pulled him over after he ran the first stop-sign, but since I *was* concerned for the public's safety, I had to come to a stop before I crossed the intersection, and he got away. As a matter of fact, I came to a stop at each and every intersection he went through. That's why it took me three intersections to catch up to him before I could finally pull him over." The judge smiles and says,

"Guilty. All fines are doubled." The motorist snaps at his attorney, "You asshole!"

...And Nothing But The Truth

The first time I ever had to testify in court was over a traffic summons. Well, over a bunch of traffic summonses. We had stopped a gypsy cab driver for picking up a fare who had hailed him in the street. This is illegal, as is operating a 'for-hire' vehicle without the proper class of driver's license and insurance. I mention, in passing, that it's also against the law to refuse to provide driver's info to the police upon demand. This particular cabbie had done all these things, and more.

I'm in the summons part of Kings Criminal Court waiting for my case to come up. The place is like an auditorium with about a hundred people waiting to have their cases heard, or for the most part to simply plead guilty and pay their fine. I suspected that I might be in for a little trouble when, after having accepted guilty pleas from several different people for 'selling alcohol to a minor' and levying fines, the judge realized that the gentleman standing in front of him pleading *guilty* had been issued his summons by the same cop who had written all the other alcohol summonses. "Wait a minute," he boomed, "Is this officer trying to use up all his tickets before the end of the month? Dismissed!" I guess that when you're playing to a packed house, you gotta give the people what they want to hear.

My case comes up and the cabbie wants a trial. We're all sworn in by the judge. We started with the summons for operating a vehicle without 'for-hire' insurance. The judge asked me, "Did you ask him for 'for-hire' insurance?" I said, "I asked him for his license, registration and insurance—" The judge interrupts: "Did you ask him for 'for-hire' insurance?" I said, "You honor, he wouldn't give me anything." He's getting pissed. "Officer, that's not what I asked you. Did you specifically ask for *'for-hire'* insurance or not?" I thought about it for a second. "I don't remember, but probably not. Like I said, though, he—" The hand goes up (must be a judge thing): "Dismissed." I figured that it wasn't a good time to tell the judge we had to yank this guy out of his car and handcuff him. We actually had to use the dozens of old summonses in his glove box to identify him, that's how uncooperative he was.

Then we looked at the summons for 'accepting a hail'. I told my story. The cabbie told another. He had even brought his sister and her husband to the courtroom and said that he was picking them up at the time. Total bullshit. I had never seen them before in my life, and I told the judge so. When I said, "Your honor, he has a different version of the truth than I do," he replied very sarcastically, "You just let *me* be the judge of that." I wonder how he would've reacted to the word 'perjury'.

We didn't even look at the rest of the summonses. The judge asked me if I had anything else to offer in the case and I told him there were two other officers with me at the time but they weren't present in court. In a very condescending tone, he said, "Well, maybe we'll take a look at that next time. All dismissed." I could feel my face getting hot, sort of like as if I had just gotten slapped in front of a hundred people in an auditorium.

Of all the people to ride the elevator with, who's standing there grinning at me but the cabbie and his 'family'. Maybe it wasn't too professional of me, but I looked at him and said, "What are you smiling at, fuckhead—I'm getting *paid* to be here. Are you?"

Act II

'You can fool some of the people some of the time - and that's usually enough to make a living.'

Anonymous

Dead On Arrival

Corpse. Stiff. Cadaver. All terms for a dead human body. Anyone who watches television or reads murder mysteries can give you another term: DOA. Those letters stand for 'Dead On Arrival'. This was always quite clear to me as a kid watching TV and reading books. It seemed straightforward enough. As a cop, though, I started thinking about it. Does it mean he was dead on *his* arrival at the hospital, or dead on *your* arrival at the scene? Subtle difference, if you think about it.

I'm a brand-new sergeant on patrol in Brooklyn one night when we got a radio call about an injured person at the Smith/9th Street subway station. I tell them we're responding. Then the dispatcher said something I've never heard, either before or since: "If you can't wait for the ambulance, you can take him to the hospital in the RMP [jargon for police car]. Well, my heart's beating a bit faster with that little message.

We screech up to the station and jump out of the car. Inside the subway, the token booth clerk points us toward the victim. There's this guy laid out on a bench. His eyes are rolled back in his head. We can see this because his eyes are open—they're also dried out. In his hand, which is laying limply across his chest, is a dagger. My partner says, "Holy shit, Sarge, he's fuckin' *dead!*" Well, it certainly looks that way. I get on the radio and say, "Central, we got an unconscious, uh, apparently seriously injured victim of a crime here." I figured someone else could say he was dead.

What I didn't realize was that I just upped this to a major caper. The dispatcher put a 'rush' on the ambulance, the detectives are coming, the duty captain is coming, everybody in the world is coming.

The first cops on the scene after us were from the Transit Police Emergency Medical Rescue Unit, our own emergency service. They start working on this guy, but they've got no pulse, no nothing. The ambulance shows up and the paramedics take over. They're shaking their heads too until one of them does this thing with his knuckles on the victim's chest. I found out later it's a test for 'deep pain response'. He did this a couple of times and our victim suddenly sits up. Turns out he was totally ossified drunk, and his story was that he was looking at this knife his friend had given him when he must've fallen asleep on the bench.

I don't remember what I told the dispatcher, but I distinctly remember saying, "Why's everybody looking at *me?*"

Ain't Love Grand?

There's no way to tell war stories without throwing in an occasional doozy. Those of you who are under eighteen years of age should not read this one unless you are accompanied by an adult. There, now I'm off the hook.

There was a cop in District Thirty whose well-earned nickname was 'Rambo'. While he certainly wasn't the sharpest knife in the drawer, he was good people, and definitely the guy you wanted behind you if you needed help. He wore a rack of medals above his shield that was disproportionate to his time on the job.

One day Rambo had the post at the Boro Hall subway station in downtown Brooklyn. He made an arrest for first-degree robbery, a great collar. He locks up a bald-headed black skell for robbing this white Wall Street yuppie at knifepoint in the men's bathroom. Like most homeless criminals, the guy was a real dirty, stinky pain in the ass. Like most yuppies, the victim was an annoying, self-righteous pain in the ass. Both were taken back to the district office.

For a serious crime such as robbery, even when an arrest was made the district detectives would conduct an investigation. First, they interviewed the victim of the robbery, the yuppie. He made it clear, very clear, that he wanted the man who robbed him punished to the fullest extent of the law. And he knew the law. After all, he was a taxpayer, and he paid our salaries, et cetera. We've heard it all before.

When the detectives interviewed the suspect, the stinky, bald-headed skell, the story took on a twist: "Robbed him? *Robbed* him?

That muthafucka robbed me!" Veteran police officers are used to hearing denials from perpetrators; even those caught red-handed sometimes swear they didn't do it. We've heard this all before too. "Muthafucka say he give me ten dollars I let him suck my dick, then the fool don't pay. The man owe me ten dollars! I want my damn money!" *Eh?*

The detectives re-interview the victim. He reiterates his story, that the guy robbed him at knifepoint in the men's room. "Sir, are you aware that filing a false police report is a crime in the state of New York?" The yuppie gets all excited, "What are you talking about? I was robbed, and I want that man arrested!" The detective was very cool: "Sir, are you aware that patronizing a prostitute is also a crime in the state of New York?" The guy almost has a stroke. "What? *What?* That's outrageous! What's your badge number? How dare you—" The detective interrupted, "Excuse me sir, what is that?" and pointed to a big, wet spooch stain on the lapel of the yuppie's Brooks Brothers suit. Heavy pause: "Well, I won't press charges if he won't..."

The Criminal Mind

I'm taking the 'A' train home one night from Brooklyn after working a four-to-twelve tour. The train is pretty empty. At Euclid Avenue, these two guys get on the train and I immediately sized them up as being up to no good. They didn't disappoint me. They look around as if they own the place, then they check the cars on each end of ours. I'm just minding my own business like any other passenger. They zero in on this little Chinese guy. Perfect. One sits down next to him while the other stands guard. "Yo, man, you got any money?" He apparently doesn't speak English, thinks this is a friendly greeting and smiles away. I glance over and the lookout gives me a hard look meant to tell me to keep on minding my own business. I take the hint and look away, back to my passenger act. "C'mon man, I wanna get some juice. You got a dollar?" The victim-to-be is nodding and grinning, not comprehending. Now, under the law, a police officer doesn't have to wait for a crime to actually be committed in order to take action, as long as he reasonably believes one is *about* to happen. I eye them again, and the lookout says, "Yo, what are *you* looking at?" Well, that was all I needed. "I'm looking at *you*, motherfucker," my shield in one hand and Roscoe in the other.

The statements made next served well to give insight into the thought processes of the street criminal. Bear in mind that I was sitting right there from the time these two first got on the train. The lookout, his brazen challenge to me thrown back in his face, blurted out:

"I didn't *do* nothin'!"
"You didn't *see* nothin'!"
"I ain't *with* him!"
"I ain't *here!*"

That's what he said, word-for-word, no shit. I flagged a passing train-patrol cop at the next stop and we took both knuckleheads and the would-be victim off the train. Click, click, two under. "You guys like to play games? Now you're gonna play *my* game." While I was legally justified in intervening when I did, they had yet to commit a crime... tonight. I called in a warrant check. As we waited for the results, the guy who had been asking for the money got very quiet. Turned out he was wanted by Nassau County. Gee, what a shock. I had the cop issue a summons for harassment to the lookout, and my cuffs stayed on his buddy. The Chinese guy was oblivious to all of this (I found out later he was *really* Chinese, like right off the boat). I called the local district and told the desk officer I had one under arrest for an outstanding warrant. There was a long pause on the phone—"You're off-duty and you've got an arrest for *what?*"

This particular desk officer and I weren't exactly friends. I was a sergeant, but he was a lieutenant—and I wasn't looking forward to this. I brought my prisoner into the district, and there he is, behind the desk like a statue, just looking down at the desk blotter. As I stand my prisoner in front of the desk, he says to the lieutenant, "We wasn't *really* gonna rob that guy..." Oh, thank you.

When the Revolving Door Gets Stuck

So, I've got my off-duty arrest for harassment with an active warrant from another jurisdiction thrown in for good measure. My prisoner has just made a pretty incriminating statement right in front of the desk officer. I'm searching him, and under his jogging pants he's got another pair of jogging pants, and... hey, wait a minute—how many pairs of pants is this guy wearing? Five, count 'em, *five* pairs of pants, all different colors. How come? Thin clothing in layers for warmth? No. Advanced perp technique. Multiple layers of differently-colored garments are worn so that after a crime, you simply strip off a layer and now you don't fit whatever clothing description the cops are looking for.

I know this desk lieutenant doesn't like me at all, but what must've sounded like an extremely hoop-de-scoop arrest when I first called him on the phone was now magically appearing right in front of his eyes to be a fairly savvy piece of police work. This is good, because otherwise he'd fuck me around for sure. "See, I had to lock this guy up. Good collar, eh?" He nods his head, "Sure is." I ask, "So, who are you gonna assign to process the arrest?" It was customary that when a sergeant made an arrest, that a police officer was assigned to do all the paperwork and to transport the prisoner. The lieutenant smiled at me and said, "You." I said, "Oh, come on, you're not still pissed about that time I lost my fucking hat, are you?"

So, I'm down in Queens Central Booking. The routine at the time was that you'd drop your prisoner off downstairs at QCB, then you'd go upstairs and sit down with an assistant district attorney to draw up the court papers. When I explained all the circumstances to the ADA, he was very happy with the arrest. In fact, he was kinda disappointed that we weren't able to charge the guy with attempted robbery since it was pretty obvious that's what he was up to. We call the victim on the phone and his American sponsor shortstops the call. Just as well since the victim apparently spoke no English at all; he was an exchange student or something. The ADA explains the case to the sponsor, telling him that we need the victim to come down and sign the papers to press charges. "No way," he says; he doesn't want his foreign guest involved. I get on the phone and tell him he's *already* involved, and that had I not intervened when I did, that he'd be trying to explain to the embassy why this guy got killed while he was sponsoring him! Tough talk, but no dice. The victim's not coming in. No matter, I'll call Nassau County. I get a Nassau detective on the phone and he says, "You got him? Great! When can you bring him out here?" I explain that I'm an off-duty transit cop with no car, and ask if they could pick him up. "Sorry, no, we don't have anyone available to take a drive out there..." Looks like I'm stuck. The ADA says, "Well, okay, we'll see what happens. Sit tight."

So I sit. The ADA goes home at the end of his shift and I sit. Nobody knows what to do with this case, and I sit. Every time I try to get it moved, it's Catch-22: they can't prosecute without a complaining victim, but they can't release the prisoner because there's an active warrant issued for him by another jurisdiction. And I sit.

When the first ADA I dealt with came back on duty for another shift, I lost my temper. "Will somebody around here make a decision with this fucking case?" The supervising ADA comes out of his office and admonishes me, "Officer, just lower your voice!" I turn on him: "That's *Sergeant* to you, buddy, and while you guys all went home and slept, I've been sitting here making about a million dollars in overtime for absolutely nothing! Am I gonna die here, or what?" After this little outburst, we finally worked it all out. The Queens DA declined to prosecute, and the Nassau detectives consented to our releasing the prisoner. All in writing. What a shame, because this guy really was a piece of shit.

Seventeen hours after this caper started, I'm about to go home. Well, not so fast! The procedure required that I release the prisoner personally. Okay, no biggie. I go downstairs to QCB with the release papers. "What do you mean, he's not here?" They tell me that he was taken to some precinct stationhouse for overnight lodging. "You mean I gotta go *where?*" Remember, I don't have a car—but at this point I do have a beard. I demand to talk to the QCB supervisor.

Who comes out, but my old buddy and former squad sergeant. "Oh, am I glad to see you!" I tell him the whole silly story. Shaking his head, he says, "Sorry, Tre, rules are rules. I wish I could help you." I'm on my knees begging him. "Well, maybe we could make an exception just this once, but... there's one thing I need from you." Relieved, I say, "You name it, Stan, whatever you want!" He smiles and asks: "Who's your hook?"

Another Shaggy Dog Story

Back in the late 80's the Transit Police Department was publicly embarrassed when a memo from a district commander appeared in the newspapers. It seemed that the memo confirmed what the department had always adamantly denied—that there was, in fact, a summons quota. This memo spelled out in great detail how many tickets were expected each month from the cops, as well as what would happen if they failed to make the number. Of course, the department's response to this scandal was to declare the commander a rogue and drum him out of the corps. They made him retire. It's a good thing they did, too, because the guy must've been nuts. Everybody knows there's no such thing as a summons quota. And there's no such thing as the Mafia, either.

Incredibly, right on the heels of this nonsense, the department issued another internal edict: All officers assigned to RMP duty will perform a minimum of two 'ejections' per tour. Translated: If you are assigned to a police car (which is a desirable assignment) you'd better throw at least two people off the Transit Authority's property during your shift, or else tomorrow you'll be walking instead of riding. These people still have egg dripping off their faces over the summons-quota memo being leaked to the press, and here's another 'no such thing as a quota' quota, in writing.

Ejections were an enforcement option that could be used instead of writing tickets. Simply put, the cop would tell the person to leave the subway. If the person didn't leave, the cop would physically throw the person out, like a bar-room bouncer. Generally, we reserved this option for those who were obnoxious, drunk and disorderly, real stinky, or otherwise not summonsable for whatever reason. Doing an ejection could be very hazardous.

One of the good things about ejecting people was that the cop did not need to identify the person on the ejection report. If the person's name was known, fine. The name would go on the report. If the cop didn't have a name, he would simply check the box marked 'unidentified' and list a brief physical description of the person on the report. Cops, being cops, quickly figured out a loophole in this procedure. I'm not saying that any cops turned in fake ejection reports; let's just say that some of these 'unidentified' people would be pretty hard to track down...

One night in 1989 I'm on patrol in Brooklyn with Booger. We get a call of a 'vicious dog' inside the subway at the Bedford/Nostrand station. We get there and find this big German shepherd roaming around the mezzanine. He's not vicious, but he's also not leaving. Now, Booger's a good cop, but he's also a good man. He used to be a preacher. I never saw him mistreat anyone or anything. Some cops might've kicked the dog or even sprayed him with mace to get him out of the station. Booger goes upstairs to the car, comes down with a sandwich, and bite-by-bite lures the dog out of the subway. We close the gate and move on.

Later that night we're sitting in the car and Booger's writing up an ejection report. I asked him what he was doing since I didn't remember ejecting anyone that night. He mumbled something; I didn't hear. I looked over his shoulder and saw him writing, "...adult male, wearing a brown fur coat..." Oh, Boog.

Famous Last Words

One of the scariest crime scourges of the eighties was the rise of the so-called 'wolfpack'. This was when a group of young men (usually teenagers) numbering anywhere from three or four to sometimes well over twenty, would simply go on a rampage, attacking people at will. It was kind of like army ants on the march because they would pretty much destroy anything and anyone in their path. Nobody really ever knew why this phenomenon came to pass in the eighties, or for that matter, why it eventually subsided. Just an aside—the term 'wolfpack' came to be considered politically incorrect by the end of the decade. It was replaced in the news media by the expression 'wilding,' like it was an event or something. Apparently, they felt it was okay to say that someone *acted like* a vicious animal, but you couldn't say someone *was* a vicious animal. The philosophical difference was lost on me, having seen the innocent victims too many times. In any case, this particular social problem, like so many others, tended to gravitate toward the New York City subway system.

One night we received an urgent radio broadcast of a wolfpack robbery on board a Brooklyn-bound IRT train. The robbery was reported at Fulton Street in lower Manhattan. I knew something was up when the politically-incorrect dispatcher started calling cars from the adjacent district as well. The broadcast was, "...twenty males robbing and assaulting passengers on a southbound train. Perp number one—male wearing a green coat, NFD [no further description]. Perp number two—male wearing a dark coat, NFD. Perp number three, dark clothing, NFD. All other perps, NFD." The fact that there wasn't very much information was to be expected. In an emergency, they'd broadcast whatever info they had, however incomplete. On my way to the Clark Street station in Brooklyn Heights, the first station in Brooklyn for IRT trains coming from Manhattan, I flagged down a precinct car and told them I had a wolfpack on an incoming train. They followed me and called for their friends on the way.

Henderson (his first name—really) had the post at Clark Street. No dummy, he stopped the incoming train with a flashlight signal and was holding it outside the station when we arrived. When I say we, I mean WE. Without exaggeration, I brought about a thousand city, housing and transit cops with me. We signaled the train's motorman to enter the station just far enough so that the first door cleared the tunnel entrance. He did, and we opened that door with our secret transit cop keys, leaving all the rest of the train's doors closed. You'd be amazed at how many cops can flood onto a subway train through one door...

The train was moderately crowded, and in technical police terminology, 'nothing was going on'. The passengers were all just sitting or standing, watching with New Yorker boredom as we swept through the train, with me and Henderson in the lead. About halfway through the train, Henderson says, "Hey Sarge, you see those two guys in the next car?" He pointed out that they were taking off their dark-colored jackets. As we entered that train car I told a couple of cops behind us to stay and watch them. The rest of us continued through the train, finding absolutely nothing by the time we reached the last car. We returned to he car with the two guys who'd been taking off their coats.

I asked the dispatcher if there was anything further on the descriptions. There wasn't, but there *was* a victim in Manhattan. I'm looking at all these perfectly normal-looking people in this train car, all looking very innocent and saying nothing. I'm also looking at about half the police officers in Brooklyn. I know this is pretty thin, but... "You two—stand up." I tell the cops who were watching over them, "Take them." Click, click, two under. There's mumbling from the other passengers, and someone behind me curses. I turn and ask, "Is there a problem here?" A passenger says, "Yo man, this is messed up." I ask why, and he says, "Because they didn't *do* anything!" I asked, "How do you know?" He says, "'Cause they were with me!" It got real quiet in that subway car. "Take him, too." Click, click...

Reader's note: Despite the fact that his eyes were nearly swollen shut as a result of the beating he suffered, when the Manhattan transit cops brought the victim to Clark Street, he was able to positively identify at least *some* of his assailants.

Smoke Signals

We had no choice but to resort to flagging down precinct cars sometimes, because for whatever reason, District Thirty was the only district we knew of that didn't equip its cars with portable NYPD radios. The only explanation we were ever given for this is that we covered too many different precincts—but we believed the real reason was that they just didn't want us getting involved in 'street shit'.

Larry and I were cruising down the block when we saw a gaggle of precinct cars flying all over the place. We had no idea what was going on (since we didn't have their radios) so Larry wisely skirted what appeared to be the epicenter of the emergency. We drove down a side street a block away and people were scurrying everywhere. Something was definitely going on here. We pulled up alongside a woman running down the middle of the street with two kids in tow.

"Hey lady, what's going on?" Without breaking stride she said hysterically, *"Omigod omigod he's got a gun they didn't get him he's gonna kill us!"* All the precinct cops were chasing her husband. "Get in!" She told us he ran out the back of the building when the cops showed up. "Thirty Robert, central, we got a man with a gun, have CPO [city police officers] meet us at, uh... standby!" There was a precinct car coming down the block. We flagged them down, and within ten frantic minutes, the enraged hubby was in custody.

We said goodbye to the precinct cops and drove away. I picked up the radio to give the happy ending to the story, "Thirty Robert, central." The dispatcher exploded: "THIRTY ROBERT, WHAT'S YOUR LOCATION? WE'VE BEEN TRYING TO RAISE YOU FOR FIFTEEN MINUTES!!" I answered, "Sorry, we've been busy..."

Battle of the Sexists

People see female cops today and no one gives it a second thought. It wasn't always so. Historically, women in the police department weren't considered to be the equals of men; they performed specialized and limited assignments only. In the early eighties, though, the titles 'Patrolman' and 'Policewoman' gave way to 'Police Officer' when for the first time, women were assigned to general patrol duties. This change was not without controversy, and the issue of women on patrol was marked by a tragic milestone in 1984 when a transit cop in Brooklyn became the first female officer in the United States to be killed in the line of duty.

There's no doubt that the women had a hard way to go in the beginning. It seemed that any actions they took (or failed to take) were Monday-morning quarterbacked by the male cops. That in itself wasn't really unexpected, but there usually wasn't any middle ground on the resulting calls. The female officers on whom male judgment was being passed were now unfairly labeled to one extreme or the other: either incompetent and cowardly, or brilliant and heroic. If only police work was so neatly black-and-white.

During the time I was a sergeant in District Thirty, the Transit Police Department was engaged in an experiment known as 'Team Policing'. It was an unsuccessful attempt to modify the existing 'Community Policing' programs which were then in vogue to fit our subterranean environment. One of the technical aspects of this was that the district was sub-divided into separate sectors, and so were the cops.

Marilyn had one sector; I had another. While I wouldn't go so far as to call us rivals, there was certainly an aspect of competition between our sectors. She was a good sergeant, but was also officially designated as a Great Cop. I remember the first time I heard the cops talking about her: "Oh, Marilyn? She's a great cop, man! This one time, Eddie had this EDP [emotionally-disturbed person] down on the tracks, right, and he's rolling around with this guy, right, and fuckin' Marilyn, she just jumps right down on the tracks with him..."

Okay, maybe it was petty of me, but after hearing the "Marilyn and Eddie on the Tracks" story for about the hundredth time, I had to ask: "How come I never hear anybody saying what a great cop Eddie is?"

Violation of the Haberdashery Act

One night there was a robbery at the Franklin Avenue subway station. The robber jumped to the tracks and ran into the tunnel toward the Nostrand Avenue station to escape the cops chasing him. Rather than follow him into the tunnel, they immediately put the job on the radio and let all the other cops know what was going on. Now the cops at Nostrand Avenue are waiting for the guy. The only problem is that somewhere about halfway between the two stations is an emergency exit—a stairway leading from the tunnel area up to the street, where it looks like just some kind of grating on the sidewalk. Larry and I, being expert subway coppers, know all about the old emergency exit trick. We drove over to the exit between Franklin and Nostrand. The cops at Franklin Avenue then gave out a highly improbable description of the robber over the radio: he was wearing an orange jacket and red pants. No shit. Like you couldn't spot a bad guy dressed like that. No matter, really, because *anyone* popping out of that emergency exit was getting grabbed.

We must've sat on that exit for forty minutes. It was a social thing; we're actually hanging out with cops from the local precinct telling war stories. While we were doing this, other cops are riding trains back and forth between Franklin and Nostrand looking for this guy, but he's apparently in the wind. Finally, someone called the whole job off. Time to take a report and resume patrol. The precinct cops leave. We're standing in front of a Chinese restaurant getting ready to leave ourselves when Larry tugs on my sleeve and says, "I don't believe it." Inside the restaurant is a guy with an orange jacket and red pants. We do our best not to show any interest or reaction while I call the other cops on the radio to see if they still have the robbery victim with them at Franklin Avenue. They do, and I tell them we're about to stop a suspect at our location.

So, we walk into the restaurant with money in our hands like we're about to order dinner. We walk up to the take-out counter, looking at the overhead menus, right behind our guy who's doing the same thing. Without warning, he's got a gun stuck in his ribs from behind: "Hello..."

The restaurant is perfect for a show-up identification; it's all windows and brightly-lit inside. The car with the victim pulls up and has a perfect one-way view of our guy, who can't see anything outside the restaurant because it's dark out. We're quite pleased with ourselves and we're just waiting for the victim to confirm that this is the robber, which seems to be a mere formality at this point. "No good," they tell us on the radio. *What?* That's right; the victim said it wasn't the guy.

I don't know what's worse—that a person could be so terrified of a criminal that they'd refuse to identify him, or that there could be two people out there with that kind of taste in clothing.

The Great Stagecoach Robbery

We never had enough cops to cover all the assignments we needed to. One day, I realized that we always assigned a cop to the Clinton/Washington subway station, but nobody seemed to know why. In Transit Police jargon, an assignment like this was known as a 'fixer'. But why Clinton/Washington? "The Pratt Institute is right upstairs..." Okay, but so what? We hadn't had any reported crimes there for as far back as anyone could remember.

Well, this was *my* sector. If we were going to do this team-policing thing right, then by golly, *I* was going to decide where my people were assigned. No more of this, 'we always did it this way'. My cops would be assigned where the crime was. I cancelled the fixer at Clinton/Washington.

A couple of days later, when I came in to work after my regular days off, another sergeant met me at the door: "Tre, did you pull the fixer at Clinton/Washington?" I nodded, "Yeah, why?" He had a real serious look on his face. "We had a robbery there last night." Big deal. "I got a lot of robberies to worry about. What's so special about this one?" He says, "A couple of mutts took all the passengers off the train at gunpoint, lined them up against the wall, and robbed everybody." I notice a small group of sergeants and cops has silently gathered around us and is anxiously awaiting my response. Never at a loss for words, I said, "Everybody?"

No Hard Feelings

The DeKalb Avenue subway station is located right underneath the back end of the Albee Square shopping mall. We used to have a big problem with groups of young hoodlums doing robberies in the subway and escaping into the shopping mall, and vice-versa. The other end of the mall opened onto Fulton Street, a generally crowded thoroughfare and another good escape route.

One night, Eddie and I responded to a report of a robbery at the closed end of the DeKalb Avenue station. A couple of foot cops also show up. It's the same old story—a group of mutts beat the crap out of someone, took all his money and jewelry, and then ran into the back end of Albee Square. I ask the victim if he'd come with us into the mall to find these guys. My streetwise partner says, "We do that, Sarge, these boys gonna be history, right out onto Fulton Street." I ask if he's got a better plan. He does; we all go into the huddle.

Eddie and I drive around to the front of the mall on Fulton. We get out of the car and call the other guys on the radio, "We're in position, come on through." They bring the victim into the back end of the mall and start walking toward us. Next thing we hear on the radio is, *"Coming your way!"* Moments later we see, through the crowded mall, two young men running toward us while looking back over their shoulders. The other cops were right behind them. When they spotted us, they both get these 'oh, shit' looks on their faces—we were between them and good ol' Fulton Street. In a scene reminiscent of a football drill, they tried to get past us to break for night-time daylight in the street. Sorry, fellas, no luck this time! I tackled one, Eddie got the other.

I handcuff my guy and pick him up off the ground. As he stands up, the biggest handgun I've ever seen in my life falls out of his waistband. It was a nickel-plated Smith & Wesson .41 Magnum revolver with a six-inch barrel, fully loaded with jacketed hollow points. Now it's our turn to have the 'oh, shit' looks—this cannon would've perforated our body armor with ease.

Anyway, we're getting ready to leave the mall with our prisoners when an angry group approaches our car and tells us that they take exception to the terrible way we've treated these two fine young men. I tell them that if they have a problem with us, to feel free and make a complaint. We drive off to the district just a few blocks from the mall.

We're in the command processing the collars when the group shows up at the door. They're inside now, talking to the desk officer, telling him all about our misconduct, our brutality, et cetera. They demand blah, blah, blah... In walks Dominick, who's done for the day and about to go off-duty. As he's passing the disgruntled group, he does a double-take, walks right up to one of them and says, "Hey, don't I know you?" Click, click. Dom locks the guy up for a past robbery committed with—you guessed it—a big, silver revolver. Strangely enough, the group is now satisfied with our performance of duty. They say they've changed their minds about filing a civilian complaint, and they leave.

Don't let the door hit you in the ass.

Still Waters Run Deep

One night the token booth at the Bedford/Nostrand subway station got robbed. The clerk was able to give a fairly good clothing description of the bandits, and the search was on. Booger and I are driving around the neighborhood hoping to spot them. For a transit cop, making an arrest on a booth robbery was better than if you caught the guy on the grassy knoll. After all, we *did* work for the railroad barons.

We're driving up Classon Avenue when we pass by a bodega. We just caught a quick look, but inside the store were a couple of guys who seemed to be wearing what the clerk had described. We stop the car, call for back-up, and go inside. We've got our guns out, and as we enter I announce very calmly, "Everybody—hands up." Everybody's hands go up. "You three, face down, on the ground." Down they go. No commotion, real smooth. So smooth, as a matter of fact, that another customer then paid for his purchase at the register, asked if he could go, and when I nodded, he left the bodega. The guy behind the counter resumed eating his sandwich and watching whatever he was watching on his little black & white television. What, are we in the twilight zone?

Our back-up arrives. I tell the three guys on the floor, "Okay, gentlemen, put your hands behind your backs." I gesture to the cops to start cuffing them. One of the guys on the floor asks politely, "Officer, why are we being arrested?" I tell him, "You're not being arrested. Don't worry, if you didn't do it, we'll take the cuffs off. We're just bringing someone over to take a look at you 'cause you fit the description from a robbery." While still face down, he asks quietly, "Uh... which robbery?"

What's your shield?
Unit, What is your shield?
Come back
with that shield?
She's got
to be kidding
10-13!
10-13!!

Wolf! Wolf!

The most serious radio call in any police department is when an officer needs assistance. That high priority is not as self-serving as it might seem at first. Somebody who'd cause an armed police officer to call for help would obviously present an even greater danger to any citizen. Furthermore, if a cop gets his ass kicked, how is he going to protect the public? So, next time you see the cops up on the sidewalk doing ninety miles an hour with lights and sirens going, please get out of the way—they're doing it for you.

One time as a cop, I had the post at the 69th Street/Fiske subway station in Queens when there was a radio signal 10-13 [officer needs help] at the Elmhurst Avenue station. My station and Elmhurst are both one stop away from the Roosevelt Avenue complex, although on different subway lines. I run downstairs and commandeer a passing car. All we've got to do is drive along Roosevelt Avenue for about four or five blocks, make a quick right onto Broadway, go another two blocks, and I'm there. My adrenaline is pumping but the job is called off as we turn onto Broadway. The cop's okay, I thank the motorist, and I catch a '7' train back to my post. No sooner am I back at 69th Street than there's another signal 10-13, this time at Roosevelt. I run downstairs again, commandeer another passing car, and I'm off to Roosevelt. This time I made it. Here's what happened: The cop at Elmhurst is struggling with someone who's resisting arrest. He radios for help (the first 10-13). A woman on the train sees that the cop's in trouble as her train pulls out of Elmhurst, so she jumps off at the next stop and dials 911. There was a bit of a language barrier and all they got was that she was at Roosevelt and a cop needed help. They put out another 10-13 at Roosevelt. It all became clear when the cop from Elmhurst, his prisoner locked in the car, came running into Roosevelt in response to the *second* 10-13 and ran into the woman who had called 911 on his behalf, who was thrilled (in whatever language she spoke) that he was okay...

One time as a sergeant, I responded to a radio call of an officer needing assistance at the Kingston/Throop subway station in Brooklyn. The dispatcher said the call came from 911. We used to get a lot of bogus 911 calls, but you still had to go. A whole bunch of us show up, find nothing, and I call it off. Less than a minute later, the radio starts again, "All units, Kingston and Throop, signal ten-thirteen *from the officer!*" Pretty hard for that to be fake. We're all running around in circles looking for the cop in trouble when I realized that we never heard any call from a cop over the radio. "Central, did this call come over the air?" The dispatcher said, "Negative, it came from the signal desk." Okay, hold it. Hold everything. I yell for all the cops to gather around—there had to be a dozen or so. "Was anyone on the phone with the signal desk before?" One cop raised her hand: "I was making my ring, I told them I was at K and T, when that first thirteen came over." Hmmm... "Then what happened?" She says, "I told them, I gotta go, I got a ten-thirteen, and I hung up." And the cop on the signal desk, thinking she was in trouble, ran over to the radio dispatcher and said, "I was just on the phone with a cop at Kingston and Throop, she needs help!"

And on either of these jobs, had there been a third call we'd have done it all over again.

Impatience Is The Better Part Of Valor

I've always hated working on the Fourth of July. The following excerpt from a 'request for departmental recognition' may explain why:

"... both officers were in the RMP on the corner of Flatbush Avenue and Nevins Street when an apparently disturbed individual ran through heavy holiday traffic to cross Flatbush Avenue and approached the RMP. He was rambling about "men following him" and that they were "trying to kill him," while gesturing toward a vacant newsstand. The man then frantically tried to enter the RMP, but was unable since the doors were locked. Suddenly, the man ran around to the front of the RMP, pulled a butcher knife from his jacket and began waving it, still raving incoherently about men trying to kill him...

Although both officers were relatively safe while in the RMP, for fear that the man in his deranged state would attack passersby or be struck by an automobile, both officers exited the RMP and approached the man. Using extreme caution not to further agitate the individual, Officer A calmly ordered the man to put the knife down. After a brief, tense moment the man complied. Officer A immediately seized the knife from the hood of the car, while Officer B quickly placed the man in handcuffs for safety. The man was later removed to a psychiatric ward by NYC EMS."

Now, let me tell you what *really* happened. 'Officer A' was Booger. We were on our way to get something to eat. It's about 8:30 pm, we've been running around all night and we're both hungry. I see this nut job coming up to the car. The reason the doors were locked is that 'Officer B' (me) was just a little quicker than Mr. Wackadoo. It's a holiday weekend, there are cops on every street corner, and this guy's gotta fuck with us on our way to lunch? I tell Booger, "C'mon, let's get outta here!" It was as we tried to pull away from the curb that he ran around to the front of the car and pulled the knife. "Aw, shit!" I got on the radio and called for EMRU [Transit Emergency Service] to come quick. The precinct cops on the corner can see something's obviously going on; I tell them on the loudspeaker to stay away, the guy's got a knife. We'll just sit tight and wait for them to come with a net to throw over our friend.

I don't know if I mentioned it before, but Booger's a big man. Big men get hungry. And it *is* lunchtime. Before I realized what he was doing, he's getting out of the car. "*Boog!*" Too late—he's out on his side, scolding this loon: "Okay, fella, quit foolin' around. Put that knife down!" The precinct cops started running toward us as I covered my eyes...

After the guy was in custody, I assigned the precinct cops to take the guy to the hospital, touching off a pissing contest between us and the precinct. Everybody starts calling me on the radio. Hey, this whole thing was a street job anyhow, and we *still* hadn't eaten. To hell with the calls; as soon as the ambulance departed for Bellevue we drove over to a nearby McDonald's. While we were waiting for our food, some guy starts choking to death on a cheeseburger. This night is really getting to be a pain in the ass. We did the ol' Heimlich maneuver and saved his life. Between them dogging me on the radio, and the fact that we were starving, we left without doing any paperwork or even getting his name.

I managed to straighten out the flap with the precinct, and we were later awarded 'Letters of Merit' for disarming the knife-wielding nut. Personally, I would've rather gone to a barbecue, ate hot dogs and drank beer.

Imperfect Match

Transit cops would deal with token-booth clerks, and token-booth clerks would deal with money, but transit cops would not deal with money. Not ever. Guard it, yes, even escort it, but never touch it. You weren't even supposed to think about it. We had some pretty peculiar rules concerning the Transit Authority's money. One of my personal favorites was the patrol guide procedure on 'revenue escorts': The cop was to have no glove on his shooting hand; the service revolver was to be unlocked and ready to draw. The best part was that the procedure spelled out that the cop was to "remain alert and ready for attack at all times" *while escorting the cash...* Not surprisingly, some took that to mean it was okay to be brain-dead the rest of the time.

Every so often a token-booth clerk would come across counterfeit money. Their procedure required them to call us. Our procedure was baffling. One part of it said, "Members [transit cops] shall not presume to be experts on counterfeit currency." Then why call us?

One night my guys called for a patrol supervisor to respond to a possible counterfeit situation. I get there to find two cops holding a very indignant passenger. They look embarrassed and motion to the token-booth. The clerk lets me in and tells me the passenger tried to pass him counterfeit money. "Show me." He gives me this dollar bill. Hmmm... It looks good to me. He starts babbling like an idiot about the serial numbers. I have no idea what he's talking about. He snatches the bill back and says, "Look, look! The two numbers, they don't match!" I looked at the bill again. He's right—they don't match. The bill was also taped together down the center. Evidently, someone had torn a couple of singles in half and taped the halves from two different bills back together, probably by accident. Good grief.

I left the token booth with the 'bogus' bill and walked up to the passenger my cops were holding. I looked him right in the eye and said, "Let me see your socks." Dead silence. Blank stares. *Nobody* got it. Look, if he's got two different halves taped together, then somewhere there's another buck made of the *other* halves taped together, like the joke about the guy wearing one blue sock and one brown, who says, "And I got another pair at home just like it..." Oh, forget it.

I gave the passenger back his dollar and said, "Pay the clerk with something else before I shoot him. Good night."

Karma

There's a saying: 'What goes around, comes around.' Don't know if it's true, but...

Things always seemed to happen when one shift went off duty as the other one came on. One afternoon, just as we were starting our 4x12 tour, the cops at the Franklin Avenue subway station called for help. Franklin Avenue was at the boundary between two districts. It was District 30's last station; the next one belonged to District 33. Since the distress call came from the cops themselves, everybody went, day tours, four-to-twelves, both commands, everybody.

There had been a shooting aboard a crowded train. In the understandable melee that followed, four guys got locked up and were taken back to district thirty. Several more, including one with a gunshot wound, were taken to Long Island College Hospital.

I'm at the hospital with a couple of cops and the gunshot victim. We were still piecing together what had happened, but something about this victim struck me as a little off. Call it a hunch, intuition, whatever, I just didn't like his demeanor. I told the cops, "Listen, these guys aren't under arrest—yet. Do *not* let them out of your sight, okay?" Then I told one of the cops to start taking the report. He shakes his head, points to his collar brass and says, "Hey Sarge,

I'm from thirty-three." I point to my stripes: "Yeah? I'm from thirty. Now take the fucking report!"

The transit detectives showed up at the hospital and I left. Some time later, back at the district, I found out the whole story—it seems that one crew had tried to rob another, but one of the intended victims had a gun and shot one of the would-be robbers. The 'victim' that I had bad vibes about was in fact a bad guy, and he and his friends were arrested by the detectives at the hospital. Of the four guys who were brought to district thirty, with the exception of the actual shooter who was held on weapons and assault charges, all were released.

The desk officer and I were discussing the incident and I mentioned that on top of everything else, one of the cops from the other district had tried to weasel out of doing a simple report like I asked him to. The lieutenant shook his head. Just then, the phone rang; it was the desk officer from the other district. They talked for a few minutes, and after my lieutenant hung up he asked me the name of the cop who didn't want to take the report. I told him. "What balls," he laughed, "His boss was calling to make sure we didn't cut him out of the commendation request." Coincidentally, the concerned lieutenant from 33 was the same guy who threw *my* commendation request (the shootout with the stolen van) in the garbage can the year before.

Reader's note (for one reader only): If you should happen to be reading this story, well gee whiz, I'm real sorry about, uh, what's that cop's name again? Heh, heh…

That Grass Ain't So Green

We were checking the subway station at Lafayette Avenue when we found some old skell asleep on the platform, just lying on the concrete. Actually, at first we thought he might be dead but we quickly figured out he was just snoozing. He was pretty old and worn-out looking so we were as gentle as we could be when we woke him up. "You okay, sir?" Here's a guy with piss and shit all over his ragged clothes, and we're addressing him as 'sir'. I've found things to work much more smoothly that way. He stirs, realizes that we're cops, and says, "I'm okay, officers, thank you." I tell him, "Listen, you can't sleep here, okay? It's too cold, you could freeze to death." He says, "I'll be leaving now," and starts to gather up his possessions, which amounted to the rags on his back and a plastic bag with some empty cans in it. We just stood by, waiting quietly, since it took him a few minutes to get moving. When he was ready, we asked if he had someplace to go, someplace warmer. He assured us that he did—probably lying—and thanked us for our concern. As we're walking him out of the subway station we're making small talk about the weather. Then, the old skell says, "Boy, ain't that something 'bout Cristina Onassis?" The story in the headlines was that the heiress to the multi-billion dollar Greek shipping fortune had committed suicide. He was just shaking his head, "She got all that to live for and she kills herself. Hmmph."

Apocrypha

Every transit cop who ever worked a day on the road has had someone come up and ask if they could come into the subway without paying. The explanations given for the request varied, but after a while they all sounded the same. Different cops had different ways of handling this. Some would fall for any story; some wouldn't budge for even the most heartbreaking tale. Most of us fell somewhere in the middle. Usually, it worked out okay. If someone was pulling your leg and got away with it once, fine—Mother Transit didn't get her buck. If they came to the well too often (like twice), you'd simply have to settle for the satisfaction of telling them to take a walk.

Like the famous Five States game, it was pretty much accepted that you could torture someone a little bit as long as you planned on giving the person a break. One of my personal favorites was, when someone asked to get on for free because they had no money, to ask them to empty their pockets and prove it to me. Many declined: "You got no right to search me!" I'd smile and say, "You're right—

and you got no right to take the subway unless you pay the fare." This routine backfired on me once when a girl emptied her purse on the turnstile at my request, and out fell two marijuana joints. She got so hysterical thinking she was going to be arrested that I almost called her a taxi cab just to get rid of her.

District Thirty was located in the subway station at Hoyt-Schermerhorn, right near the Brooklyn courthouses. At least once or twice a day, some lowlife would knock on the door and ask with a straight face to get on for free, because "I just got outta jail." I'd always ask with an equally straight face, "Oh yeah? What'd you get locked up for?" Most didn't want to say. I'd insist. "Uh, they said it was robbery, but..." My usual response was, "Get the fuck out of here before I lock you up again." What a prick, huh?

One night, the knock on the door was a jailbird with a note, something that had just started recently. It was a pre-printed form letter from a Legal Aid attorney which said that so-and-so was just released from wherever, and to please admit him/her to the subway for free. I asked, "This guy's your lawyer?" He nodded. I jotted on the back of the note, "Give your client a token, you cheapskate," and signed my name. After a while we didn't get any more Legal Aid form letters.

My favorite story is one which I heard from 'a friend'. Some cop in Brooklyn (not me) is standing there when this guy comes up and says, "Officer, can I come in for a minute? I just want to talk to my boy over there." The cop can see someone sitting on a bench on the platform. "Him?" He says, "Yeah, him." What the hell, the cop figures, there's no train coming, and he lets him in without paying. This cop (not me, I swear) wasn't born yesterday, though, and he watches the guy walk down the platform and sit down next to the person on the bench. Soon enough, he comes walking back out. "Thanks, officer." A few minutes later, the man who was sitting on the bench comes up to the cop and says, "That guy just robbed me..."

Reader's note: If you'd like to know what 'apocrypha' means, look it up. I had to.

Interacting With The Ridership

Unlike many police departments across the country (and some across the street) the New York City Transit Police Department never had a problem with corruption. That's not to say we were scandal-free, we just had different problems. Rumor had it that we were prone to, uh, violence.

Since these were nothing more than rumors I won't dignify them with any sort of explanation. I will, however, tell you a joke that floated around for years. Ready?

> Q: How many transit cops does it take to throw a guy down a flight of stairs?
>
> A: None. He fell.

Reader's note: Hey, don't get excited. It's just a joke…

Be Vewy, Vewy Quiet…

Working in 'plainclothes' means not wearing a uniform or any other badge of office. This is not really the same thing as working 'undercover'. The subtle difference is that the undercover cop is usually trying to infiltrate some type of criminal organization. While that task has it's own inherent risks, the undercover cop is generally acting according to plan which hopefully doesn't include taking unexpected police action. On the other hand, the plainclothes cop is out on patrol, which means potluck. Sometimes, the plainclothes cop's worst enemy is his brother officer in uniform. Sometimes.

District Thirty had been plagued by a rash of armed robberies in the downtown Brooklyn area, all apparently committed by one lone gunman. It was starting to seem as if the bandit was thumbing his nose at us, and everyone wanted to collar this guy. We were flooding the area with cops, including plainclothes teams. Considering the unreliability of the Transit Police communications system, this was potentially a recipe for disaster, especially when it rained. After all, when the string between the tin cans got wet, the message sometimes got garbled.

It was a dark and stormy night, and Rambo was assigned to plainclothes at the Court Street subway station downtown. This particular station was as far underground as a coal mine and had a large freight elevator to bring passengers up and down from the platforms to the street level. Right next to the elevator was a stairway with about a million flights of stairs. On occasion, the robber used the stair/elevator trick to make good his getaway.

The job comes over the air of a 'man with a gun' at Court Street. Could it be our bandit? Nobody wants this guy more than Rambo. Everyone's riveted to the radio as we're all flying toward Court Street.

The dispatcher finally obliges: "Male white, thirties, wearing a black 'Motley Crue' tee-shirt, blue jeans, NFD." There's a long pause, and the patrol supervisor comes on the air: "Central, advise everyone that sounds like one of our plainclothes units!"

Rambo is no fool. He knows that a confrontation between armed police officers is a cop's worst nightmare. He takes up a position by the entrance to the staircase down to the platform level, and with his shield hanging around his neck, his anticrime color band on his wrist, his portable radio in one hand and his revolver in the other, he waits for uniformed backup to arrive. In the meantime, the bandit can scratch the stair trick off his list.

The first train that pulled in had several uniformed cops on it. They ran over to Rambo, who began to tell them his battle plan. The dispatcher came over the air again with the description of the gunman. The cops started laughing: "Hey Rambo—look down."

Heavy metal is a respectable form of music, listened to by all manner of people. Really.

Count Your Change

Here's a story I heard years ago that may or may not be true. Either way, I thought it was pretty funny...

As the story goes, some old skell got run over by a train. Although he miraculously survived he was taken to the hospital with some very serious injuries. The transit cops handling the accident did a thorough job, but for some reason unknown to the riding public, they would not restore subway service. The whole scene is frozen. This dragged on for some time until some boss showed up and wanted to know what the problem was. The cops took him aside and said, "We can't find his arm..." Upon overhearing this conversation between the cops, some other skell—apparently a drinking buddy of the victim—busts out laughing: "Boy, he ain't seen that arm since *Ko-rea!*"

From The Mouths Of Babes

One of the day-tour cops became a minor celebrity when he stopped a farebeat who attempted to pull a gun on him. Paul's ex-Marine fist was like a cinderblock, and a loaded 9mm was taken away from the beat, along with a large sum of drug money and a beeper. The news crews were waiting for Paul when he came out of court—not because it was the first time someone had tried to gun down a New York City cop, but because it was probably the first time for this particular farebeat—he was all of thirteen years old.

We all kidded Paul, but it really wasn't funny. The worst part about it was that the budding young thug was released on recognizance by a Family Court judge before Paul was even finished with his paperwork. It's a good thing we kept the gun.

Later that evening, there was a knock on the side door of the district. This was the one that all the losers used to knock on when they were trying to bum a free ride, so I always opened the door prepared. There's a guy who looks to be in his late twenties, and a little kid, maybe twelve or thirteen, tops. The guy's got a really grim look on his face. "Can I help you, sir?" The kid says, "Yeah, I want my gun back!"

It took me a second, but I realized that *this* was the little desperado who tried to draw down on Paul. Wow. He's not even into puberty yet! I ask the adult, "Who are you?" He's the older brother: "My mom sent me down here to find out if it was true, to find out if he got arrested today." Now my head is spinning. This kid, a juvenile drug dealer who tried to pull a loaded handgun on a uniformed cop, was released by a judge *on his own recognizance!* Junior pipes up with, "They said if I brought this ticket here, you'd give me my shit back." After what must've been a long pause on my part, I ask, "How old are you, young man?" He looks me straight in the eye and says defiantly, "Thirteen." I said, "Oh yeah? Well, you're just too fucking *young* to get your shit back."

The only satisfaction we could get in this minor (pardon the pun) miscarriage of justice was that, apparently, this little kid stood to receive more punishment from his superiors in his drug-dealing organization for losing the gun, the money and the beeper than he was facing from the courts.

Sticky Situation

In the heart of downtown Brooklyn you'll find the Jay Street subway station, with two of the borough's major subway lines, the 'A' and the 'F'. Since it's also transfer point between these lines the various trains would sometimes wait there in the station so that passengers could make their connections. The station is right underneath the headquarters of the Transit Authority, so I'm sure it's perfectly safe.

I'm strolling along one evening rush hour with my two cops when this guy comes up to us, identifies himself as an off-duty cop, and tells us that some people are being robbed in the front of the 'F' train that's parked there. Hey, nothing we can't handle. We start walking toward the front of the train. In hindsight, it would've been better had we told the conductor to close the doors.

Just before we came to the end of the train there was a flurry of movement, like we flushed a flock of birds out of the bushes. A couple of guys bolt out of the train and fly up the platform stairs. How did they see us coming? A couple more guys who had been sitting on the steps took off after them. They must've been the lookouts. Now the chase is on.

Danny and I are right behind them. We're moving pretty quick for two big guys. We fly up the stairs after them, leaving Danny's partner and the off-duty in the dust. Now we're on the mezzanine level. At this point I have to mention that the Jay Street station is huge; it stretches for several blocks underground. Danny and I are sprinting, and we're so close the bad guys can't even look over their shoulders, because if they slow down by one bit, they're bagged. Incredibly, they made it through a highwheel, a one-way revolving door used at some subway exits. That highwheel's spinning like an airplane propeller and we hit it right behind them, exploding through it together—*"Holy shit!"* Now we're flying toward the exit stairs leading to Fulton Street, but they're opening the distance. This is not good. As wild as the highwheel feat was, we're still packing way too much gear to be chasing a bunch of guys in jeans and sneakers. As we hit the last stairway I realized that they were gonna give us the slip. Well, we had run too far, too hard, and there was no way I was giving up that easy. In anger and desperation I screamed, *"Eeeyahhh,"* and threw my nightstick at the guy I was about to lose. Pow. Got him! Ha, ha, ha! Then I threw up.

Danny's partner wasn't sleeping while we were running. He had called for the cavalry on the radio. As I climbed up onto Fulton Street gasping for air I see lots of lights and hear sirens coming from every direction. Like an idiot I start running again. I don't know where Danny is; I think he croaked. A police car down by Livingston Street has got someone stopped. I stagger down there to see that it's one of the guys who fled from the train. Great! "Not so fast," the lieutenant in the car says, "You ain't puttin' him in *this* car!" Seems that in his panic to escape, the guy pooped his pants. Well, now I don't feel so bad about blowing my lunch, anyway.

After he ordered some other car to take our slightly exhausted and extremely smelly prisoner back to the district, I went back to the subway station. One of the district cops is standing there—with the guy I nailed with the nightstick. I was just about to ask why he wasn't in handcuffs when I saw the shield hanging from his neck. Brooklyn-Queens Plainclothes Task Force. Ooops…

I went to apologize about the little nightstick thing, and my cop is shaking his head, telling him, "Yo, man, this sergeant, he's *always* beatin' on the brothers. He hit you with his stick? Word! I never see him beatin' on the *white* cops. I'm tired of working for him! And *sore*, too."

Dummy Up

Supposedly, when you're no longer assigned to patrol duties it's easier to 'stay out of trouble'. I thought I'd be relatively safe while a captive of the training division, working in an office.

Pete and I were cops together in the late-night train patrol unit. We're working together again in training, but I'm a sergeant now. I never had any illusion of that protecting me, however—the common denominator for many of the people in the division was their similar educational backgrounds, and for the most part, rank wasn't that significant.

We were doing some training course for emergency situations at the Transit Museum in downtown Brooklyn. For one of the exercises, we needed to use this life-sized CPR dummy we had borrowed from somewhere. It seemed that the best way to get the dummy to the museum was to put it in the back of a police car and drive it over with us. After all, it's the same size and shape as a person, where better to put it than a car seat?

We all pile into the police car. Since I'm the boss, I sit up front. Pete sat in the back with another instructor, with the dummy sitting between them. We're driving down Tillary Street and the traffic starts to get congested. This is the heart of downtown during the afternoon, what did I expect? Well, it's safe to say I didn't expect what happened next. There's a commotion behind me; I almost jumped out of my seat. I turn around to see Pete punching the shit out of the CPR dummy. "Pete, what the fuck are you doing?" He's going to town on this poor dummy. People in the other cars are, uh, noticing this. Now he's got the dummy by the back of the neck and he's bashing it's head into the partition between the front and back seats of our marked blue-and-white police car. The other cars are swerving as we pass them in traffic, they're slamming on their brakes, they're wishing they had video cameras. They think this is something? Wait 'til they see what I do to Pete when I get my hands on him...

The Transit Museum is located directly underneath a tall office building on Schermerhorn Street. I didn't stop yelling at Pete until we got there, although the yelling was starting to get mixed with laughter, because I had to admit it was pretty funny. I know I'll be hearing about the 'incident' later, but it's too late now, it's done. Might as well laugh. "Okay, you dummies, bring your cousin downstairs, and quit screwing around." I went downstairs myself to get set up for the class. I'm down there a long time—and they're still upstairs. I went back up to the street to see what was keeping them, and I find there's a gathering crowd of maybe thirty people all looking up at the skyscraper. The roof turret lights of our police car are on, flashing away silently. The people, all passersby, are real quiet except for murmurs of, "He musta jumped." Pete's in the middle of the crowd, also craning his neck to look up... with our CPR dummy laying on the ground next to him covered by a sheet with the feet sticking out.

Office suicides are bad, but office beatings are worse. Ask Pete.

Pen Pal

One of my co-workers in the training division, John D., was a sarcastic, political maneuverer who had mastered the art of the stab in the back. He had carved out a veritable office empire and nearly everyone was intimidated by him to some extent. Not me. As a matter of fact, the beginning of our professional friendship can be traced to a brief but telling moment in time. He was imperiously walking down a hallway as if it were his, and as we passed, rather than offer any type of a normal greeting, he simply turned his head away and muttered under his breath, "Putz." Nearly simultaneously, I mumbled, "Fag…"

For all his bullshit, John really was an expert in the field. For some mysterious reason I think he took a liking to my way of doing business. He never stabbed me in the back—to the contrary, on several occasions he was actually quite helpful—however, there was simply no getting past his mean-spirited edges. Once, while I was working on a project in Manhattan, he became somehow involved from his kingdom in Brooklyn. I don't recall the specifics, but in response to his inimitable methods I sent him a handwritten note via department mail:

> "John,
> I noted with some interest that you had taken the time to get involved with the [whatever] project, and that you had even mentioned several items to Inspector Smith at the weekly staff meeting. Upon careful consideration I found your input to be very helpful. As always, your expertise and experience has served to enhance the quality of the training offered by this division, and I'd like to thank you for taking the time out to contribute to the improvement of a project that I'm solely responsible for. Although I will receive the credit for the success of this particular project, I do feel obligated to acknowledge the integral role you've played from behind the scenes, and to thank you for helping me with my own professional development as a training supervisor as well.
> Tre
> / signature /
>
> p.s. – Fuck you.

He told me later that he got a kick out of my little note. Someone else told me his coffee came out of his nose.

School Daze

For six months in 1991 I was an instructor at the NYPD Academy, teaching transit recruits. The recruit curriculum consisted of four basic subject areas: Law, Police Science, Social Science and physical training. It had not changed much since I myself was a recruit at the Academy. Maybe that's because only six years had gone by...

The good news about being an instructor at recruit school is that you've got the perfect audience for telling war stories. Recruits will believe just about anything. Of course, even their gullibility limits can be exceeded, if you really work at it.

The bad news is that I was a police science instructor. That's 'police science' with a capital 'yawn'. For the most part, police science is the study of departmental rules and procedures. Like, what form do you fill out if such-and-such happens, and who gets which color copy of said form, *ad nauseum*. The stuff was deadly boring to read, let alone to teach. The worst part about it was that they actually expected me to look at the lesson plans before I'd teach classes. Can you believe that?

One fortuitous aspect of teaching police science was that for some reason the Academy made the recruits lug their patrol guides back and forth with them at all times. Maybe it had to do with building strong muscles or something. Anyway, it worked out great for me, because if one of my students asked me a question in class that I wasn't able to answer off the top of my head, I'd simply say, "I dunno—why don't you look it up?" Hey, I already passed *my* sergeant's test.

I'm not sure that all my students appreciated the wisdom of my methods, though. After one particular classroom question, while they were all grunting to get their patrol guides off the floor, I heard one recruit officer express her disapproval by sucking her teeth. As she had not yet been a police officer in the field, I was sure that she didn't realize that her little form of non-verbal communication was one universally despised by cops since it was nearly always used only by mutts and morons, so I didn't want to overreact. "Are we suffering from dental problems, Officer Smith?" She's confused:

"Huh?" I said, "Looking something up in the patrol guide is what police science is all about." Thus endeth this specific lesson—or so I thought. "Well, I've taken police science before, and it was nothing like this." All the other recruits looked up from their books upon hearing this amazing response. Pleasantly, I ask, "Where did you take police science before?" With a smug face she announces, "John Jay College of Criminal Justice." I'm impressed. "Well, Officer, when John Jay gets their *own* goddamn police department, we'll do it their way. In the mean time, look it up!"

Subway Olympians

This story isn't really a war story. I'm including it here mostly because it involved one of my better comebacks.

Every year, competitors from law-enforcement agencies throughout the state come together for the State of New York Summer Police Olympics, to compete in events such as archery, horseback riding, judo, tennis, bowling, track and field, you name it. I was a member of the New York City Transit Police Pistol Team.

We were a force to be reckoned with. During the years that I shot we won a bunch of medals. More importantly, we had a lot of fun. We considered ourselves to be, well, different from our fellow competitors. To put it bluntly, a lot of the guys we shot against were tight-assed hillbillies who took the whole thing a little too seriously. Many of them wore department-issued team shirts, shot company ammo, and even competed on job time. We were there on our own time and expense, and really looked at the whole thing as just a great excuse for a three-day party.

We used to do things that were simply not common. For example: target scoring in competition is generally done by the person shooting next to you, who happens to be your competitor (the thinking is that'll keep it honest). If it's debatable as to whether a particular shot, say, is an 'eight' or a 'nine' most of these guys would make it an 'eight'. I shocked a fellow competitor once with our brand of sportsmanship—while scoring his target, I took out my .38-caliber pencil, jammed it through the questionable hole in his target, and said *"Now* it's a 'nine'." I doubt he would've done the same for me.

So, we're shooting in Albany during the summer of 1991. I'm locked in a ferocious private competition with my teammate and good friend, Kenny. He's Chinese. You'd never know it, unless of course, you looked at him. Anyway, we had been shooting neck-and-neck, with Kenny just edging me out. This, by the way, was more important to us than the actual competitive match we were officially engaged in. For those of you who may not be familiar with competitive pistol shooting, it looks like this: about fifty guys stand side-by-side on some big field and everyone shoots at the same time at a row of paper targets, also side-by-side, kinda like the lanes in a bowling alley. When the shooting is over everyone walks up to the targets together and they count the holes. As already mentioned, you don't stand next to your own teammates. This particular bright and sunny morning (well, okay, like most other mornings) I'm pretty bleary and red-eyed from the night before. We're scoring our targets, and Kenny, my arch-rival, is about twenty guys away from me. He had shot really well, and in a shocking violation of the stuffy range etiquette, he rips his target off the post, waves it at me and yells, "Hey, look at this, sucker! Ha, ha, ha!" There was an uncomfortable silence. Then I yelled back, "Yeah, well *you* don't have to squint!"

Not entirely coincidentally, I have a beautiful daughter who was conceived during an Olympic weekend in Syracuse, New York. When she was born, as sometimes happens with babies, she became jaundiced. I called Kenny on the phone. I said, "My child is yellow." After an awkward silence, I added in my most menacing tone: "Keep looking over your shoulder," and hung up.

Increditable

The New York City Transit Police Department became nationally accredited in 1991. At the time, it was the second largest department in the country to be so accredited, and the only such police department in New York City. 'Accreditation' was a process by which a police agency would comply with some very detailed standards and requirements outlined by a self-appointed association of police experts. Upon satisfactory inspection by this association and their subsequent approval, the agency in question would thus be deemed 'accredited'. When the Transit Police accomplished this milestone in '91, we began sporting 'accredited' decals on our police cars, and 'accredited' pins on our nametags. When we would explain this stuff to our brother officers in the NYPD and the Housing Police, their general response was an amused, "So what does that make us? Fakes? Amateurs? Unqualified?"

Before you start to think that I'm not in favor of accreditation, I'd like to mention two things: First, there is ample precedent for self-appointed associations being involved in monitoring or otherwise positively influencing a profession (for example, the American Medical Association). Second, although the point of this story is the apparent silliness of the paperwork involved, some real improvements were enjoyed by the Transit Police as a result of the accreditation process. It just wasn't enjoyed by me.

Here's a simplified explanation of how it works: In all police departments, cops walk their beats. That's it. Now, in an 'accredited' department, the first thing they've got is a written rule that says, 'Cops walk their beats.' Then, they've got a written procedure designating someone who ensures that the cops are in fact walking their beats. Finally, they've got a training course that teaches the cops how to walk correctly. Of course, in order to have a training course, you have to have a lesson plan. Here's where I come in. I worked in the training division for about three years. For two years and three months of that time, it was involuntary servitude. It's not that training was that bad, it's just that I worked for an ambitious, one-way scumbag whose footprint was on the backs of the necks of all of those who helped him rise through the ranks. Ahh, but I digress. Anyway, quite a few of the written accreditation standards were directly related to training. We, as well as everyone else, worked very hard to complete our share. The cars got their decals. Our boss got promoted. We got more work to do.

In 1992, fresh from our success with national accreditation, the Transit Police undertook the challenge of attaining state accreditation as well. Same principle, different group of people. Most importantly, different *paperwork* saying the same thing. But hey, the state people had this little medal for everyone to wear over their shields that said, 'State Accredited'.

I was a training supervisor at the NYPD Academy (answering to the Transit Police training division) when my boss told me to rewrite a stack of lesson plans and course materials, "when you're not busy." When I'm not busy? "Like when I'm home and off-duty?" I took a look at this stuff—it was the exact same thing we had just gotten finished doing for the national accreditation committee the year before. I pointed this out to my boss and asked why we didn't just submit the same materials we used for the nationals. He said, "All the stuff for the state is in a different format, so you can't use the material from the nationals. You still have to do all these lesson plans." I said, "*Do?* Don't you mean *re-do?* Let's cut the bullshit, okay? When you teach a course you only use one lesson plan. It's just like rules and procedures. We're not gonna have one set of procedures when we're going for national accreditation, and then change the procedures next week when we go for state, are we? Or maybe I should call the national people and tell them that all the shit we did for their inspection is going in the garbage can. Maybe they'll help us peel those fucking stickers off the cars!"

Brilliant and logical argument, but I ended up doing the new lesson plans anyway. We ended up getting state-accredited, we got our shiny new medals to wear above our shields, *plus* we kept our national accreditation stickers, to boot. And speaking of boots, I finally got my transfer—not to where I had wanted to go, exactly, but...

Field Training

In January 1993 I was ejected from the training division and landed on the Rockaway peninsula, at the most remote outpost of the Transit Police: District 23. All is good with the world as far as I'm concerned. Then a new class of recruits graduated from the Police Academy, and as far away as I was, they *still* managed to find me.

We had a shortage of field training officers. Lucky me, somebody remembered: "Hey, you used to be in training, why don't you take the new guys out?" So, four probationary officers follow me like baby ducklings to the subway station on the island of Broad Channel. I explain to them that we'll be doing what's known as a 'Violation Enforcement Patrol'. The plan is simple—we spread ourselves out along the platform, and when a train comes in we each look in and inspect the car that's in front of us to see if there's any law-breaking going on. "Everybody got it? Good." Here comes a Rockaway-bound train. We're all in position along the platform. The train pulls in, the doors open up, and at this time of the afternoon more people are getting off than are getting on. The doors close and the train pulls out. Well, that was easy enough. One of the regular district cops was riding on the train; we waved to each other as the train left. As the crowd of exiting passengers thinned, I checked the platform. One, two, three… Uh-oh.

I called the district cop on the radio, "One of my kiddies escaped. He's on the southbound 'A' with you. Make sure he's okay and send him back, alright?" He laughed, "Ten-four, Sarge." I thought it was pretty clear what the plan was, but then again, they *are* new. You have to accept mistakes from them as they learn. I've just got to hold my breath until our dunce comes back.

A northbound train from the Rockaways pulls in after about ten minutes. Number four is not on it. Out comes the radio, "Hey did you send him back, or what?" I tell the district cop to take a ride back to where number four got off. Now, I'm getting worried.

The trains run about twenty minutes apart and we had to wait for the next northbound. When it finally came, the cop radioed me that he found the probie and he was on his way back to Broad Channel. That's a relief. I'll get whatever explanation he's got when he gets back.

The train pulls into Broad Channel and number four gets off. I'm just standing there silently with the other probies. He walks over with a sheepish look on his face and salutes me. He's so new he's standing at attention. I returned the salute and ask quietly, "Where were you?" He says, "Gaston Avenue." That was the first subway station in Rockaway. Forget about why he *left* Broad Channel in the first place, I want to know, "Why weren't you on the *last* northbound

'A' from Gaston?" He says, "Well, I had to inspect the post, Sarge." Inspect the post? This kid has got one day on the job; he's not allowed out by himself! "Officer, give me your hat." He gives it to me and returns to a position of attention. I examine it carefully. It's brand-new, with a shiny visor and a bright silver cap device. I turn it over in my hands several times in silence, then I gripped it by the visor, tested the feel of it, and *Pow!* I whacked him right across the top of his head. "Don't ever do that again."

After all, I am a state-certified training officer. Nyuk, nyuk, nyuk.

The Frame

There's a young kid who struts around Rockaway like he's a tough guy. I see him hanging around with the wrong crew and trying to look cool with the girls. If they could've seen him when I first met him a few years back, they'd laugh him off the street.

We were riding the last train home one night after a quiet tour working anticrime. A couple of kids get on the train a car ahead of us and they seem a little too concerned about the other passengers on the train. This interest in itself is enough to raise *our* interest, so at the next stop when they moved a car ahead, I followed. My partners knew I was watching someone so they in turn watched me. We did the leapfrog gig a couple of times, and as the train was pulling into the last stop at Beach 116th Street, one of the kids starts doing what I kinda hoped he might—he starts scratching his initials or whatever onto a train window with a rough stone. This type of graffiti vandalism is pretty annoying, so I pounce on him with my shield in my hand: "Police! What are you doing?"

This kid can't be more than fourteen years old. He drops the stone, gets all panicky and says, "Nothing! I wasn't doing anything!" My partners now circle in for the kill. "Oh, yeah? What's this?" When confronted with the evidence, he does the slightly unexpected —he takes a deep breath and goes, "Waaaaaahhhhhhh!"

We've got him inside the district and he's carrying on something terrible. I mean, snot coming out of his nose, everything. The way he's crying, you'd think we were torturing him. As we're getting the information necessary to prepare a juvenile report and ship him home, it also becomes apparent that he feels we've somehow mistreated him. "What's the matter with you? Why don't you stop acting like a baby?" He gets a grip on himself (finally) and says, "You set me up!" I almost fell off my chair. "What are you talking about, I set you up? I saw you do it!" With a straight face, he says, "Yeah, but *still*…"

Wildlife

Woody was what we referred to as a 'spent round'. He was only in his thirties, but he looked way, way older. Something must've happened to him, and it probably happened in the subway…

The boys and I were in the command processing a bunch of farebeat collars one night. Woody wasn't into the arrest scene, he was just in the district on his meal break. We were all just sitting around bullshitting in little coffee circles when he mentioned something about turtles. My ears perked right up. From across the room, I interrupt: "Hey Woody, you say you got turtles?" He says, "Yeah, why? You?" I say, "Yeah, sure! I got an Eastern Painted. What do you got?" He says, "Oh, I got a couple of different kinds. I just got a musk turtle last week. Ever see one of those?" The other guys are quietly frowning as the conversation takes this odd turn. Kevin says, "What are we, in a fucking playground?" I snap at him, "Ah, shut up. Woody, what kinda tanks you got, anyway?" He says, "I got a couple of fifties in the basement, but I built a pond in my backyard." I'm laughing, "You got a *pond*? Oh, man, can I sleep over your house?" He chuckles and says, "Only if you wear those pajamas with the flap in the back."

Our Own Worst Enemies

You'd think that with all the crap cops have to put up with from the public that we'd at least give the on-duty cops a break when we're not working. Unfortunately, sometimes that's not the case.

Some cops are so stupid they almost beg to get locked up when they're off-duty. Like the guy who blows the red light with impunity to impress the girl in his car, even though there's a marked police car sitting right there with two cops who don't know him from a hole in the wall. Or the guy who has to make sure that people see his gun as he's getting out his wallet to pay for his slice of pizza. Gee, we're all so impressed.

Booger was getting our coffee and I'm sitting in the car waiting for him. I see a scruffy guy, mid-thirties, at the payphone on the corner of Franklin Avenue and Fulton Street. He sees me looking at him, and while I wouldn't exactly call it a dirty look, he didn't seem to be too thrilled that I was watching him. As he turns back to the phone, I see the barrel of a handgun poking out from under the bottom of his waist-length jacket. So, I wait for Booger to come back to the car, and I tell him there's a 'man with a gun' standing on the corner. We walk up on him and our guns come out, down at our sides. "Keep your hands on the phone, okay?" He does. I reach over, pull his revolver out and drop it in my coat pocket. Very low-key operation so far. We holster our guns and I ask, "You got a permit or something for that?" Now, I'm getting a definitely dirty look. "I got a shield." He shows me his ID. I hand him back his gun and say, "Sorry, guy." As I'm walking back to the car, he yells, "Yeah, well you coulda asked first!" Bear in mind that not only am I on-duty and in full uniform, but I'm also a sergeant. I walked back over to him and said, "Officer, you better get a shorter attitude and a longer coat."

Then there was the guy we saw walking down Liberty Avenue one hot summer day. He's wearing dress slacks, a silk shirt with buttons open down to his stomach—and the butt of a gun sticking out of his waistband. What a stud. We stop him, and surprise, he's 'on the job'. I inform him that his gun is drawing just a little bit of attention, and he says almost absent-mindedly, "Oh, yeah, I just got this holster..." and walks away without adjusting his appearance at all. I didn't have the energy to deal with such a dope, but I'm sure some other unit did.

Steve M. told me a story that wins first prize. He's on late-night train patrol and he sees this passenger who appears to be carrying a gun. It's a middle-aged guy in a suit who also appears to have been out partying a bit. Steve walks up to him, literally with his hat in his hand, and says, "Excuse me, sir, are you carrying a gun?" Turns out the guy is some big-time veteran detective, and for the next ten minutes Steve's got to listen to his red-eyed bullshit about how "cops nowadays ain't as streetwise as they used to be." When *he* was a rookie, he'd never simply walk up to a man with a gun; what if he was a bad guy and had just robbed a bank, blah, blah, blah... Steve stood there and politely listened to this very public criticism of his patrol skills, as did all the other passengers. When the detective finished dispensing his free advice, Steve said, "Well, thank you sir, I appreciate it." With his left hand, he put his hat back on his head. With his right, he put away the snubnosed thirty-eight that he had been holding the whole time inside his hat. "Have a nice night."

You Can Never Go Home Again

I grew up on a small street named Hurley Court. For some unknown reason, one side of this street was paved and one side was just gravel. I lived on the gravel side, which, according to neighborhood lore, was 'the wrong side of the tracks'.

There were only three houses on the gravel side, and my best friend Willie lived in one of them. Like mine, Willie's dad was a cop, but that didn't matter—we were determined to wreak as much havoc as we could. Phoney phone calls, garden hoses introduced into basement windows, paper bags containing dog poop set on fire and left on doorsteps with a ring of the doorbell, et cetera. Proudly, we pioneered the technique of nighttime deposits of live crabs in milkboxes. Who knew that morning milk delivery would go the way of Mitch Ryder and the Detroit Wheels? One of our crowning achievements was the summertime launch of an 8-oz. skyrocket right through one of our neighbor's windows. Both our jaws were hanging as the missile disappeared. Then, we heard the muffled thump and all the windows on that floor briefly lit up. We laughed. We ran.

Willie and I had a pact, which, although not foolproof, served to confuse our pursuers more often than not. If one of us got caught in a follow-up investigation into some mysterious neighborhood occurrence, whoever was on the hook would finger the other one. Since this was agreed upon in advance there were no hard feelings. Besides, there was the added benefit that when the other one was caught as a result of the snitching, the fact that the grown-ups believed they had somehow driven a wedge between us usually softened the punishment. Of course, none of this worked if we got bagged together.

One day I happened to be in a police car in the vicinity of my old neighborhood, so I figured I'd take a trip down memory lane. We drove slowly since the surface of the street was as bad as I remembered it. Before I could get all teary-eyed at seeing my childhood home, a woman came running into the street, flagging us down. My partner and I instantly crank up the readiness dial to a heightened state of alert. "What's the problem, ma'am?" This old woman starts yapping about all the potholes. Before my partner could express his annoyance that she approached us as if this was an emergency, which it clearly wasn't, I started laughing, "Lady, this street was like this twenty-five years ago!" She says, "And how would you know?" I point at my old house: "I grew up here!" She looks at the house, then at me, then back at the house. Then it clicked. "Ohhh, you little bastards used to throw rocks at my dog!" I smiled and said, "Nah—that was Willie."

A Face Only A Mother Could Love

Beer makes some people brave; it makes some people stupid. Some people are lucky enough to have it both ways.

Two young chowderheads were feeling their beer-muscles one night on Beach 116th Street. They were starting to get a little ugly, so one could only assume that they were unable to get laid. Now *that's* hard to believe... They were looking for something to focus their energies on when they noticed a guy looking at them, standing with a small group of people in front of the subway station. Apparently they took this as a challenge to their manhood because the next thing you know, one of them says, "What are you looking at, you chink fuck?" I guess they didn't like the answer he got, because now the two of them walk over, and one tries to kick him in the groin. Well, the guy *was* Chinese—and he was also a member of the Rockaway Beach Transit Police. For whatever reason, these two geniuses had decided to pick a fight with a plainclothes team coming back from a sweep. What happened next, happened with astonishing speed. Rather than bore you with technical details, let's just say they got 'beaten up and taken to jail'.

We've got them inside the district and it starts to dawn on one of them that they've made a terrible mistake. He calms down and his arrest proceeded normally. His buddy, on the other hand, is still causing a problem. He's handcuffed but he tries to kick us. This just *won't* do. He had no one to blame but himself for the injuries he suffered when we put an end to his childish and immature behavior.

So, now we've got to take him to the hospital, and to our surprise, it turns out he's only seventeen years old. He's about six feet tall, two hundred pounds, with a crew-cut, moustache and goatee, and tattoos on both arms. Okay, and a footprint on the side of his head. Anyway, since he's a minor for medical purposes, we had to get his parents down to the district.

His family lived close by and his mother came down within ten or fifteen minutes. Whatever it is he's been drinking, we'd like to buy some, because he's *still* going off in the cell. They're explaining to his mother at the front desk that he's been arrested and you can hear the commotion coming from the back where the cells are. He's shaking the cell bars like a gorilla, screaming at the top of his lungs, "I'll kill all you motherfuckers, let me outta here! Yo, money, I'll kick your fuckin' ass! Cocksuckers!" His mother walks into the cell area and it was like somebody flipped a switch—he's suddenly meek and subdued. As he hangs his head, looking down at his feet, he mumbles, "Hi, Ma…"

She wheels on us with fire in her eyes and says, *"What have you done to my baby?"*

The Piss Ranch

For a geographically huge area, District 23 had comparatively few subway stations. It also had very few public restrooms. Understandably, this led to a rather common violation of law. So common, in fact, that Woody christened the place 'The Piss Ranch'.

Many passengers couldn't hold it in anymore after being stuck on some pretty slow trains all afternoon, and they just did what they had to do. Since we had to spend all day there, we were usually quite unforgiving, and a lot of tickets were written for 'Urinating in Public'. Before you get too sympathetic here, I'd like to point out that most people would seek out the relative privacy of the back side of a stairwell on our elevated platforms before committing their dastardly crimes. We always wondered why none of the other exiting passengers ever seemed to realize that it wasn't raining, yet they had to descend through curtains of 'water' drizzling across the stairways leading down to the street.

Woody used to address his fellow cops as 'piss ranchers'. Once, I made the mistake of calling one of our probies a piss rancher, and Woody politely corrected me, "He's a piss cadet." He did this with the utmost respect, since after all, I was a piss foreman.

When the news of my impending promotion came down, Woody was one of the first to shake my hand: "Congratulations! Now you're a piss manager."

Act III

'They say hard work never hurt anybody,

but I figured, why take the chance?'

Ronald Reagan

These Little Town Blues

Say 'New York City' to most people and they visualize Manhattan with its famous skyline, hardly a selling point if you spend your time underground. When I was promoted to lieutenant, I was involuntarily assigned (emphasis on 'involuntarily') to the district covering the east side of Manhattan, from Chinatown to Spanish Harlem, District Four. Since I was not only a subway cop, but a small-town Queens subway cop, I had reservations as to whether I would be able to cut it in the big city. But hey, if I can make it there, I'll make it anywhere...

Much to my surprise, Manhattan turned out to be quite a fun place to work. The concentration of people made for an interesting variety of police customers—lots of bad guys to catch, victims to help, and most importantly, spectators to entertain.

One of the major urban crime problems that I struggled to cope with was the dreaded Immigrant Peddler. These guys used to ride the trains and sell stuff to the passengers. They had all kinds of devilish toys, some of them wind-up, some of them battery powered. All were brightly colored. They even had sales pitches which, if you listened closely, you'd realize were memorized fragments of a foreign language (English). Very subversive, indeed.

I came in one day and took over the desk to assume control over a major police operation, the processing of the arrest of a peddler. It seems that this gentleman was not only violating statutes of the NYC Administrative Code by selling goods without the proper licensing, but that when confronted by the authorities he pretended not to speak any English at all—like I was born yesterday. As a Desk Officer, it was a simple case to crack. I reached out to our highly skilled bank of interpreters to chip away at his clever facade and obtain the information necessary to issue him a summons. What was not so simple was, what the hell do you do with forty-six baby red-eared green slider turtles?

A side note on one insidious aspect of this case: When I eat at work, I pay. If I arrested you and you offered me money to let you go, I'd add on charges for bribery. One of the better traditions of the Transit Police is that we've always been incorruptible. I was deeply ashamed when I caught myself thinking that I could probably slip a turtle or two into my shirt pocket without anyone noticing...

Being pure of heart and highly disciplined, I quickly put these thoughts out of my head and contacted the local humane society to take custody of all the baby turtles. They agreed to take them, but said we had to deliver. I assigned one of my most trustworthy officers, John J., to be the delivery boy.

John is standing outside the district office in the Union Square subway station, in full uniform, with a big plastic tray full of turtles, waiting for his ride to the animal shelter uptown. An out-of-towner walks by, sees him and figures this is just one more sight to see in the Big Apple. "Oh my, you've got turtles!" To his everlasting credit, John throws his arm up, protecting his charges from public view. "Ma'am, step back please. These aren't just turtles—they're Transit Police drug-sniffing turtles." She starts squealing, "Oh, Mary, Bill, come quick, see this! They've got police turtles!" And the crowd starts forming...

Numba Sixteen

I know, I know, Manhattan is the center of the universe. Fine. I don't care how many trendy restaurants there are, the food is still too goddamned expensive. When you work in the city every single night you can't afford to be spending fifteen or twenty bucks for a piece of toast with some bean sprouts and chive butter.

There was a little Chinese restaurant upstairs from District Four, near Union Square. I found the place as a result of being assigned as the desk officer. I couldn't leave the desk, but everyone at the command said not to worry, this place delivers. Even a small order? Yeah, no problem. They've got a menu at the desk. Okay, I look at it. Hmmm... How bad could they screw up 'House Special Chicken with Fried Rice' anyway? I decided to take a chance with my $3.75 and call in the order. Within fifteen minutes, this little guy comes into the district with my food. I gave him five bucks, and it really wasn't bad!

I'd get the desk about twice a week and I'd almost always end up ordering my dinner from this place. "Hello, this is the police. Can you deliver an order to Union Square in the subway?" The voice on the other end would immediately ask, "Wha' you wan, numba sixteen, hot an' spicy?" I must have a distinctive voice. That number sixteen was delicious, though. After a while, every time the delivery guy would come in, I'd give him *six* bucks. That's how good it was. They used to throw in these little dragon-fire red peppers that we'd challenge each other to eat. "Hey, you ain't supposed to eat those, they're like a fuckin' garnish or something!"

About the only time I didn't get my 'numba sixteen' was when he'd come into the district with a food order that nobody would claim. District Four was a *big* command, with something like three hundred cops. It was usually a madhouse, at least on the four-to-twelve tour that I worked. Still, it didn't seem right that he would come down to deliver a five-dollar order and whoever ordered it would fail to own up to it for whatever reason. He'd just stand quietly by the door, wasting his time as we'd yell, "Hey, Chinese food, up front!" Without realizing it, I let him stand there for about fifteen minutes one night. Nobody came up and he just left without saying anything. I felt bad when I noticed he had left. After that night, if no one came up within a few minutes, I'd end up buying the food myself before I'd let him leave. Sometimes my pot-luck order was okay, but it was never as good as 'numba sixteen'.

One day I had to come in early for some reason or another and I was looking to kill some time without going into the district. I'm walking around Union Square when I notice the little Chinese restaurant that I've only known from a name on a menu. What the hell, maybe I'll go in and see how they make 'numba sixteen'. I go in, walk up to the counter to order, and this guy in the back working the wok says, "Hey boss, how you doing?" The little guy who had been delivering my food was the *cook*!

If anyone tells you not to tip, that it's covered by their paycheck, don't believe it.

Mail Call

From time to time, citizens would write to express their concerns, to complain, or just to give thanks for a job well done. If specific cops were named in a thank-you letter, they'd get a copy of the letter placed in their personnel folder as an 'attaboy'. If the letter was a complaint, well...

This one is in my folder. I'm not sure how to categorize it.

Dear Chief Smith:

I am writing to bring to your attention the fact that you have several officers of superior ability working in the 4th District (Union Square, Manhattan); specifically, Officers Jones, Johnson and Nehoc. It's certainly possible there were others who escaped my attention. I only regret that I had to make their acquaintance under the following circumstances.

On August 24th, 1993 I was assaulted by a 16-year-old punk, with at least one accomplice, on the IRT #6 train near Bleecker Street. After an exchange of words, this miscreant struck me above the eye with brass knuckles. Despite the attempts of myself and a bystander to detain him, he was able to escape, along with his accomplice. A passerby was kind enough to guide me to Officer Jones, who broadcast a description of my assailant. After I was treated by an ambulance crew, I got into a police car in the hopes of finding the perpetrator. Presently, it was reported on the radio that Johnson had detained a suspect. I immediately identified the suspect as the degenerate that had attacked me. Quite frankly, I was amazed that the officers were able to pick out this villain from among the many that litter this city. One accomplice was also arrested. I would like to know why I was never asked to identify him. I never mentioned it to any police officer at the time because I was too distraught to think of it then. Was he immediately released?

Other than that, Lieutenant Nehoc went above and beyond the call of duty by buying me a shirt to replace the bloodstained one I was wearing. In general, I was impressed with the professionalism exhibited by the above-mentioned officers. I wish I could say that the effective police work of these men has removed a menace from our streets. However, everyone knows that with the screwed up legislators, judges and juries in our society in general and our state in particular, these scum will likely escape the punishment they justly deserve.

Sincerely,

/ signature /
John Q. Axengrinder

Now, let me tell you what *really* happened. Mr. Axengrinder was riding the train, minding everybody's business. These two inner-city kids also on the train were acting like typical teenagers. Evidently, this offended Mr. Axengrinder's sensibilities, and he told them so. Although it's debatable just exactly how he meant it, his choice of words (*"you people..."*) didn't sit too well with the kids. Perceiving an insult, they in turn commented on Mr. Axengrinder's apparent ethnicity. Tempers flared, and Mr. Axengrinder got bonked in the head.

I didn't know the whole story when he got in my car, but since we thought it was possibly a bias-motivated incident we handled it quite seriously. Everybody was brought back to the district and an exhaustive inquiry was conducted. So exhaustive, in fact, that we intended on running lab tests on the bloody clothing to determine whose blood was where. Despite the fact that he was demanding a federal investigation and even though he had a light jacket with him, Mr.Axengrinder refused to give up his shirt until I got him a new one. Our final conclusion: The incident was not, in fact, motivated by ethnic bias. Mr. Axengrinder was just a very annoying person.

Reader's note: Our chief wrote a nice letter in reply, thanking Mr. Axengrinder for his concern. I, on the other hand, hired him as a staff writer.

Language Barriers

Working in Manhattan was certainly not what you'd call dull. About the only thing you could count on was being surrounded by more people than you had ever seen in your life, or would ever want to.

One afternoon Jimmy and I were in the car somewhere near Houston Street (pronounced 'How-ston'—this ain't Texas) when there was a disturbing call on the 'division' radio. That was the radio used by Big Brother, the NYPD. Like our radio, theirs was divided into geographic zones. The call came over clear as a bell: "Uh... central, can I get an ambulance to (XXX) Canal Street?" There was no mistaking the commotion in the background of the transmission. The dispatcher said, "Unit, be advised, you're on the wrong division." What that meant was that the cop had the little knob on the top of his radio set to the wrong channel. The location he gave was also across the transit district boundaries somewhere in District Two. Jimmy gave me a look; I nodded. It sounds like this cop's got a problem. We were headed that direction anyway... The next transmission was the cop requesting an ambulance forthwith. The background noise sounded really bad and once again the dispatcher told him he was on the wrong channel. Jimmy gives it the gas, we're going fast. The next and last transmission we hear is the cop calling for help, hurry quick, help! Now we're up on the sidewalks to get around traffic. At this point, we tell the transit dispatcher that we're responding to a division radio call for assistance at (XXX) Canal, since it appears likely we may soon be wrecking our car.

We pull up to the location simultaneously with the precinct patrol supervisor and the precinct anticrime car. The address is a storefront and we have to wade through the literally hundreds of people thronging five or six deep across the sidewalk in an endless stream. The door's locked. We bang on it, someone buzzes us in, and we flood into the place. Turns out it's a jewelry store shared by several different merchants. All the glass counters are facing each other and there are video cameras aimed every which way. There's a young woman on the floor bleeding and unconscious. There's fingerpointing from behind the counters; everyone's screaming in Chinese, apparently accusing each other of having done the 'El-Kabong' on her, and the poor cop who called for help is caught in the middle. We've got absolutely no idea what's going on and unfortunately, neither does the cop. As we're trying to sort things out (which is very difficult with everyone pointing fingers and screaming in Chinese) we hear the English phrase we all understand: "He got a gun!" All fingers now point at one guy. All the guns in the world suddenly come out of their holsters and everybody dog-piles onto said guy. The glass counters smash, the Chinese cacophony intensifies, and now the cops from District Two who heard *our* call on the transit radio come running up outside. They can't get into the store, they see all of us in a melee on the floor with our guns drawn, so they're picking up a garbage can off the street and are about to use it as a battering ram to take down the storefront. I catch a quick look at Jimmy, who laughs, "What the fuck are we doing here anyway?"

Reader's note: The story was it was a gangster shakedown gone bad. The crime guys took the collar, the girl lived, and Jimmy and I went back to the subway, where it's safe.

License To Kill

Police officers are entrusted by society with an awesome responsibility. We are authorized to use deadly physical force, and we carry the equipment necessary to do just that. Sometimes.

Desk officers are also encumbered with massive responsibilities. Without going into all the technical aspects, let's just say that we're too busy to answer the phone. When I had the desk in District Four, I never took phone calls personally, there were just too many other things to do. The cops would screen my calls carefully. One afternoon, one of my faithful shortstops tells me, "It's Officer Smith, he wants to talk to you." I give the cop a dirty look and he says, "I don't know what he wants; he says he'll only talk to you." I take the call.

"Hello, Lou, how you doin'?" This guy's gotta be kidding. "I'm fine, officer, what do you need?" He says, "Uh, I hate to bother you, but I left something in my locker today when I went to patrol..." I'm really not in the mood for this beating around the bush bullshit. "What'd you forget, your hat, your memo book, what?" Long pause: "My gun." Now I'm very interested in this conversation. "Where are you right now?" He says, "125 and Lex." Not only our most distant post, but also one of our toughest. "You got a partner?" He says yes. "Okay, right now, hang up and come back to the command. Right now, okay?" 125th Street and Lexington Avenue was a priority post which was supposed to be covered at all times, but this was a special circumstance. "Both of us?" he asks. Not one to overreact, I banged the phone receiver on the desk about a half a dozen times, then I screamed, "No, give your partner the combination to your locker and send him back to get your gun! Get your ass back here right now!" After I slammed the phone down, I started to worry—this cop was as dumb as a shoe, and I *did* give him two different set of instructions...

Fearless Leader

The best thing about being a police lieutenant is that for the most part, you get to do whatever you want. Few captains get involved with the nuts and bolts of policing, and in the field a lieutenant is usually the highest ranking officer actually 'on patrol'.

Solo supervisory foot patrol was a uniquely transit assignment. The NYPD doesn't even let sergeants go out by themselves, let alone lieutenants. One of my favorite assignments has always been to go out on patrol in uniform, on foot and alone. That's why I'd give myself that assignment—it's good to be king.

So I'm walking around one afternoon. I decided to visit the cops at Grand Central Station. Whenever a boss would visit cops in the field, it was standard practice to sign their memo books indicating the time and place of the visit (cops keep a chronological record of activities in this memo book; they're supposed to write down everything they do). Anyway, after I signed their books, I then decided to move on because it was miserably hot in Grand Central. Hey, it wasn't my post, why should I sweat it out?

I'm walking west on 42nd Street when I hear a foot pursuit on the radio. A few blocks further west from me, they're chasing some purse-snatcher up from 38th Street. They give a pretty good clothing description over the air. Hmmm... If the guy gives them the slip he might pop up on 42nd Street, and if I'm lucky, he'll be so tired from running that I'll probably be able to catch him. Now I'm striding with purpose, trying to get closer so as to be able to spring my trap.

As I'm crossing Fifth Avenue this guy in a suit comes over to me and says, "Officer, come quick! People are getting robbed in there!" He points to the front of a building on Fifth Avenue. I ask what he means by 'getting robbed'. He says, "There's a guy inside with a gun, and he's sticking up the place!" Yeah, that's robbery alright. "Now?" I ask. "Right now!" he says. Well, fuck me.

I ease up alongside the glass doors and grab a quick peek inside but I can't see anything. On the transit radio, I say, "Four lieutenant —priority, central!" The dispatcher tells everyone to clear the air and answers me. "Central, I got a signal 10-30 with a firearm, in progress, (XXX) Fifth Avenue. Gimme an 85 [help] forthwith." I hear the dispatcher beep the alert tone a few times, then he puts out my location correctly. At least everybody knows where I am. Oh well, here goes nothing. I take another peek, pull out ol' Roscoe, take a deep breath, and go on in.

I find the victims of the stick-up inside. The gunman's gone, having run out the back a minute before I came in. Whew, that's a relief. Since my transit radio doesn't work inside buildings, I tell the people I'll be right back—I duck outside to tell the dispatcher, "Central, (XXX) Fifth Avenue is in the past, the perp is gone. Slow everybody down. Give me a minute, I'll put out a description." Now, I could swear that I heard the dispatcher acknowledge me. I go back inside to talk to the victims. As I'm getting the descriptions, I hear sirens coming from all directions. Oh, shit! I run back outside and all these cop cars come screeching up. As my radio comes back to life I hear the dispatcher beeping away and putting out a distress call on my location. "Central, I said it's in the past! Call it off! Call it off!" Apparently, he had tried to raise me, and when I didn't answer him right away (because I was in the building and didn't hear him), he assumed the worst and had sent the cavalry. A little embarrassing for me, but it was probably the right thing to do under the circumstances.

One of those cavalry charges, all four transit cops from Grand Central, came running up huffing and puffing seconds after I called it off. I said hello, but then went back to the matter at hand which was putting the robbery victims into police cars to drive around to look for the bad guy. Once that was done I turned to the transit brigade. They had run several blocks on a very hot day to back me up, and I was grateful. "Hey, thanks a lot, guys. Let's go get some sodas or something." Everyone agreed that was a good idea. Since they were all off their assigned posts now, I figured, "Might as well give all of you a scratch first." This way nobody gets into trouble. They take out their memo books and offer them to me for my signature. I take the first book, and as I sign it, I glance at the cop's last entry: 'To 5th Ave, assist Lieutenant.' The next book: 'Enroute to 5th Ave, rescue the patrol supervisor.' Eh? I look at the cop but I sign. Jimmy hands me his book: 'Squeals for help, 5th Ave...'

If Looks Could Kill

There was another lieutenant in District Four who I got along with about as well as anyone did, and that was not too well. This guy was a scary dude. One of the running jokes about him was that he was a dead ringer for the actor Al Lewis, better known as 'Grandpa Munster'.

One day we had a prisoner with what appeared to be some funny money so I called our friends at the U.S. Secret Service. I neglected to tell the desk lieutenant since I didn't feel like arguing about it with him. Anyway, a couple of agents came right down to the district in Union Square to take a look at the money, and promptly told us it wasn't counterfeit after all. I thanked them and apologized for wasting their time. Like any true law-enforcement professional, one of them said, "Hey, no problem, that's our job, you can call us anytime." Hmmm... These two agents seemed like regular guys, so I said, "Well, while you're here, you feel like going along with a gag?" They looked at each other for a second with raised eyebrows... "Yeah. What do you got?"

The plan: To go up to the front desk and chew out the desk lieutenant with a routine about how they're big-time federal agents, how dare we waste their time with petty bullshit like this, and boy, if we ever call them again for anything, et cetera. I told them that the other lieutenant was a real grouchy bastard and he deserved a little sunshine. Or maybe even a threat of an income-tax audit. We're all laughing as they agree to do it. The two agents 'got into character' and then swaggered up to the front desk.

They took one look at Grandpa Munster glaring at them silently from behind the desk and they came back to me and said, "Nah, we'd rather take a bullet for the President..."

Live, From New York...

Jimmy and I threw on our civilian jackets and snuck away from the desk to grab something to eat one Saturday night. As we walked back to Union Square with our food, we couldn't help but notice the Emergency Medical Rescue truck parked near the top of the stairs.

Downstairs, we see the gathering crowd on the mezzanine. Hearing no music, we correctly figure it's no concert. With lunch firmly in hand, we squeeze through the circular crowd to see the show—this guy, butt-naked, squatting on the concrete and talking to the EMRU cops—with a real big knife in his hand. To the bewilderment of the gawkers, Jimmy and I put our food down and silently joined the inexorable 'two steps forward, one step back' ballet with the Rescue cops. When he felt the moment was right, nature-boy suddenly leaped, and was just as suddenly bagged and tied.

While the applause was dying down, we notice another blue scuffle taking place a little further down the mez. The post cop is struggling to cuff somebody. The traveling road show relocates, and we discover that *this* poor soul just didn't want to keep on living.

I requested two ambulances on a borrowed radio, telling the dispatcher that they were both for 'emotionally-disturbed persons'. After a time, the ambulances arrived, and as they departed, I informed the dispatcher of their respective destinations. Confused by the two different hospitals, the dispatcher asked for a clarification. "Uh, no, central, they're not together... Why do you ask?"

Zzzz

Early in 1994, I managed to make the move from Manhattan back out to Queens, where I belong. I landed in District Twenty in

Jackson Heights, which is basically where I started as a cop. On a side note, everybody kept congratulating me. I never thought Queens was *that* great—then I found out that everyone thought I had just been promoted to lieutenant. I didn't have the heart to tell them that I had been a big-city lieutenant for a year already.

My first week back, who shows up in the district but a plainclothes team I knew from Manhattan. "Hey guys, what are *you* doing out here?" Lots of handshakes, laughter, et cetera, and they say they're part of a task force sent to Queens for some minor turnstile crime condition. "Try to stay awake, okay?" We all laugh and make the snoring sound.

It wasn't a half-hour later that I'm responding to a frantic "10-13, shots fired!" from my old friends. Seems they were minding their own business (okay, in a donut shop, what's the difference) when these two guys got into a heated argument. Not knowing that they were cops, one guy suddenly decided to settle the beef by unexpectedly pulling a gun and blasting the other guy a few times. The team did a phenomenal job—they apprehended the shooter after a foot chase and took him into custody without any cops firing a shot, plus, they recovered the murder weapon.

I surprised my new co-workers in District Twenty by taking charge of the crime scene upon my arrival and running the entire job from that point on. Transit cops *never* ran street homicides, especially brand-new lieutenants! I told the task force people, "Well, you know, nothing hardly ever happens in Queens..."

Now, That's Good Eatin'!

I don't know if it was my years in the Navy or my travels across the country, but for whatever reason, I consider myself to be a *connoisseur* of fine foods. Either that, or I'm just, uh... a pig.

One night out in Rockaway we had a seafood festival. John Z. had brought in a bushel of what he said were 'lobster tails'. We had a barbecue, and as we sat down to eat it became apparent that those were no ordinary lobsters. "Ow! You bastard!" Before long we were all bleeding. There just didn't seem to be any way to get them open without cutting or stabbing yourself with their spines. "You dummy, these ain't lobsters, they're *rock* lobsters!" I have no idea what a 'rock lobster' is, but boy, they were good. I was able to hold a pen within weeks.

When I worked in North Queens, which is definitely much more civilized in terms of available food, I'd occasionally get a rise out of people I was working with by stopping at street vendors and ordering 'monkey on a stick'. If there was an off-beat or unusual cuisine to be had, I'd have it. The foreigner the betterer.

As my tastes became known to the cops I worked with, some would try to cater to me. One night, Doc was going out for food. He asked what I wanted; I said, "Surprise me." He brought back the most exquisite red snapper I've ever scarfed down. Except for the tail, of course. They were just starting to hold roll call for the late-night train patrol cops as I finished the big fish. The sergeant conducting roll call had no idea what had happened to cause him to lose control of his group as I nonchalantly walked across the room behind him... with the tail of the fish sticking out of my mouth.

Just like in District Four, when I worked in District Twenty there was a little Chinese restaurant at the top of the stairs which I used to eat at quite frequently. This place was really Chinese, though, with very few non-Asian customers. Everybody in District Twenty used to make fun of me because at one point I used to eat at this place almost every night. They would make me anything that I asked for, and I rarely ordered off the menu. One night as I ordered my dinner, anticipating the abuse I would get when I went downstairs, I said, "Do me a favor, give me one of those too, okay?" Hey, I was a good customer—no problem! I told them to just put it in on top of my food order. I walk into the district with my dinner to the expected comments of, "Oh shit, what's he got tonight?" I stop at the front desk and start yelling, "Why doesn't everybody mind their own business and leave me alone? What's wrong with what I eat? I eat Chinese food just like everyone else! Here! Here! You want to see?" I throw my bag of food down on the desk, open it up, pull out the duck's head and start waving it: "It's just regular Chinese food!" They were *running* away from the desk.

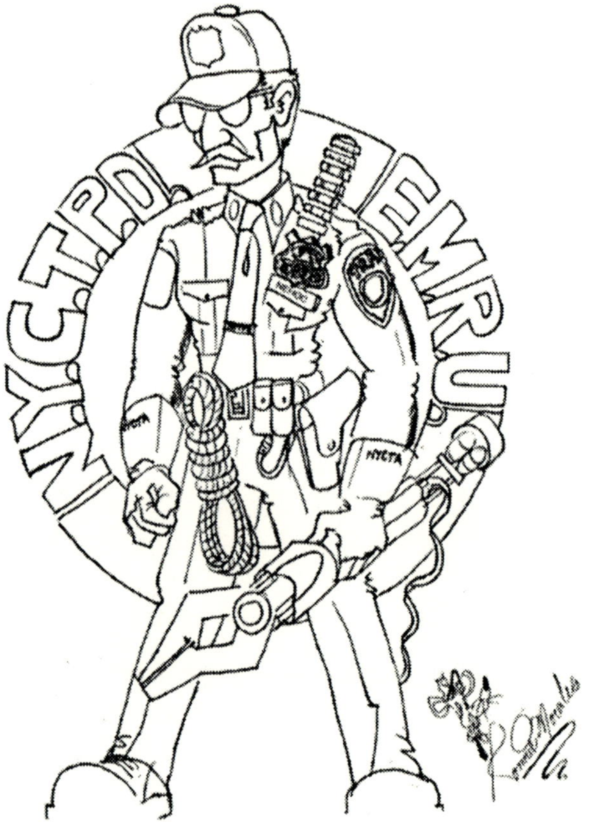
N.Y.C.T.P.D.
E.M.R.U.
NYCTA
NYCTA

Henry the Caveman

The New York City subway system used to be plagued with minor criminal vermin known as 'turnstile tamperers'. These guys made their meager living stealing subway tokens, either by breaking into the turnstile, or by jamming it up with something, waiting patiently, then putting their mouth over the coin slot and vacuuming out any tokens deposited by unknowing passengers. Some of them also possessed keys to the exit gates. They'd let in the passengers and pocket the tokens. These guys were more of a financial nuisance to the Transit Authority rather than a real menace to society. To the transit cops, they were a real pain in the ass, not so much for the crime statistics they would generate but because for the most part they were sub-human cavemen armed with metal implements, emotionally disturbed with their brains fried on crack cocaine or other substances, and they generally carried bizarre communicable diseases such as tuberculosis, hepatitis, HIV, et cetera. Oh, did I mention that many were as inclined to fight as to flee? Luckily, most of these guys are now past-tense, probably as a result of their swinging 80's lifestyle. They certainly aren't in jail.

Henry was arrested by one of my anticrime guys for about the thirtieth time in his criminal career. When he was brought before my desk, he was very cooperative... and very quiet. The cop told me when they grabbed him he put something in his mouth. He personally had arrested him several times before. The last time, Henry stuck his tongue out at him as he was being released with his appearance ticket. There was a razor blade on his tongue. It had seemed important to Henry to let us see that—that the razor was in his mouth the whole time that he was our guest. So, this time, it seemed important to me to ask him, "What's in your mouth?" Silence. "Open your mouth." Nope. Caveman no speak. Fine. "Fuck you, then. Stand there." Our hand-held metal detector yelped when we put it near Henry's head. I called for Emergency Medical Rescue to come to the district and told them I had a prisoner who had probably secreted a weapon in his mouth, but that he wasn't causing a problem—no rush. Henry stood at the front desk rear-cuffed rather than continuing the arrest process which normally entailed being uncuffed and placed in a holding cell. And he stood there. About an hour later, he said, "I have to go to the bathroom." I said, "Oh yeah? Open your mouth." Caveman no speak. No open mouth, either. And caveman stood there.

When EMRU showed up, I told him again to open his mouth. Caveman no speak. Well, they say that it's the amps that kill you, not the volts. Fifty thousand volts later, Henry spits out a few tokens and a key. This was disturbing for all of us, but probably more so for Henry, who still hasn't gone to the bathroom. Our metal detector continues to go off near his face. "Open your mouth, asshole!" Caveman no speak. Another lightning bolt and he spits out a few more keys. It was an emotional moment for all of us. One of the EMRU cops tells Henry that the next shot is going on his family jewels. He didn't see the cop hand me the Taser's battery before he put it to his crotch. Caveman speaks—then faints—without opening his mouth! The metal detector is still going off, so when Henry wakes up he gets zapped a third time. He spits out a few more things, and the detector is *still* going off! No shit. Caveman wins; we can't do this anymore. We sent him to the hospital under guard. He refused to keep still long enough to be x-rayed—for about six hours, anyway. The cop's attention span must've finally gotten used up, because the next thing that happened was that Henry innocently submitted to the x-ray, which showed nothing. Caveman wins again, and goes to the bathroom.

Don't Bank On It

Sometimes transit cops will get involved in strange capers not normally associated with the subway system. Like the cop who had the foot post at the Woodhaven Boulevard subway station, right underneath the Queens Center Mall. He hears a loud crash, goes upstairs, and finds himself handling a vehicle accident. I was a little annoyed when he called for a supervisor since I figured, what's the big deal? It's just a car crash, guy.

It seems a city bus driver lost control of the bus while making the turn onto Queens Boulevard. The bus blasted a car, which blasted another car, which blasted yet another car. Not finished, the bus then creamed a police car, mounted the sidewalk, flattened a row of mailboxes, nailed a few pedestrians, and crashed into a bank. Other than that, though, it was just routine.

Since I was the first boss on the scene, or possibly because it was a Transit Authority bus, or maybe because I'm a schmuck, I somehow ended up running this mess. The precinct boss helped me coordinate traffic diversions, the Fire Department Rescue and NYPD Emergency Service units opened up the bus like a tin can, and Emergency Medical Service ambulances evacuated the numerous injured to several different hospitals. The NYPD Highway Accident Investigation Squad showed up and did a preliminary investigation, and a precinct unit prepared the actual accident report. The Transit Authority accident investigators showed up to examine the bus, which I refused to allow them to move until I was able to get the building architect and a Department of Buildings inspector on the scene to assure me that the building wouldn't collapse when we pulled the bus out. And, hey, let's not forget about the United States Postal Inspectors who came to take custody of the now very flat mail.

As you can imagine, this whole thing was a major and dramatic scene which took several hours to successfully resolve. Once again, New Yorkers pulled together during a crisis and showed our true character and virtue under pressure. Well, most of us, anyway.

There's always somebody who just doesn't get it. I'm not shocked anymore, but I'm always amazed. It's near the end of this whole incident, as a matter of fact, so near that there's a monster crane ready to yank the bus out of the building. We've still got all the traffic diverted, and we've got police lines (yellow plastic tape that says, "Police Line—Do Not Cross") strung up all over the place to keep the pedestrians back while everybody works. I'm standing there admiring our operation when this woman, about fifty to sixty years old (and unless I miss my guess, probably named 'Sadie') just lifts up the police line and starts walking toward the bank. "Excuse me, ma'am, where are you going?" She dismisses me: "I've got to go to the bank." I had to physically stand in her way to make her stop. Remember, this scene still looks like downtown Beirut. "You *can't* go to the bank now. Would you please go back over there?" I gestured to the street where she had entered the police line. She gets pissed off and says, "I always use this bank. Why can't I go to the bank?" Irresistible: "Because it's a drive-through window now!" She says, "That's not funny."

Shit Happens

Every so often, a particular criminal provokes a reaction from the police. One such criminal insisted on snatching purses and handbags from subway passengers at the 67th Avenue subway station in Queens. He didn't do it once or twice, he did it a whole bunch of times. So many times, in fact, that the entire district's patrol strategy changed gears to catch him.

Without going into detail about the strategy itself, let's just say that the crucial position was manned by our most experienced anticrime cop. He shall remain nameless for security's sake, but his initials are M.M.

The operation had been in full swing for quite some time, involving quite a few cops, when from my safe position behind the desk I hear M.M. calling for a car on the radio. He doesn't sound happy. As usual, our dispatchers have to ask twenty questions, including: "Twenty crime, what do you need the car for?" M.M.'s answer was garbled and unclear. The dispatcher asked again. M.M. fairly shouted into the mike: "For an area search, okay central?" A chain reaction then began inside the district. First the chuckles, then someone started giggling, and within short order we're falling off our chairs. This fuck just hit again—right underneath the noses of our crack anticrime team.

Upon hearing the crime team report a negative result on their canvas, one of the district detectives gleefully radioed to have the victim brought to the command to look at photos. "Yeah, fine, ten-four!" Ouch! Is that smoke coming out of the radio?

When M.M. came in with the victim, it was pretty obvious that you could fry an egg off his face. Nobody said a word. This is, after all, serious police business. No more time for fun and games. You could hear a pin drop as M.M. walks the victim past the desk and into the detective's office. He came out alone a moment later. Nobody's saying a word. Finally, M.M. says through clenched teeth, "This woman got hit right on the platform, and she didn't scream or nothin'. Not a goddam sound." The tension is unbearable, and I for one can't take it anymore—"Well, that's probably 'cause she didn't want to *wake the po-lice!*"

Reader's note: I'm not really concealing M.M.'s identity for security reasons. I'm doing it because he cut off his blond pony-tail and joined the Highway Unit, and I'm afraid he'll give me a ticket if he ever catches me...

Louie The Lump

If there was one thing that I hated more than having to take the desk, it was having to take the desk after Louie. The closest thing I ever heard to anyone actually sticking up for him was, "he's got like twenty-three years on the job." How he managed that will always be a mystery to me. To be as kind as I can be, let's just say that Louie's alleged mind was seldom, if ever, on his work.

An off-duty transit cop was in a shootout one night in the District 20 area and had lit up a couple of guys with her 9mm Glock. I knew someone who was involved, so I actually knew most of the details before I came to work the following afternoon. Lucky for me, because I was supposed to relieve Louie on the desk. As usual, the turnover I got from him was sloppy and incomplete. He didn't even mention the shootout, but knowing him, it was possible he wasn't even aware of it. We're in the locker room and he's changing to go home. I asked if anything else was going on. "Oh, yeah, there was a shooting last night, so you might get some chiefs coming by." Really. "And?" He doesn't stop getting dressed, but now he does have a confused look on his face: "And what?" I'm going to kill him. "You said there was a shooting and there might be some chiefs coming by. What am I supposed to tell them?" He says, "That there was a shooting... Hey, I don't know, it happened on the midnight!"

I'm sorting through all the junk on the desk that Louie should've taken care of before I relieved him, and I'm trying to figure out how to get even. While I was going through the property locker I found an off-duty .38 revolver belonging to the cop involved in the shooting. It was standard practice in the Transit Police to temporarily hold all of an officer's weapons for safekeeping at certain times, like if the cop was in a shooting, was hospitalized, got arrested, et cetera. He should've told me that this gun was in the locker, but I'm shaking my head thinking that he probably didn't even *know* it was there. Hey, wait a minute...

One thing I learned about Louie was that he was actually more nervous than he was dumb. As shaky as he was, you think he'd pay more attention to what he was doing. He's walking out the front door and I ask him if there were any guns in the locker. He stops at the door for a minute, "No, I don't think so." Perfect. "Louie, you fuck, I find a gun in there, I'm going to shoot you with it, okay?" Laughing, he turns to go as I pull out the envelope with the snub-nosed .38 revolver. "Oh, shit, what's this?" He stops laughing. "Louie, are you crazy? What is this *doing* here? This is Officer Smith's gun! It had to go down to the ballistics lab! The District Attorney's office just called—oh, man, are you in trouble!" His eyes popped out of his head, and he was standing there stuttering as I pocketed the keys to the locker and stepped out for a cup of coffee.

It's not like I helped to push him over the edge or anything, but I think twenty-three years service is enough for anybody.

Stay In Touch

It was nearly the end of our tour when the report of a 'man with a gun' came over the air. We were almost there when two of our guys got broadsided by Mr. Magoo who apparently was unable to see their brightly-flashing police car. It all became clear when I interviewed him and noticed the hearing aid in addition to the coke-bottle glasses. Oh, well...

They weren't hurt too bad, but their car was totaled. We needed the Fire Department to cut them out of their steel accordion, and the whole thing took quite some time. Not too long after our scheduled tour of duty had expired, my radio starts squawking, "Twenty lieutenant, 10-1 [call the district]." I sent one of the cops to check all the payphones on a nearby street corner. No luck, all out of order. Again, "Twenty lieutenant, 10-1." I asked the Emergency Service cops if they had a cell phone; they did but it too was out of order. The duty captain arrived, and we couldn't figure out how his phone worked. "Twenty lieutenant, 10-1 forthwith!" This is starting to get irritating. "Yeah, central, I would if I could, but there's no phones out here!"

When I got back to the district about an hour later, the midnight desk lieutenant was hopping mad. "What the hell was going on out there?" I explained that there just weren't any phones. "You gotta keep the desk officer informed! You shoulda sent somebody to go find—" I cut him off: "Listen, number one, I needed everyone I had on the scene. Number two, who the fuck you think *you're* talking to?" Okay, so we're not the best of friends.

Within a couple of days, the midnight lieutenant published a directive advising everyone of their responsibility to notify the desk officer immediately of all details regarding any major incident, *or else*. The only thing missing from the rather heavy-handed directive was a picture of a skull and crossbones. The four-to-twelve sergeant was turning out the troops that night and I heard him reading the directive. I interrupted his roll call to apologize for the nastiness of it. "Look, fellas, this is kinda my fault. The other night when they wrecked that RMP, I didn't call right away and Lieutenant Smith almost had a baby. He can't do shit to me, but he *can* hurt you. So, do yourselves a favor—if you can call, call. I know it's hard sometimes, but do the best you can." With that, they hit the road and I took the desk.

About a half hour into the tour, I get a phone call from the sergeant. "This car took a red light right in front of us and wouldn't pull over. We finally got it stopped, and the driver is high as a kite." I'm listening patiently but I really don't know why he's calling. It sounds like a ground-ball. "Anyway, we've got her under arrest right now, so I figure we'll—oops, gotta go!" Now I've got a dial tone. Then the police radio starts beeping: "All units, twenty sergeant's got a foot pursuit, Queens Boulevard and 65th Street..."

It seems that while his partner was busy searching her car, the sergeant noticed a nearby payphone. He left the handcuffed woman in the back of the police car while he went to call me and she decided to climb out the window and take off, leading them on a several block chase. I can't say he didn't try to keep me informed, but I really wasn't all that interested. Well, not at first, anyway.

Gorgeous George

Doc and I are sitting in a police car parked on 82nd Street just south of Roosevelt Avenue in Jackson Heights, enjoying our cafe con leche. We both notice the two guys get out of the jeep parked a few spots ahead of us, and we both immediately make them as cops. One of them walks over to our car.

He shows me his identification, the five-pointed star of the U.S. Secret Service. "What's up?" He says that they're about to execute an arrest warrant inside one of the little storefronts on 82nd Street. I ask if he'd like us to go in with them, and he says thanks, but no thanks. "Look, we're just having coffee. You want us to leave, we're outta here, not a problem." He says, "No, no, actually, I want you to stay right here. If we have any trouble inside, we're going be coming out of there in a big hurry, you know what I mean?"

They go in. In my rear-view mirror, I see a uniformed cop come walking up. It's George. He had the post in the elevated subway station behind us on Roosevelt Avenue. Now, George is an unusual guy. He's been on a couple of 'true-story' television cop shows and he's been in the newspapers many times. He's like, uh, a hero cop or something... but all the other cops say that he's a legend in his own mind. He's not a bad guy or anything—the truth is, he's an aspiring actor and screenwriter. For him, I guess, the job really *is* living theater.

"Hi, George, what's up?" He salutes and says, "Nothing, boss. I just saw you from the station. Anything going on?" I tell him, "Nah, we're just relaxing." I catch a quick look at my partner, and I see he's looking at me real hard. All the color has gone out of his face. Uh-oh. Suddenly, I get the picture. Our friends are going to come running out of the storefront with some South American drug lords chasing them with machine-guns. George is going to visualize his Academy Award right here, and Doc and I are gonna get cut to ribbons in the crossfire.

"Ah, George, do me a favor, okay, and go back to your post now." He's visibly hurt by this unexpectedly rude request—I had just told him we were on a break, but now I'm telling him to get lost. He's walking away with his tail between his legs, and I feel bad. "Hey, George, wait a minute. Listen... the truth is, we're here on a stakeout with the feds. They're inside executing an arrest warrant, okay, and the whole thing is about to go down right now. It's all pre-planned, so we can't, uh, have any strange faces involved. You understand, right?" He's still got that lost puppy look on his face for a second, then he breaks out in a grin, "Yeah, right. See ya!" He walked away laughing.

I'd hate to be remembered as insensitive, especially after getting killed.

Dead Pan Handle

Even a stopped clock is right once in a while. A corollary of that theorem: It wasn't really Louie's fault *this* time.

Periodically, the Transit Police would launch some type of crusade against peddlers, beggars and panhandlers. One of these particular crusades involved the denial of 'Desk Appearance Tickets' to certain repeat offenders who had made the hit parade and were included on one of our scofflaw lists. One of these menaces to society had been nabbed on Louie's tour. The cop called downtown and was mistakenly informed that this particular guy was not to be given a DAT, and as a result, he was sent to Queens Central Booking. Shortly after I relieved Louie on the desk I found out that this prisoner, a 54-year-old loser, had taken sick at QCB and was now at the hospital. I asked Michele, my anticrime sergeant, to take a ride over and check on the situation.

Michele was one of my best sergeants, but her sense of humor was dry enough to choke a camel. Sometimes this would confuse me. One time, I had sent her to a typical subway job; a passenger had stumbled into the side of a moving train and was knocked to the platform. Actually, that's just a routine aided case, but anytime a train was physically involved in an accident we would send a police supervisor. She called me on the phone from the scene and said,

"You're not going to believe this, but apparently he's a little, uh, intox..." I chuckled. "No kidding. So is he okay, or is he going to the hospital?" She said, "Nah, he's dead." I laughed. "No, really what does he got, a knot on his head, or what?" She said, "Well, okay, he's got a knot on his head too, but he *is* dead..."

So tonight, she calls me from the hospital. "He had a heart attack and he's in the intensive care unit." *This* is not good. A drunk getting killed by accident is one thing, a prisoner dying in police custody is another thing entirely. I'm almost afraid to ask: "Michele, is he likely to die?' Long pause, then she answers, "I guess." Shit! I tell her to come back to the district right away. As I hang up the phone, I tell one of the cops to whip up a DAT and to load up the Polaroid camera.

Michele comes in and I stuff the camera and the appearance ticket in her hands and tell her, "No fucking way is Louie's prisoner dying on my tour. Get back to the hospital and issue him a DAT before he croaks!" At this point, I still wasn't even aware that this prisoner had been denied a DAT by mistake, that someone downtown had simply misread something. As far as I knew, I was breaking the rules, but it seemed to be the lesser of two evils.

Michele comes back a while later and tells me, "He's a free man." She hands me the district copy of the appearance ticket and the Polaroid photo which we were required to attach to it, and walks away. I glance at the photo and do a double-take. The guy's eyes were closed, he had tubes in his nose, down his throat, et cetera. "Damn, Michele, you take this picture before or after they buried him? It looks like he's DOA!" She comes over to the desk and takes the photo, looks at it carefully and says very seriously, "No, he looks *good* in that picture..."

Luck Of The Irish

Spend enough time in the subways and sooner or later you will encounter a passenger who goes head-to-head with a train. There are three basic types of accidents: First, there is the 'man-under'. This is where the person is run over by the train. A 'man-under' can be quite gruesome and is usually (but not always) fatal. Second, there is the 'space-case'. This is where the person falls into the very narrow gap between the moving train and the platform. The effect is no less horrible than that of a 'man-under' and the results are often similar. The third and last type of accident is the 'dragging'. Subway car doors do not open like an elevator's when they close on something, say, an arm or a leg. When they close, they close. The only thing that opens them is the conductor's key. If the conductor doesn't see that someone is caught in the doors for whatever reason, that person will pretty much stay caught in the doors as the train pulls out. If the person is inside the train with an arm sticking out, that's one thing. If the person is outside the train with an arm caught inside, well... The one thing that all three types of train accidents have in common is that the train *always* wins.

One night I responded to a report of a 'person struck by a train' at the Steinway Street subway station in Astoria, Queens. When I got there, the medics were already in the process of removing the victim to the hospital. Since it was not at all clear what had happened yet, I assigned Andrew to go to the hospital in the ambulance with the victim, who was apparently still alive at this point. I had to start the investigation into the accident. As a matter of procedure, we treated these accidents much in the same way we would treat a major crime scene, not only because they usually involved fatalities but because sometimes they actually *were* crime scenes. I didn't know which way this one was going. I went down into the subway as the ambulance took off.

Downstairs, I find the victim's friends, a group of college kids from the Midwest who were visiting the Big Apple. They don't know how it happened, so I ask them to tell me the story from the beginning. It seems they were going to the city for some night-life, they were waiting for the train, Mary was looking to see if the train was coming and she got hit by the train. That's it, that's their story. I was just about to ask if they all went to Moron University when I realized that they were on the wrong side to go to Manhattan. I ask them if the accident happened on the other side; they say no, it happened where we were standing. Hmmm... I'm no expert on trains, but I do know that they can be real sneaky. The subway is pretty noisy, but it's often deceptive as to which direction the noise is actually coming from. Mary and her out-of-towner friends were waiting for the train on the wrong side and heard one coming but didn't see one, so Mary leaned out over the edge of the platform to see further into the tunnel, and *whammo!* She was looking the wrong way and the train hit her in the back of the head. Not only did she never see it coming, but neither did her friends. That's why everyone was confused. I thought I'd heard it all.

I took Mary's friends to the hospital, and Andrew is with her in the emergency room. Now, I don't know if it's because of his prematurely gray hair, his Irish brogue, or simply his pleasant disposition, but Andrew's got a good way with people. They're working on her and he's in there talking to her, giving psychological first aid while the doctors sew up the gash on her head. He steps away to talk to me. "She's going to be okay," he tells me, and he starts to explain what he knows about the accident. I tell him what I've figured out and we both had a good laugh. He had all the information we needed for our reports, so it was time for us to leave. He tells me that there's just one more thing he's got to do and he goes back into the treatment area where her friends are consoling her. "Well, Mary, I have to go now." She says, "Oh, thank you so much for everything. You're wonderful, Andrew!" I think she's in love. "There's just one last thing," he says as he pulls out his memo book, "could you please give me six numbers between one and fifty-four?"

You Shoulda Seen The One That Got Away...

For a time, the Transit Police Department was in the fishing business (they called it 'sweeping' but I always felt that was a misnomer). We would go out in teams to lock up all the farebeats we could catch, and as soon as our nets were full, we'd go back to the district to do the arrest paperwork. We'd usually end up releasing our 'catch' with appearance tickets, provided that they weren't wanted.

1994 was a great fishing season in Rockaway Beach, and I came back for it like a true sportsman. Every night, we would go out and quickly fill our nets with ease. There were only about a half-dozen of us on the district fishing team but by the end of the summer we had made like something over a hundred and fifty arrests. With a few exceptions all of these arrests were effected without incident. We always treated our prisoners with courtesy since they really weren't arch-criminals. We'd process the arrests right in the holding cell area, and for the couple of hours it took to do the paperwork we were generally very pleasant and sociable. Our prisoners frequently struck up new friendships with each other while they were our guests. Sometimes, we'd have a real lively group and it was almost like throwing a party. More often than not, they'd actually thank us at the end of the night.

Part of the arrest process involved conducting a 'warrant check' on the person in custody. This was a search of the city, state and federal law-enforcement computer networks to see if anybody was looking for your prisoner. Every once in a while you would come up with a 'possible hit' which you'd then attempt to confirm. As with any computer database, the information was not always accurate or conclusive—just ask anyone who has mistakenly been listed as having bad credit or something ("I'm sorry, Mr. Smith, but according to our records, you're deceased...").

I suppose that having the name 'Jose Rivera' in Spanish is something like having the name 'Joe Smith' in English. Mr. Rivera was a perfectly pleasant farebeat. He worked hard as a waiter, and not having too much money he hopped over the turnstile to save a buck and a quarter. He had good identification, said he'd never been arrested, and it looked like he'd be out the door in two hours. That is, until the federal computer check said that he was a 'violent felony offender' wanted by the Seattle Police for narcotics trafficking. Hmmm... It's probably not him. The machine just searches by name and certain other bits of info we feed it; I'm sure there's probably something we can use to show that they're looking for a different Jose Rivera. We print up the warrant information and there's not too much there. Well, let's check height and weight, that's an easy one. Five-foot-eight, a hundred and fifty pounds? Shit. He *is* 5'8", one-fifty. Well, that's probably as common as his name. Anything else? It also says, 'scar, chin.' We go back to the holding cell. "Hey, Mr. Rivera, could you come over here for a second?" He comes up to the bars, and I ask, "Uh, what's that?" He says he got it from shaving.

We asked him to tell us every place, every address he ever lived at, back to when he was eighteen years old. He tells us, place by place. All New York or Puerto Rico. He could be telling the truth, but now we're starting to wonder if we've actually got somebody after all. They can be real cool under pressure, these arch-criminals. So, we call Seattle. I explain on the phone, "We've got someone in custody here who pops on a Seattle warrant. I doubt it's your guy, but I'm looking for more info so we can rule him out." The girl on the phone says, "Okay, no problem. Can you classify his fingerprints?" I bust out laughing and say, "Classify his prints? You kidding? You're lucky we can *take* his fucking prints!" There was a long pause on the other end, then she says, "What department did you say you were with, lieutenant?"

After I finished convincing her that we really were the police, the Seattle cops came through for us. It took a while but she managed to fax me a photograph of the narcotics trafficker they were after, and it was *not* our Mr. Rivera. Our guy was nervously waiting in the cell, all alone, since the other prisoners had long since been released. It's almost four in the morning. I come into the cell with a copy of the computer printout of the arrest warrant. As he read it, it looked like his eyes were gonna pop out of his head. Then I handed him the faxed photo of his West Coast namesake. I apologized about the delay in releasing him and told him he could keep the photo as a memento.

He thanked us. Profusely.

The Giz

Everybody loves the Giz. That's not his real name, of course. Anyone who's ever crossed paths with him in the Transit Police will know who I'm describing regardless of the name. The Giz has been on the job for over thirty years. When I was a mere smurf the Giz was my lieutenant; now, we work side by side in the Rockaway Beach Transit Police. The Giz is an average-sized guy, maybe a little short. He's got blond hair, a face from Ireland and a smile for everyone. He's got earrings and tattoos and parts of his body pierced that I don't want to know about. He comes to work sometimes covered with beach sand and even pieces of seaweed. It's entirely possible he might actually be a leprechaun.

One minor detail about the man strikes you fairly soon after you first meet him—he doesn't speak English. Well, not more than a word or two consecutively, anyway. His very name, Giz, is short for 'gizmatoid', which he uses as a kind of general-purpose noun. It's normally open to the listener's interpretation as to exactly what he's referring to. Wide open.

Some minor samplings of this foreign tongue:

Police supervisors frequently have to sign documents. Most of them say, "I've gotta sign this," or words to that effect. The Giz: "Let me whip a hammer on it..."

The borough commander's staff visited the district, and the Giz was laying low. Nobody knew where he was for a while. When he finally surfaced, he asked, "The bushels gone?"

You'd never know it to look at him but the Giz was a ferocious copper, and in his day was known to 'put the wood' to the bad guys. We usually don't let him out anymore, but not too long ago he did respond to a police emergency: he jumped out of the car with his stick in hand and asked a baffled precinct cop, "Where are the frogs, lad?" I do believe he intended on sliding a little wood their way.

"Check the valve." Huh? "Check the valve!" Translated: What time is it?

The Giz was at a community meeting and some particular crime problem was being discussed. When pressed for an official position on the subject, he said something like, "Uh, we'll send a couple loose units to pinch the goose." He doesn't go to community meetings too much anymore.

The most famous Giz-matism takes some explaining to set up: The Transit Police Department was a fairly centralized operation. Every recorded incident was given a serial number called a Central Number (CN# for short). In order to complete a job, a transit cop had to make a barrage of telephone calls, no small challenge in the subway. The two things the cop needed were the desk officer's 'classification' of the incident, and the CN#. First, call the desk officer. Then, call downtown, and the CN# would be given by someone who'd record the details for posterity. Finally, the cop had to call the desk officer back with the CN#. The predictable loop which often occurred was when the desk officer would withhold his classification pending a CN#, the guy downtown would refuse to give the CN# pending a classification, and the poor cop would get caught in the middle.

One night a young train patrol cop got involved in some trivial incident. He called the desk officer and described the whole thing. The Giz listened patiently, then told him, "Ah, make that a YGC." The cop dutifully calls downtown to get his CN#, relates the details of the story, and tells them that the desk officer classified the job as 'YGC'. They were just about to give the kid the CN# when they realized they didn't know what that meant... and neither did the probie cop.

Since they still held the coveted CN#, they told him to call back the desk officer to get an explanation for the 'YGC'. The kid calls the Giz back with his hat in his hand since it was not wise to piss off a desk officer. "Sir, it's Officer Smith again, I'm really sorry to bother you. I just got off the phone with downtown, and they wanted me to call back, uh, because they said they don't understand, uh, they don't know what's, uh, what's a YGC?" The Giz took no offense; he laughed and replied, "You got cock!"

YGC has become such a venerated expression within our command that members have actually used it, much to everyone else's confusion, in official police radio traffic.

Funny thing, when I'm out drinking with the Giz, the language barrier disappears completely.

Doubles, Anyone?

Everyone knows that the average person is not a criminal, so what then could be the source of our high crime rate? The recidivist, of course! To recid, in Latin, means to fuck up again. Most of the people cops lock up have been locked up before by other cops. Every so often, we get the cheap thrill of catching the same person twice.

Sweep

The Mott Avenue station, like most, has a bunch of public telephones on the mezzanine. We were doing a fare-evasion sweep there one night when this guy jumps over the turnstile and walks over to the phones. We grab him. His story is that he came in to make a call, a common excuse (most of these callers just coincidentally board the first train that comes in). Problem is, there's also a whole bank of phones right *outside* the turnstiles. Click, click, one under arrest. This guy kept crying all night long about how we were wronging him, to the point where the other honest beats in the cell told him to shut up. They actually started throwing shoes at him, he was so annoying. Like the rest of them, he was given a desk appearance ticket to answer for his heinous crime at some future date.

Two days later at the same Mott Avenue subway station we were sweeping again. Some guy jumps over the turnstile and walks over to the phone. We walk up to him. Normal police procedure calls for something like, "Police, you're under arrest." He turns around—it's the same whiner we locked up two days ago. "Don't you say a fucking word!" He didn't.

Bernie
Rockaway Beach is a beautiful place, except for what's commonly referred to as Rockaway riff-raff. Like Bernie. A local drunken asshole, he normally causes disturbances which require police attention. I'm not against alcohol, but I think some people shouldn't drink—especially those who like to fight with the cops when they're hammered. Bernie loves to fight. We locked him up (again) one night after some minor stupidity and rather than beat the snot out of him (which he deserved) we found an even better way to abuse him: he was brought in handcuffed, full of piss and vinegar. All he wants is to go a few rounds with any or all of us. I told him we were too busy to pummel him. A couple of the boys literally sat on him while we wrote him a summons for disorderly conduct. When the ticket was written, we stuffed it in his pocket, uncuffed him, threw him out like the garbage, then locked the district's front door. To be ignored bothered him worse than a beating would have.

Oh, yeah?
One night we were involved in a canvas for a robbery suspect with the anticrime cops from the precinct in Far Rockaway. Canvassing means driving around looking for a bad guy, usually

with the victim in the car to point him out. The crime guys have the victim in their car. About ten minutes into this thing, they radioed for another unit to meet them. We were right down the block and were there in a New York minute. The crime sergeant has someone in cuffs, and he's screaming bloody murder. No fight, just noise. I asked the sergeant if this was the guy we were after since he didn't really fit the description given by the victim. He says, "Oh, no. I locked him up a few months ago for carrying a gun. I seen him tonight while we were canvassing and he ducked behind a building, so I stopped him and asked him what's up. He says, 'Nothing. I ain't got no gun; you can check.' So I did, and he's got another gun." The guy was just pissed at himself that the sergeant called his bluff. The dispatcher asked if everything was under control. Everything except us laughing and the guy cursing...

Artiste

Two collars I love to make are robbery and graffiti. Robbery because it's a savage affront to normal civilized behavior, and graffiti because it's an arrogant expression of contempt for the rights of others. Rarely do the two coincide, but one night the planets were properly aligned. We're parked under the busy elevated subway station at Lefferts Boulevard when this young man comes up to the police car and tells us he's just been robbed. We started asking the basic police questions, and he mentions that he thinks they went into an apartment building around the corner after they robbed him. I tell him to jump in the car, and off we go. He directs us to a building on 117th Street and Liberty Avenue. Using skills we picked up from our friends in the housing police, we search the building and find three guys on the roof getting high and doing graffiti. Turns out they're the guys who robbed our victim. Click, click, three under. Such was the quality of our police work that two of the three pleaded guilty to first-degree robbery not long after the arrest.

Months later, we were cruising down Liberty Avenue when there was a radio call of a guy spray-painting graffiti at 116th Street and Liberty. Who do I see fitting the description but the guy I locked up on the rooftop several months earlier who had refused to plead. He was still in deep shit over the earlier robbery and was out on bail awaiting further court appearances. He was less than happy as I locked him up again for graffiti and he uttered this brilliant statement—"You know, I'm gonna stop coming around here." Oh, break my heart.

Red Light, Green Light, One Two Three...

We're stopped at a traffic light on Cross Bay Boulevard. There are three lanes in each direction plus turning lanes with arrow lights. Now, some New Yorkers think that they're smarter than everybody else when they're behind the wheel, and they just *have* to get wherever it is they're going. All the rest of us are just out sightseeing. Well, while the rest of us sightseers were obeying the traffic signals, this one guy, obviously in a big hurry, figures out that while the turning lanes have their green arrows, everybody else has a red light. Being smarter than everybody else in addition to being in a big hurry, our hero decides to pull into the 'left-turn only' lane when the green arrow came on, but instead of turning, he blew the intersection light and went straight ahead. A perfect crime except for that he didn't see the other car coming in the opposite left-turn lane. *That* driver foolishly thought that when he received his green arrow it was safe to make his turn. Apparently, he's not as smart as our guy. There was a big screech but no crash. To help fill the embarrassed silence after the screech, we threw in a couple of woops on the police siren.

This guy tries to tell us that the light had just gone yellow-to-red real quick, that's why he took the intersection. "Honest mistake, okay?" We point out to him that he took the intersection from the 'left-turn only' lane. "Yeah, well, that's because the light changed so quick, the guy in front of me stopped short and I had to swerve around him into the turn lane." In addition to being smarter than everybody else, he apparently thinks he's smarter than us dumb transit cops. Rather than ask him why he couldn't stop in time if the car in front of him could, we simply pointed out to him that we were sitting at the light and saw him pull out of his lane *after* he had come to a stop. While he was temporarily at a loss for words, we also pointed out to him that his driver's license was suspended and he was now under arrest. "Hey, wait a minute! You guys are transit!"

Even though he's in handcuffs in the back of a police car he's still trying to explain how he had done nothing wrong at the intersection. He talked all the way back to the district. And he talked. And he talked. We bring him in front of the desk and he's still going. Enough already. "Hey, listen—number one, you're locked up, so save your breath. Tell your story to the judge. Number two, who cares *what* you think? If you could *drive* worth a shit, your license probably wouldn't be suspended in the first place!" There's a long pause, and he says, "Yeah, that's true, I guess..."

Family Connections

We got a call of an 'off-duty PO needs help' on board a train. Since the call was coming from the train crew, it was less likely to be bogus than if it had come from 911, and half the police department shows up. It turns out to be a real call.

Apparently, two guys had gotten into a fistfight on the train, and an off-duty cop jumped into the fur ball. Now, it's all over. We've got everybody separated and off the train. Since it was rush hour we released the train to continue on it's way. I asked the off-duty cop what happened. Turns out he didn't know what started it, he just broke it up. I ask one guy what happened; he said the other guy started it. I ask the *other* guy, and he tells me the opposite. What else is new?

Both of them have got cuts, bumps and bruises, but neither is seriously hurt. One guy's in his thirties, clean-cut and well-dressed, apparently coming home from work. The other one's a little younger and dressed in street clothes. I'm kinda leaning toward believing the older guy, but I've see too many peculiar incidents to fall for a stereotype. I have the cops bring them together, and now I'm holding court:

"Gentlemen, I don't know what happened here or why, so let me explain what's going to happen next. Whatever I do, I'm going to do the same thing to both of you." The older guy says, "That's crazy! Look at me," and he gestures to his bloody and torn clothing. "Yes sir, I understand that, but I don't know who's fault that is. If either of you claim to be injured, I'm going to arrest both of you on assault charges and let a judge sort it out." They both think it over for a minute. "Are either of you hurt?" They're both okay. "Fine. Then you'll both be getting summonses for disorderly conduct." The older guy says, "Wait a minute, why do I get a summons? *He* started—" I cut him off with, "Would you rather get arrested?"

The cops separate them again to identify them and prepare the summonses. I see one of the cops is having a little trouble with the younger guy. "Is there a problem here?" The cop doesn't buy his identification. I don't either. He's starting to doubletalk. I tell him, "Listen, if we can't ID you for a summons, then we're gonna lock you up instead." Now he's sweating because he knows I'm not kidding. He's trying to explain, and he says, "You can call my aunt, she'll tell you who I am!" I ask, "Who's your aunt?" He says, "Mary Smith." Like I'm supposed to know who that is... Well, as it happens, I do. "John's mother?" He says, "Yeah!" I said, "That's Joe's mother, too, right?" Now, he's smiling with relief, nodding his head. Click, click, one under. We had locked up John *and* Joe before—not exactly the best choice of character references. I voided the summons on the older guy and gave him my sincerest apologies.

And would you believe it, Mary's nephew had a warrant out for his arrest? Go figure.

Say What You Mean, And Mean What You Say

Before I can tell this story you need to know some background to 'set it up'. A while back, Mike got into a little trouble when a prisoner he was guarding tried to hang himself. Mike wasn't anywhere near the cell area when it happened. It was actually a pretty feeble gesture on the prisoner's part with little real chance of success since he wasn't being held in an overnight lodging cell, but the one behind the front desk with lots of cops in and around constantly. Just the same, it was Mike's responsibility to watch him. He was written up and given a 'complaint'. His explanation was simple: a sergeant had told him to go put gas in one of the police cars. In other words, he was only doing what he was told. The sergeant's rebuttal was that he had just meant for Mike to take care of the car at his earliest convenience, *not* to drop what he was doing. Mike said, "When *he* tells you to do something, there ain't no ands, ifs or buts—he wants it done now." I mention in passing that the sergeant, who shall remain anonymous, was nicknamed "the General." Hmmm...

It's now a hot summer day in 1994. We get a report of a robbery-in-progress on board a train at Broad Channel. The first cop on the scene quickly informs everybody by radio that the victim stayed on the train, but two bad guys left the subway and were headed north on Cross Bay Boulevard on foot. Mike was coming down Cross Bay when he spotted them. His partner grabbed one, and the other one led Mike on a merry foot chase for several hundred yards. He caught up to him, stomped him into the ground and took a gun off him. I show up on the scene before the dust settles and order that both bad guys be kept separated. We throw Mike's prisoner in the back of my car and the other guy in the back of Mike's car. Now, the plot thickens. The prisoner in Mike's car tells us that he was just riding the train when this guy comes up to him, pulls a gun and orders him to help commit a robbery or he would kill him. "You mean you just got *kidnapped* by this guy?" That's *exactly* what he meant. He says he was on his way to meet his family when this happened. Back at my car, Mike's prisoner is going through what we refer to as 'the perp act'. He's hysterical, yelling and screaming about his innocence, and he's jumping around and kicking like he's an EDP. "Knock it off or I'm gonna get my Taser and light you up right here in the car, understand?" I didn't have a Taser, but he didn't know that—he calmed right down. We've got cops further up the line looking for a robbery victim *and* the family of one of the 'bad' guys. We found both. Not only did the robbery happen, but the second guy's family *was* waiting for him. After a bit of investigation it appeared that the second 'bad' guy was telling the truth—he was innocent. If you do the math, you'll see that that meant the guy Mike caught was twice as bad as we thought.

When the guy in the back of my car calmed down he was really just planning his next move. We get to the district, and now he's pulling the 'sick perp act'. We have to walk him in almost holding him up. He needs water, he's gonna pass out, et cetera. We toss him in the cell and in a matter of minutes he's lying on the floor. While I radio for an ambulance with as much boredom in my voice as I could muster, Mike tells the guy (who's now feigning unconsciousness), "Hey, scumbag, we called an ambulance. Go ahead and die if you want, but you're *still* under arrest."

The ambulance arrives. As they start to examine him, he goes into convulsions. He's literally foaming at the mouth. Mike and I are in the cell block as the medics are frantically working on him. We're keeping up a non-stop patter of encouraging remarks, like "That's gotta hurt," and "Hey, maybe he's got eyeball cancer or something!" They're looking at us like we're nuts. This guy is in really bad shape. Now, the medics are calling for help on *their* radio. It looks like they've got to 'intubate' our prisoner to save his life—in other words, they have to shove a hose down his windpipe. Mike says, "Wow, you mean he could go outta the picture? Cool!" The second team of medics show up and they're setting up a miniature operating room right there in the cell block. They've got needles, bottles, electronic monitors, everything. "Hey, Mike, could you do me a favor whenever you get a chance," I asked as they worked feverishly, "and go gas up the car?"

They thought we were out of our minds when we both nearly fell down laughing. I tried to explain to them that Mike had a history of doing automotive maintenance as his prisoners croaked, but they didn't get the joke.

Reader's note: Our prisoner didn't die. Mike and I took him to the hospital and watched the doctors examine him. As a matter of fact, it turned out he wasn't sick at all. It was all just an act, as we suspected. Regarding crime and punishment—he had been locked up earlier in the month for robbery and gun possession and was out on bail when we grabbed him. The housing cops were looking for him in connection with a homicide, too. Based on our investigation the second prisoner was exonerated of any wrongdoing and was released, and Mike's guy was sentenced to 7 ½ to 15 years in prison, where he will have ample time to work out and improve his health.

Anatomy Of A Killer

One of the best fishing holes we had for a while was the Mott Avenue subway station in Far Rockaway. There were many farebeats to be had there. It did present the District 23 fishing team with certain technical obstacles which had to be overcome, however. One problem was that the station was unlike any other in District 23 in that the token-booth and turnstiles were on the street level with the platforms and trains upstairs. If we were to try to reel in a fish downstairs in full public view, we might catch him but probably wouldn't get too many nibbles on the ol' hook afterwards.

Without going into detail on how we would overcome that problem, another problem would in turn soon present itself: what to do with our sweep prisoners? I had a great idea one night—we'll keep them on the empty train which is parked upstairs. Even though people in the neighborhood can see the train, nobody'll know that the 'passengers' sitting on it are actually beats under arrest.

The plan worked very well for several sweeps. Then we had the pleasure of meeting Charlie. We immediately got the impression that Charlie spent a little too much of his free time sucking on a crack pipe.

We've got seven people already under arrest, all sitting on that 'A' train quite peacefully. As with most of our sweeps it was simply business and the people we locked up just went along with the program. Imagine our embarrassment when Charlie started acting out in front of our guests. He kept getting up despite being told several times to sit down and be quiet, growing progressively more agitated each time. Finally, he jumps up and starts yelling, "I ain't no Far Rockaway faggot! I'm a killer! I'm a killer! I'm a East New *York* motherfucker!" Enough already. I gave Muggsy the nod, and he, uh, sat Charlie down. Muggsy is a big boy, and now our killer needs medical attention. "You asshole," I tell Charlie, "this was a perfectly good sweep until you fucked it up!"

We took him to Peninsula General Hospital in a police car because he was causing such a commotion we really couldn't wait for an ambulance. Besides, he really wasn't hurt too bad anyway. The PGH emergency room, like most, has two sets of double doors at the ambulance entrance. As we walk in, Charlie is still carrying on, and as we're between the first and second sets of doors he starts kicking out at the walls and anything else he can reach. Really, enough is enough. The Transit Police were well-trained in some very nasty handcuff techniques, including one known as 'pain compliance'. Well, Charlie complied alright. He's on the ground and I'm whispering in his ear, "You're in for a *real* long night if you don't knock it off, okay?" He didn't answer me, because I think he was having a religious experience. At the very least he saw lots of bright colors. He's just laying there, panting, like he's had a heart attack or something. "Come on, let's go." We picked him up off the floor and brought him to the triage area. Now, Charlie isn't making a sound other than breathing. He's as meek as a church mouse. He walks where we tell him to walk and stands where we tell him to stand. The triage nurse comes in and asks him his name. He doesn't answer. She asks what his problem is, like where does it hurt? Still no answer. She sees the trickle of blood coming out of his mouth, and says, "Okay, let me see your lip." Charlie explodes, "Lip? *Fuck* my lip, look at my motherfuckin' *arm!*"

Step Lively

One of our most unusual sweeps on Mott was noteworthy not so much because of who we caught, but how we caught them:

Our spotter came over the air with, "There's a whole bunch just went—I couldn't see, there were too many—white baseball caps, that's all I got for sure." Well, that'd have to do. Our team goes into action. Shields out, colors displayed, holstered guns visible and portable radios cranked, we stroll onto the train, only to find the other team. There were about thirty people, all wearing white baseball caps, all smiling.

"Good evening, folks. We've got room in the van for six people with ID who ain't got no plans for tonight. And, please, nobody with warrants..."

Communications Arts & Science

To call the transit police radio system 'unreliable' was an understatement. We operated with a system which was added on to another existing system used for the trains, and neither one worked too well. The department used to make public statements to the effect that they knew the system was bad (like they could ever deny it) but that we were doing the best we could—as if that public confession would absolve them of guilt. Then, to save money, they replaced the police dispatchers with civilians. Not that the cops on the radio were so great, but after they civilianized it seemed that sometimes we weren't even speaking the same language anymore. Oh, well. It all went to further the transit cops' self-image as rugged individualists, because sometimes you really *were* alone out there.

The bright spot in this otherwise bleak picture was that, as always, there were opportunities for laughter, especially when trying to teach 'central' a lesson. Even under pressure, with tempers flaring, it was possible to get in some good shots. Of course, everything was taped, and I'm not sure they had any sense of humor downtown.

Environmental Science

The far southern reaches of the transit system in Queens encompass some very non-urban areas. Part of the territory patrolled by District 23 is actually a national wildlife preserve. No skyscrapers there, but lots of plants and weeds. So much vegetation, in fact, that one of our chronic problems during the dry summer season is fire. The subway stations at Howard Beach and Broad Channel are frequently affected by smoke conditions as a result. During one of these incidents, I was having a lot of trouble communicating with the transit dispatcher. For some reason, she just couldn't understand or comprehend that I was saying 'brush fire'. We went back and forth several times. "You got a *what* fire?" "A brush fire, central." "Did you say a *bus* fire?" "No, central, a *brush* fire..." It started to get pretty silly after a few minutes. "Central, you know what a *forest* fire is? Same thing, only shorter."

Philosophy

In the early nineties, one of our chiefs had reasoned that calls coming from the Transit Authority should not be as unreliable as calls originating from 911, which were bogus with notorious regularity. Well, I'd say his reasoning was correct—calls from the TA *should not* have been unreliable, but... Our dispatchers were instructed not to accept a final disposition of 'unfounded' or 'unnecessary' when the job originated from the TA. One night in 1993, I responded to a call of a 'suspicious male' hanging out near a token booth. When I arrived the token-booth clerk pointed me toward a guy sitting on the bench. I walked over and said hello. I asked him what he was doing there, and he said, "I'm waiting for a friend, why? Is something wrong?" I told him nothing was wrong, but that if his friend didn't show soon he might as well give up since the trains were scheduled to stop running at midnight due to track repairs. He wasn't aware of that, and he thanked me. I noticed he was doing a crossword puzzle, something not real popular with the criminal element. I radioed, "Central, 10-90Y [unnecessary]." A few minutes later the dispatcher calls me back and asks *why* the job was unnecessary. Now, to have to explain a radio code kind of defeats the purpose of using a code in the first place, so I said, "Because I'm a better judge of character than the railroad clerk." I guess they didn't think that was funny, because I had to call some captain downtown to explain just what I meant.

Criminology

In a manner related to our anal-retentive centralized recordkeeping, our dispatchers used to bombard you with questions about police actions which really didn't need to go over the air. One type of questioning was regarding 'classification' of incidents. If you had an arrest or a report of a crime, they'd want you to give them the details right down to the exact Penal Law charge. Considering that even desk officers used to refer to various law books prior to classifying incidents it was a little unfair to put cops on the spot for this info, particularly if they had been physically involved in anything. One time I responded to a robbery and when I told the dispatcher that I had a victim in my car to canvas for the bad guys, she asked, "Can you advise what kind of robbery?" I said, "You know, central, a *robbery* robbery."

Public Administration

To defend our dispatchers, they were usually only trying to do what they were told. You could tell, because some of the silliest transmissions were made after a long pause—like someone was leaning over the dispatcher's shoulder and putting in their own two cents. One night we chased a train from Far Rockaway up through Broad Channel and finally into Howard Beach. I knew we weren't going to be able to catch it, so I called the precinct cops on my division radio and asked them to give us a hand. They did, and they grabbed four guys who had beaten and robbed someone in Far Rockaway. We arrived on the scene moments later and then coordinated bringing the victim over from Far Rock for a show-up. Once they had been positively identified as the perpetrators I told the transit dispatcher, "Central, four under for robbery and assault, 106 crime is taking the collars." Bear in mind this was a transit caper. About a minute later the dispatcher calls me back and asks, "Why is the 106 taking the arrests?" Good question. I answered, "Because I'm a lieutenant, and I said so."

Physiology
A District Twenty cop had locked somebody up. The guy was screaming like a banshee in the background of the radio transmission. The dispatcher asked the cop if everything was under control, if he was okay. With a real bored tone of voice, he answered, "I'm fine, central. Just an earache, that's all..."

Psychology
Between the lousy system, bad information, poor management and negative comments from the field, it must've been tremendously stressful to be a transit police radio dispatcher. That's the way it seemed one night when we were responding to a job where the dispatcher had inadvertently put out some bad information. The cops started going after the dispatcher, who then started making more errors, and the cops got even more bloodthirsty. She finally beeped the alert tone a few times and said frantically, "Okay, okay, clear the air, clear the air! All units, be advised that—that—UNNGHHHH!!!" All the cops started jumping up and down giving each other the 'high-five'. We finally made one snap.

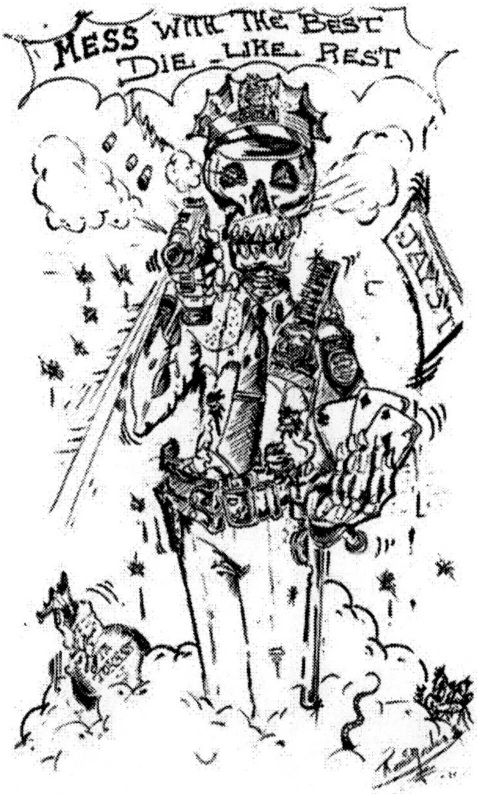
MESS WITH THE BEST
DIE LIKE REST

Kung Fool

The average transit cop was a highly trained, battle-ready fighting machine feared by criminals throughout the city (except on Staten Island). We were tough enough to patrol alone with lousy communications; in groups we were invincible.

There was a brawl one night right in front of the district on Beach 116th Street. You got used to it after a while since there's not too much else to do in Rockaway late at night. We were in the district processing a cell full of prisoners from a farebeat sweep when somebody ran in from the street yelling, "Hey, there's a big fight outside!" Kevin, his partner and I went to see what was going on. Just as we stepped out, ka-*boom*, this guy knocks Bernie into the middle of next week. Bernie, you may recall, was a local troublemaker who we'd locked up numerous times for stuff just like this. However, none of us had ever laid him out with one punch before—he was a pretty tough bastard, especially when he was drunk. Even though we've got a cell full of prisoners we decide we've just gotta go get this guy, if only to find out how to make Bernie calm down so quick.

Bernie's assailant does a fast walk down to the corner of Rockaway Beach Boulevard and hangs a left. He doesn't seem to be aware that three cops have taken an interest in his handiwork, but then again, we're in plainclothes. Kevin and his partner catch up to him at Beach 115th Street and make the stop. I'm about a half a block or so behind them. I'm not in a rush; between the two of them, they *are* a five-hundred pound gorilla. It looks like it's all over when suddenly the guy spins away from them, I hear a *thwok*, and he's running toward me.

They say police work comes down to a split-second decisions in times of crisis. I've got just about a split second to make my move here because this guy is coming at me real quick. In a millisecond I see that he's looking past me. He's running for daylight and doesn't even perceive me as an obstacle. I could tackle him... Nah. We'll probably both go flying through the plate glass windows of the storefronts. I could punch him... Nah. It might break his neck, plus I'll probably break my hand. Wait! I got it! As he sprinted past me I threw the most picture-perfect roundhouse kick and caught him square in the belly. I felt his spinal column wrap across the instep of my left foot and the impact spun me around. I'm laughing as the boys run past, "Set your watches, 'cause he's going down!" I figured ten seconds, tops.

He made it as far as the corner of Beach 116th and Rockaway Beach Boulevard and turned right. We trotted up to the corner expecting to find him around the bend collapsed like a heart-shot deer who didn't know enough to lay down and die. We turned the corner, and *shit!* He's flying up the block! He ran all the way up to the corner of Beach 116th and Beach Channel Drive, and was still going! Some precinct cops see us chasing him and now we've got a 10-13 going for a foot pursuit. We're playing a losing game of catch-up until a precinct car finally stops him at Beach Channel Drive and Beach 113th Street, about six blocks from where my kick should've stopped him. "He threw the bag over there!" Threw what bag over where? The precinct cop goes into the bushes and comes out with a nylon satchel full of cocaine packaged for street sales. None of us saw it but we weren't even *thinking* about that. We were still in a state of shock over the foot chase. Me, I'm a babbling idiot: "I can't believe he ran away. I got him. I *got* him. How the fuck did he run? How *could* he run?" Kevin says, "Hey, I even heard it! That kick sounded like a sledgehammer hittin' a fucking watermelon!" The three of us are just standing there, panting. With a hopeful look on his face, one of the precinct cops asks, "So, uh, you guys taking the collar?" I looked at the gazelle in handcuffs. He's about thirty-five years old, pudgy build, and—I don't believe it—he's wearing *sandals*. This is too much. "Nah, you want it, you got it. We got a bunch of collars tonight already." So, we gave away a felony narcotics arrest and went back to processing our tankful of farebeats.

Reader's note: I found out later what that 'thwok' sound was. Mean bastard that he is, Kevin had taken a nightstick with him. When the guy broke away, Kevin took a power swing at him and caught him right across the Achilles' heel. Good thing, too, otherwise he would've *really* left us in the dust.

Broadcast Comedy

Although I've taken digs at the transit radio dispatchers, keep in mind that the NYPD division radio dispatchers were sometimes no bargain, either. While their system was technically superior, their dispatchers were as fallible as ours. My personal gripe was that some of them would refuse to acknowledge calls from transit units unless it was absolutely necessary. Not all of them, just some. They did have one dispatcher who, hands down, was the best I've ever heard on any radio. Anybody who's heard him will know exactly who I mean.

There's some kind of FCC rule which requires all broadcasters to periodically identify themselves over the air with their station call sign and broadcast frequency. When this dispatcher would do that, he'd follow it with, "...that's NYPD Division Fifteen, we've got the 100th, the Fighting 101, the 102, the 106, Transit, Street Crime, Housing, Aviation, you need it, we got it..." Cops used to call asking, "Central, who's on this division?" just to hear this.

Most dispatchers were dry and humorless. Not this one. He never missed an opportunity to slip in a gag while he was broadcasting. Some unit had called in a plate check. "Okay, six-adam, that comes back [car's not stolen] to an '87 Toyota, two door, blue, registered owner, Ahmed Al-Khafzahoul Mujahedeen, common spelling..."

He got away with murder most likely because he was the sharpest dispatcher I've ever heard, police-wise. One night there was some kind of commotion on the air, one cop frantically calling another by his first name. That almost always meant an impending disaster of some sort. Some dispatchers would ignore an unauthorized transmission like this, or worse, would continue to broadcast routine traffic, stepping on the two cops talking to each other. Not this one. He recognized them by their voices, stopped what he was transmitting and started calling them, "One-sneu (street narcotics enforcement unit), one-sneu, you okay?" He had to call them a few times before they finally answered, but they did and said they were okay. He asked for their location and the cop got snippy, "I said we're fine, central!" He came back with, "Alright, tough guy, call me if you need me."

One of the reasons that some division dispatchers wouldn't acknowledge transit units was that we did not show on their computerized 'run-down'. In other words, we were like extras. After all, we weren't part of the NYPD. If they had a subway job they would usually assign it to an NYPD sector car. Not this one. If it was a transit job he'd call us. He even knew most of our car numbers so he could enter the assignment into his computer system. One night, he calls me: "Transit lieutenant, you on the air?" He tells me there's a 911 call for a report of some past crime, the victim is at so-and-so subway station. I was pretty far away but I tell him, "Standby, I'll get you a unit." I switch radios and assign the job to a nearby plainclothes team. Then I switch back to the division radio and tell him 'transit crime' is going to pick up the job. He says, "Ten-four, Lou, they got a car (number)?" I laugh since they're on foot, "Yeah, central, Chevrolegs." Silence. Well, *I* thought it was pretty funny... About five minutes later, he's broadcasting some routine job, "six-eddie, ten-eleven commercial burg alarm, one-eleven sixteen—what? Oh, I get it! Chevro-*legs*! *Ha, ha, ha!*"

Tree Killers

One of the definitions given in my dictionary for the word 'bureaucracy' is:

> "A system of administration marked by ...ever increasing inefficiency and red tape." (*Britannica –Webster*)

The Transit Police Department was actually a very well-administered organization. However, like any organization we did sometimes lapse into bureaucratic stupidity. One of my favorite wastes of paper was our system of promulgating new rules or procedures.

The Chief decides that nobody should stick beans in their ears. He publishes a written directive which states, "Members shall not stick beans in their ears," and distributes it throughout the department. So far, so good. Then it starts to get a little silly. The chief in charge of the 'Patrol Bureau' publishes his own directive which states, "You heard him, members shall not stick beans in their ears." Then, the chief in charge of the 'Borough' would publish... That's right, each commander at every subordinate level would in turn publish another written directive of their own telling us not to put beans in our ears. We'd end up with sometimes as many as five or six written directives all saying the same thing. Honestly, I got the message when the first chief wrote it down, but hey, that's just me.

Towards the end things started getting really ridiculous, kind of like the fall of Roman Empire. They started 'civilianizing' the department in order to get the cops out from behind their desks and to save the taxpayers' money. Their methodology was a little strange —they'd let some armed administrator retire, then they'd replace him with a civilian manager, usually at a higher rate of pay, and generally with an expanded staff! How exactly this was a savings, I'm not sure, but luckily for the taxpayers some of those civilians really knew their shit, unlike us dumb cops. The proof was evidenced by my favorite written directive of all time, put out by a new and improved civilian 'chief' shortly before our demise. This directive informed us about the need to conserve natural resources, and advised all of us to avoid wasting these precious resources by limiting our paper usage. The directive outlined several methods to avoid wasting paper, such as using both sides of the paper, making double-sided photocopies wherever possible, using the blank sides of old documents for scrap paper, et cetera. All of these were good ideas and showed great foresight. The only criticism I had, and it was a very minor one, was that this directive was published and distributed as three-page, single-sided, *doubled-spaced* document. No shit.

If it would make the now-bald rain forests feel any better, that directive made great scrap.

Knight of the Round Table

One of the trendier things they started doing in the Transit Police was to call down a half-dozen or so randomly selected officers of the same rank to have informal meetings with the chief to discuss items of mutual concern. They called these enlightening little sessions 'Round Table' meetings. Getting randomly picked for a round table meeting was generally met with about the same level of enthusiasm as was getting called down for random drug-screening.

When my number came up, I couldn't get out of it. I worked a four-to-twelve tour the night before, and had gone out fishing with the boys. We didn't finish processing the collars until about five in the morning. There wasn't really enough time to go home and take a nap, so I hung out in the district until it was time to shave, throw on the cleanest uniform I had, and jump on the train.

The ride from District 23 to Jay Street in Brooklyn was very long. It was even longer if you took the local train, which I did—hoping desperately that I'd be able to get involved in something or make an arrest—anything to get out of going to this meeting. No such luck. I show up in the chief's office to find the other lieutenants from around the city who also couldn't catch a cold. After some reunion handshakes and commiseration, the chief comes out and invites us in to his office.

I didn't know this chief personally, but every dealing I'd had with him up to this point had been fairly unpleasant. His nickname was 'Chief What-The-Fuck.' He was big on chewing a nasty cigar and yelling at people before all the facts were in. I *really* didn't want to be here.

"Good morning, fellas, come on in. Sit down—make yourselves comfortable." There's a couple of boxes of donuts on the table, and the coffee pot is brewing fresh. The chief makes some small talk with two or three of the lieutenants who he apparently knows from the past. Everything is very nice, very informal. It's gotta be a trap.

With the pleasantries completed, the chief steers the meeting to business. He's very genial, but at the same time, very focused. He wants our input on these issues. After all, we are the supervisory backbone of the department. Captains may command districts, but lieutenants actually run the show, and he knows it. I'm starting to think that maybe I've misjudged this guy. Everything he said was reasonable and intelligent. I'm exhausted from being up since yesterday, but I'm kinda glad I came here after all.

About forty minutes into the meeting, he produces a stack of paper. "I'd like you guys to take a look at these, and I'd like you to make sure that you're using them when you plan out your sweep strategies." I take a look at one of the stapled handouts. It was a statistical report of fare-evasions, broken down station by station, tour by tour. The Transit Authority used to compile these reports. The Transit Police, at least on my level, used to throw them in the garbage. Between the fact that the chief was being such a swell guy, and that I had just come from locking up farebeats all night, I decided to speak up. "Chief, with all due respect, these numbers, they're really, uh, not too good." He frowned a little, and said, "I'm sure they're not a hundred-percent accurate, but you can use them as a tool." Not a hundred-percent accurate? Ha! My fellow lieutenants are all shaking their heads, indicating agreement with me. Egged on by their support, I replied, "No sir, I mean, they're no good *at all*. C'mon, Chief, they make these numbers up! They're total horseshit! Look—here, it says that there were three hundred and seventy-two farebeats at Edgemere Avenue on the four-to-twelve. I got news for you, there weren't three hundred people using that station in twenty four hours, and I mean coming, going, paying or not! You really think we're gonna go fishing where there ain't any fish, and *not* go fishing where the fish are jumping into the boat? I'm telling you, this shit ain't worth the paper it's printed on." As I finished my little outburst, I see my fellow lieutenants nodding their heads in wholehearted agreement, with murmurs of, "He's right, Chief..." He's just looking at me, silently chewing his cigar. I mention in passing, that to be a Chief in the Transit Police, you had to be appointed by the Transit Authority.

Anyway, District Twenty's not that bad. I worked there before, so it's not like I'd get lost or anything.

My Brother's Keeper

One of my cars called for a supervisor to meet them regarding a possible arrest situation. I arrive at the foot of the Queensboro Bridge to find they've got a car-stop. Not only does the driver not have the right paperwork, but they think he might be drunk. I ask him if he's been drinking; he says he's had a few beers. I ask him to walk a straight line to the corner. On the TV cop shows, they can never do that. He does. Thinking quick, I then tell him to walk back to me—backwards. I bet he can't do that. He does. Rats. I couldn't even do that sober. So much for drunk driving. "Where's your license?" He left it at home. He swears he has one, just not with him. He says his name is David Silverberg. The only paperwork he's got is an old insurance card for the auto, but the owner's name is something like

'Vincenzo Bacciagalupe'. He says it's his uncle's car. "How can a guy named Silverberg have an uncle named Bacciagalupe?" He goes off on this elaborate line of shit about how his father married his cousin whose brother divorced his sister and remarried his... et cetera. "Okay, okay." I really don't trust this guy, so I radio in for a plate check as well as a driver's license check.

We're waiting for the dispatcher to give me the results, and Silverberg says, "Hey fellas, can you speed it up a little? I'm in a hurry." I ask him what's the rush, and he says, "I got an appointment with my work-release counselor." What? "You're a convict? You think you'll be on time if I throw cuffs on you? Then shut the fuck up. Besides, what are you doing drinking beer before you go to see your counselor?" He says, "Hey, as long as you're not doing drugs, they don't give a shit." The dispatcher tells me that the driver's license comes back clean, but the car's plates are expired. Against my better judgment, I decide to give him a break. Silverberg starts to say something, and I tell him to shut up before I change my mind.

About two hours later, the dispatcher asks me to call her on the phone. "Lieutenant, those plates you ran before? Um, the reason they came back expired was, ah, well the car was stolen..." I asked her what was the point of her telling me, since the guy was long gone. She said she figured she had to notify *somebody*. Well, now I'm pissed off. I kinda knew Silverberg was full of shit, but I never expected our own dispatcher would inadvertently help him get over. I replayed the incident in my mind. Most people mix the truth in with their lies; it makes it easier to remember the story that way. Plus, I can't imagine why anyone would tell the cops he was a jailbird in the first place, especially if he wasn't—Silverberg couldn't have been lying about that.

We take a ride over to the Queensboro State Correctional facility. I describe David Silverberg to the desk sergeant. "Wait a minute, I'll be right back." He comes back with a photograph of our guy, but the name on the photo is *Harry* Silverberg, not David. He must've given us the other name so the license check would come back clean. The sergeant told me he was in lockdown for the night. I explain the computer error with the stolen car, and tell him I want to arrest Silverberg. He says, "Why don't you just wait until morning when the other guys come for him?"

It seems that the Staten Island detectives are going to lock him up for burglary, and they had rigged a deal with the corrections people to release Silverberg from his sentence early. Our guy was out partying, celebrating what he thought was his soon-to-be walking papers. He really was in a hurry to get back to jail. He just didn't know that the minute he walks out the door tomorrow he's getting arrested again. My partner comes in and tells me he found the stolen car behind the correctional facility—parked on a fire hydrant. What balls.

I get the Staten Island detectives on the phone, offering them the additional felony charges to add on when they lock up Harry Silverberg. The detective laughed, "Good, the prick. You know who he burglarized, this fucking guy? His brother. He steals from his own brother, you believe that?" I said, "You mean his brother David?" There was a pause on the other end of the phone: "How'd you know his name?" Oh, I don't know, I just took a shot.

Smooth Move

Then there was the guy who came into the district one afternoon and said that he was afraid to go home because he had had a fight with his wife earlier, and now there's a police car parked outside his house. He wants to know if they're there to arrest him. He gives me his address and I telephoned the NYPD division dispatcher. She checked her screen and told me that a precinct sector car was at that location handling an unrelated job, a noise complaint about a barking dog or something like that.

"It's okay, they're not there for you." The guy looked like I lifted a million pounds off his shoulders. He thanked me. "So, I guess you didn't want to get locked up today, huh?" He laughed and said, "No, sir, not at all!" I said, "Don't mind me asking, but if they *were* there for you, you think it was a good idea to come in here?" He looks around and realizes everybody's been watching him. "Uh, yeah, heh, heh, I see your point..."

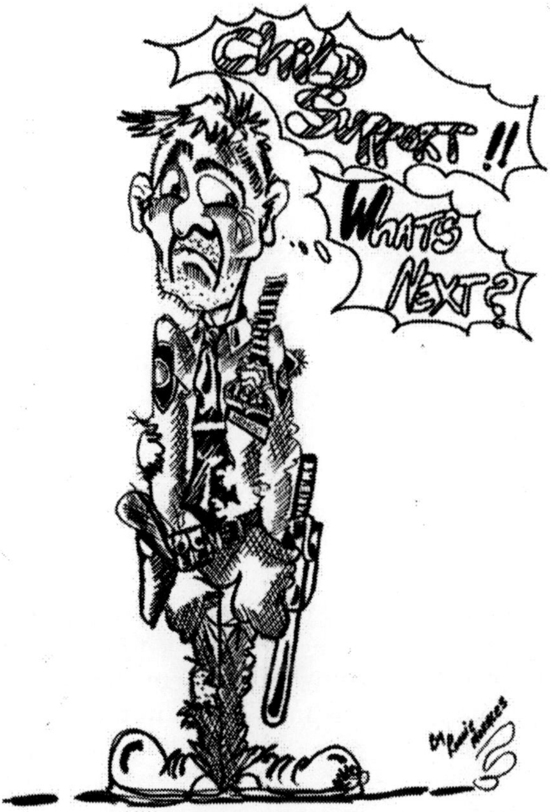
Child Support !!
What's Next?

Bear Market

By the end of 1994 it looked as if the three police departments were actually going to be merged into one. This had been proposed many times over the years but it never came to pass. This time, the Mayor was determined to make it happen and his strategy was a simple one, based on simple economics: The City of New York had always footed the bill for the payroll of the New York City Transit Police Department, and if the New York City Transit Authority refused to relinquish control of it's police force to the city, then the city would stiff them for our payroll. The people of the city wouldn't suffer any permanent loss of police protection as a result of the subsequent and inevitable layoff of over four thousand transit cops since the Mayor promised to hire us all back from a not-yet-established 'preferred' hiring list. In a political battle reminiscent of the Cuban Missile Crisis, the Mayor and the TA bigwigs were eyeball to eyeball, and we were all waiting for someone to blink.

The prospect of getting laid off was not a pleasant thought. If it did happen, would bosses be re-hired as bosses, or would we all be re-hired as cops? And at what pay? Starting pay? Even more ominous, the real basic questions of *when* and *if* we would be re-hired at all were far from certain. For those of us who were arbitrarily assigned to the Transit Police in the eighties as a result of the tri-agency hiring system, the whole thing had a nasty ironic twist.

Not too many people could go to work everyday with these thoughts, especially when the work sometimes involved risking your life. Most of us just put it out of our minds and tried not to think about it. Still, it had an effect.

There was a rush on the pension system. After having paid into it for a number of years, most of us were in a position to take out 'low-interest' loans from our own monies. If you borrowed too much or too frequently, however, there were certain tax penalties. I had borrowed before this merger thing and my accountant had strongly advised me against taking any more pension loans, but when it came down to facing the tax man if I didn't get laid off—or chasing down the people who had un-employed me if I *did*—the choice was obvious: Give me all my money now! Later, my accountant said, "What did you do? You dummy, I *told* you not to do this..."

Although the Transit Police was a trendsetter in converting to 9mm semi-automatic service pistols as early as 1990, I for one steadfastly refused the new weapon, instead opting to retain my old-fashioned Smith & Wesson .38 revolvers. I had never felt ill-equipped carrying these magnificent tools, especially since I could shoot the balls off a fly at fifty paces. In late November, 1994, I finally surrendered, and was in the last 9mm transition class offered. People wondered why I finally took the new gun after holding out so long. Simple: We bought our Glocks at a special departmental price of three hundred and ninety-eight dollars. I figured, if they lay me off, I'd sell it for market price of about seven hundred bucks.

Reader's note: I've since learned to like the Glock, but I'm thinking of selling it to my accountant. Since he's my pal, I'll probably let him have it for six hundred. After all, it is used...

The End

On April 1st, 1995, I was assigned to District 20 in Jackson Heights but was covering as the District 23 patrol supervisor on the four-to-twelve tour that night. On my way down to Rockaway, while driving south on Woodhaven Boulevard I hear the alert tone beeping away on the NYPD division radio:

"In the 102 David sector, we got a 10-30, woman being robbed at knifepoint inside the drugstore, Woodhaven and Jam, Woodhaven and Jam. 102 David?"

We're less than a block away from Jamaica Avenue. "Ah, transit lieutenant, central, give me that job. I'm right down the block."

The dispatcher is my favorite. He says, "Okay, unit to back the transit lieutenant, Woodhaven and Jam on a thirty?"

A 102 precinct sector car acknowledges and the dispatcher gives us all the info he has. Then he asks, "Lou, what's your RMP number?"

As we roll up on the robbery, I answer, "Central, that's Transit 356. Well, until midnight, anyway..."

On April 2nd, 1995, at 0001 hours, the New York City Transit Police Department ceased to exist. We 'merged' into the New York City Police Department and became the NYPD Transit Bureau.

Walk Softly, But...

One of the chronic daily assaults on the quality of life in New York City is that there's no place to park your car. Ever. Traffic is one thing, but what do you do when you can't park? Circle until you run out of gas? Of course not. You just do whatever you gotta do. Then you get a ticket. It's enough to make you want to take the test for the post office.

Prior to the merge of the New York City police departments, people used to do things with automobiles right in front of us which they wouldn't have *dared* to do in front of our brother officers of the NYPD. After all, we were just transit cops, right? Pretty silly misconception, because in reality transit and housing cops were always empowered to enforce any law or ordinance, just as the NYPD cops were.

The first thing they did after the merge was to paint all our police cars NYPD blue. The cops can still tell each other apart by virtue of some codes and numbers on the sides of the cars, but to the average citizen we all look alike. We quickly noticed that motorists reacted quite differently to us when we were driving our brand-new blue cars. I was born and raised in Queens, so I'm not unsympathetic to the plight of the motorist—but I always take advantage of the opportunity to have a laugh or two, especially at work. I'm sure I'll get into trouble one of these days...

We'd pull up to a subway station and there'd be a dozen cars parked illegally in the bus stops, on the fire hydrants, et cetera. Sometimes there'd be a driver sitting in the car waiting to perhaps pick up a subway passenger. I'd start droning away on the police car's public-address loudspeaker like a robot zombie, "*Bus stop... Nooooo parking. Nooooo standing. Nooooo anything...*" At this point, the occupied cars would usually pull out to begin the eternal circling procedure. *"Tickets. Lots of tickets. Towwwww trucks..."* Now, people would start running out of stores or wherever. Okay, so I'm laughing, but I'm not writing.

One night, one of my cops made an arrest and I had to go pick him up. We pull up to the subway station at Queens Boulevard and Union Turnpike and there's absolutely no parking due to all the illegally parked cars. I get on the loudspeaker and start going through my act. Cars start moving out and we pull in. Then this guy comes up to me, identifies himself as an FBI agent and says, "Please, we're picking someone up here, we're not staying!" It seems most of the cars were government cars. I tell him not to worry, we're doing the same thing; the loudspeaker routine was just bullshit so we could park the police car. We both had a quick chuckle and I went downstairs to get my cop and his prisoner.

When I came up a few of the government cars were pulling out. Looks like the feds got their man. My partner was laughing, "Holy shit, you missed it – they dog-piled on this guy!" As we're putting our prisoner in the back of the police car, a junior G-man runs up to me with his ID out, "Officer, officer, wait, that's my car over there, the blue one, okay, *please* don't give me a ticket..."

Bad Boys, Bad Boys, Whatcha Gonna Do...

I was on patrol one afternoon in Jamaica when there was a radio signal 10-13, a distress call from a cop. A guy had pulled a gun on a narcotics sergeant during an arrest sweep and jumped out of a second-story window making good his escape, except that the understandably distressed sergeant jumped right out the window after him. The sergeant lost him in the ensuing foot chase, but a whole bunch of us showed up so quickly in response to the 10-13 that we came to the conclusion that the guy was hiding, probably lying in the weeds somewhere. I realized pretty quickly that not only was I the highest ranking member on the scene, but that I had also announced the fact on the radio—making it pretty difficult for me to wriggle out of this one. I wasn't too familiar with the area so I asked the sergeant to draw me a map. While he was doing that, I requested Aviation and Emergency Service to respond to the scene. As soon as my map was finished, I began assigning units to positions forming a perimeter around a couple of square blocks. I ordered all the plainclothes units to leave the inside of the cordoned-off area, and waited.

The plan was simple: I figured since the guy was somewhere in the immediate area armed with a gun and laying low, we'd just seal off his escape routes and hunt him down with the proper equipment. At least it seemed like a plan to me. I had not yet been issued an NYPD manual and I had no real idea what the proper procedure was. I was going by stuff I had seen on Fox TV's "Cops"...

The guys with the shotguns, machine-guns and heavy body armor showed up. As soon as the police helicopter was hovering overhead, they began a house-to-house, backyard-to-backyard search. It took them about forty minutes and they came up empty-handed. I felt pretty stupid as I called off the operation. The helicopter flies away. My first helicopter, and it's gone. So sad. While I'm trying to figure out how to explain the whole thing, and to whom, one of the cops on the perimeter radioed me and said that a homeowner had just spotted the guy in her yard. My guess is she probably saw some of the cops searching. I asked if that was what happened. "No! She described the guy we're after, and she just saw him!" What the hell, I ordered everybody back to the perimeter and told the dispatcher, "I know they're out of gas, but if they can do it, I need aviation back at this location." Within minutes, I get another helicopter. I still can't believe they sent the *first* one, and now they're flying sorties like it's the Persian Gulf. The whole operation begins again, house-to-house, this time joined by a hungry police dog as well. The first helicopter comes back, presumably after refueling, and relieves the second helicopter. I'm really hoping we catch this guy, but... we didn't. To my surprise, nobody was pissed off at me, although I certainly felt like a subway loser. The narcotics sergeant told me, "Don't worry, I'll see him again." Yeah, and he'll be like a neighborhood folk hero.

I ran into the sergeant a couple of weeks later and he told me that as promised, he saw our friend again and he locked him up. He said the guy asked innocently, "Were all those helicopters looking for *me?*"

If The Shoe Fits

After the merge we stopped processing collars in the transit districts. Instead, we began to bring all our arrests into the precincts. This caused a little bit of friction because now the precinct desk officers had to sign off on our arrest paperwork as well as that of their own people. To minimize any hard feelings resulting from the perception of adding to their burden and to maintain tighter control over the quality of my own officers' work, since the merge I've continued to sign off on arrest paperwork belonging to my crime guys. In effect, I always act as our own desk officer even though we no longer have any such position. Hey, nobody ever said I couldn't.

The importance of properly prepared arrest paperwork became painfully evident during a Supreme Court trial case that we were involved in. The defense attorney, in his efforts to cast a 'reasonable doubt' about his client's guilt in the mind of the jury, was trying to attack our credibility by drawing attention to errors and inconsistencies in our paperwork. This was his most viable option since his client was a lowlife piece of shit who was guilty as hell.

The district attorney was going over the battle plan with me and Steve. We were examining the mountains of paper connected with the case when he said, "John Doe is black?" Steve and I both look up. At this late point in the game, neither one of us could believe that the prosecutor could be uncertain on such a fundamental point. Steve says, "No, John Doe's white. *James* Doe is black. Why?" He's holding the booking sheet for John Doe: "Well, it says here that he's black." Steve is one of the most meticulous cops I know when it comes to paperwork. "No way, gimme that!" He snatches up the flimsy yellow sheet of paper and reads it intently for a minute—then he sags in the chair. "Aw, shit." Somehow, he had checked the wrong box when he had made the arrest. Here we are at trial against a defendant whose lawyer is saying that the police have got the wrong guy, and Steve's little goof isn't going to help our case one bit. I'm thinking smugly to myself that that's why we need supervisory oversight on this stuff. Even a normally sharp guy like Steve can make some fairly dumb mistakes unless there's a good boss keeping an eye out. "Well, who's the dope that signed off on that booking sheet?" Now the two of them are glaring at me. "Oh..."

...And You Won A Color TV, Too!

Since my wife's a cop I can even tell war stories at home. The only problem is that she has this really annoying habit of 'one-upmanship'.

My wife and her partner are on patrol in Brooklyn one night when they stop for what they thought at first to be a motorist in distress. They pull up alongside the other driver and she gives him the universal signal for 'roll your window down'. Well, in New York, anyway, the signal is a circular motion with your hand while mouthing the words, "roll your window down." This guy turns on his windshield wipers. Close, but... Rightly suspicious of the fact that he doesn't seem to know how to operate his own vehicle's controls, she orders him out of the car. A radio check of the license plates, and voila! They come back stolen. Not the car, mind you, just the plates. Well, stolen is stolen, so click, click, one under.

At the precinct, the guy is swearing that the car belongs to his friend Kyle and that he legitimately borrowed it. Makes sense so far – if you borrowed a car, you'd really have no idea about it's registry (or lack of). While her partner beeps the guy who supposedly owns the car, she checks the car further. Surprise, it's just a little bit warm. The detectives from Queens are extremely excited by all of this. They want to know if she has Kyle in custody. She tells them, no, and asks why. It seems they've been sitting on his house for weeks, and they'd *really* like to talk to him.

So, she gets Kyle on the phone and tells him that she locked up his buddy for driving his car without any proof of ownership. He nervously assures her that it really is his car. She asks if he has any paperwork. Of course, he doesn't, so he starts double-talking that his father has the papers, he's out of town, et cetera. Putting on her best combination act of dumb female and incompetent bureaucrat, she tells him that if he comes down to the precinct to claim the car, she'll let his friend go. Kyle knows he really can't do that, so he balks. She nonchalantly says, "Look, I go off-duty in one hour and they won't pay me overtime. If you want to help out your friend, come on down. I'm not waiting; if you don't show up by the end of my tour, the hell with it, I'm going home and he goes to jail. You know, I'm trying to do the right thing here, but..."

Well, her double-whammy worked. Everybody is standing around the desk when Kyle peeks inside. The desk sergeant, in his best serve-the-public tone, asks, "Can I help you, sir?" Obviously uncomfortable, he mumbles something about his car. The sergeant says, "Are you Kyle?" He comes around the desk with a big smile, "Hey, thanks for coming down," and offers a friendly handshake. Kyle takes his hand, I guess out of politeness——and click, click... That easy. It seems the car was taken in a carjacking in Queens, and was subsequently used in a number of violent push-in-home invasion robberies. Kyle was a bona fide crime wave.

I'm impressed, but I still outrank her.

The One That Almost Got Away

I knew it couldn't be good when the sergeant called for *his* supervisor. That would be me. They were doing a fare-evasion sweep at 90th Street and Roosevelt Avenue. Well, I've done so many sweeps myself—what could possibly have gone wrong that I haven't seen before?

I arrive to find them standing near the prisoner transport truck. They're all a little disheveled looking. "What's up?" One of their prisoners escaped, but they caught him. He's in the truck. I ask if anyone got hurt, they all say no. I open the door of the transport truck. There's a young guy sitting in cuffs, maybe seventeen or eighteen years old, all sweaty and out of breath. "Hey, why'd you run for?" He says he was scared. "You been locked up before?" He shakes his head no. I'll bet. "Well, now you're in even more trouble, stupid." I close the door and turn to the sergeant, "Okay, no big deal. Just add on an 'escape' charge when you do his paperwork. I'll see you later." I start to leave and the sergeant, a twenty-year veteran, says, "Uh, can I talk to you for a minute?"

It seems that they were trying to consolidate trips with the truck. The plan was that the truck was going to take the prisoners to the precinct and on the way back, they were going to stop and pick up coffee and donuts. The team chipped in and had the money ready. Makes sense to me. "So?" So, while they were getting the prisoners ready to be transported and giving the money to one of the cops with the truck, the guy made a break for it. All hell broke loose, they had to chase him down, et cetera. "Okay, I get it. What's the problem?" The sergeant is starting to get all red in the face. He says, "We can't find the donut money. I think he stole it."

For the second time, I opened the door on the transport truck. "Alright, stand up!" We search the kid head to toe looking for the missing twenty bucks. He's got something like twenty-seven bucks on him. "Eh, what's this?" He's also got the 'prisoner's property' form which the cops filled out when they first arrested him, crumpled up and stuffed in his pants. It's not a receipt; the prisoner doesn't *get* a copy of it. Plus, it says he only had had seven bucks and change. Amazing. This guy not only stole the cops' donut money as he was making his move, but he also had the presence of mind to steal the property form which had his name on it. "Scared, huh? You're full of shit." I tell the sergeant to charge him with Grand Larceny, a felony, and to voucher the property form and the twenty bucks as arrest evidence. He tells this to the cops and it sets off an undercurrent of mumbling. "Hey, Sarge, then who's gonna buy the donuts?"

Friendly Competition

Back in July, 1995 I had a real busy month in District 20 in northern Queens. It seemed every time I went out, somebody got arrested for robbery. By the time the month ended thirteen unlucky bandits had gotten scooped up as a direct result of my coming to work. We did have to let three go afterwards, though, because the victim in that case lied to the cops. Hey, that's not my fault; the capture was still legitimate based on what we knew at the time.

My lovely bride was working as a sergeant in the NYPD Transit Bureau, Kings Task Force. Very impressive title for what was basically nothing more than our old late-night train patrol unit! And I may have mentioned to her once or twice about my exploits as a crime fighter, but it's not like I was bragging or anything. I just mentioned it, uh, a couple of times, that's all.

A few months later, just as things had gotten pretty quiet where I worked, they started to pick up for my wife out in Brooklyn. She grabbed four guys for a robbery one night. "Great." A few nights later, she grabbed five more. She told me the story, then said, "That's nine for the month, and the month's not over. What's the number to beat, ten?"

Hmmph. "Actually, it's thirteen. Also, you gotta look at the number of incidents—you're getting them four and five at a time. You really only had two captures, there were just a lot of bodies each time. I had to catch *mine* one and two at a time, and it took me *seven* incidents to catch thirteen." She looks at me carefully for a minute then says, "Actually, it *is* ten. You had to let three of them go." She can say whatever she wants, but I'm not bowled over by the fact that she had two, count'em, two incidents, and caught everybody involved. Everybody gets lucky once in a while. I may have mentioned that to her, too...

Before the month was out, she responded to a report of a robbery at the Liberty Avenue subway station. The victim was waiting in the street as she pulled up. He had gotten robbed by four guys down by Livonia Avenue and had jumped on the bus to get out of there. My wife tells him, "Get in," and they take a ride back to where the robbery happened. It's a little after two in the morning when she spots one of them standing on a street corner. Click, click, one under. They throw the prisoner in a precinct car and keep looking. A guy peeks out of a doorway to see what's going on. "There's another one!" Click, click, two under. What are the chances of that happening? "Sarge, we going in now?" She says, "Not just yet." They keep looking. A few minutes later, someone else peeks out of another doorway. Click, click, *three* under. Now, you know they're not leaving. It's about twenty after two when the victim says, "You're not gonna believe this, but..." Click, click. In a time span of about fifteen minutes, my wife made four separate apprehensions for armed robbery, bringing her total for the month to – *thirteen.*

Women.

Wrong Place Squad

In 1995, the NYPD announced with much hoopla that they had formed an elite 'cold case' squad manned by only the best of the best detectives, and they would take only the cases which mere mortals had been unable to solve.

Not to be outdone, as soon as I managed to claw my way back to the Rockaway peninsula, we formed a 'wrong place' squad, led by the illustrious Jack B., former U.S. Marine and present-day stand-up comic. He believes in properly positioning himself so as to get maximum results with minimum effort. He made three arrests in 1995, each a finely-crafted masterpiece of police work.

Wrong Man
We responded to assist a housing cop in foot pursuit of a robbery suspect—a male black about twenty years old, six feet tall with dreadlocks wearing a white tee-shirt, green pants and brown shoes. The housing cop lost the guy around Beach 56th Street in the projects. Jack arrives and promptly finds a male black about twenty years old, six feet tall with dreadlocks, wearing a white tee-shirt, green pants and brown shoes—carrying a .380 automatic pistol. Jack locks him up. We get the housing cop on the scene to confirm that this was the guy he had been chasing for the robbery. It wasn't. The guy was just minding his own business and had poor taste in clothing. Jack had scooped up the unluckiest gunman in Far Rockaway.

Wrong Place
For a time, Jack was exiled to the midnight shift as a result of having been caught trying to scam a day off. He had told his lieutenant that he had an emergency, that his girlfriend was in the hospital. The lieutenant gave him the day off, then called the hospital to check Jack's story ("Jenny who?"). So, it's about a quarter after four one morning, and Jack was uh, shall we say, on his lunch break—yeah. He was on his lunch break, and he hears screams coming from the subway station. Once a Marine, always a Marine. He leaps into action and discovers a guy with a stocking pulled over his face dragging a girl to a deserted stairwell. Jack locks the guy up for attempting kidnapping. I interviewed the girl later and she said, "That cop came out of nowhere!" Well, that's true...

Wrong Man, Wrong Place

There was a robbery on the mainland and the suspects were believed to have escaped on a train to the Rockaways. Once again, Jack leaps into action and stops a train on the island of Broad Channel. Searching the train, he spots his quarry—a guy with a loaded, sawed-off 12 gauge shotgun. Jack locks him up, and boy, was the guy pissed off. Not only did he *not* commit the robbery, but he was also the kidnapper Jack locked up earlier in the year. Might as well stayed in jail. You can run but you can't hide.

Reader's note: Stay tuned for excerpts from departmental commendation reports taken from the personnel folder of Jack B. Be forewarned, they are not for the faint of heart.

Dinosaurs

Policing has probably always been a seniority-driven profession. This has certainly been highlighted in New York City as a result of the fiscal crises of the 1970's. The city came so close to going bankrupt that it had to resort to some extraordinary measures to remain solvent. One of these measures was the laying off of several thousand cops in the mid-seventies. The police departments didn't hire any new officers at all until the eighties. When these new officers did join the force, there was an enormous gulf in seniority between the post-layoff cops and the pre-layoff cops, who became known as Dinosaurs. When I joined the Transit Police in 1985, there were many dinosaurs walking the earth. We feared them. Now, they are nearly extinct, and we abuse them.

I used to work with a housing lieutenant. We were discussing the layoffs and other ancient history. He mentioned that he came on the job in 1974 with the last class hired which did not get the axe. I made the comment, "Well, you lucked out, right? You didn't get laid off." He replied, "Yeah, I lucked out. How'd you like to be dead-last for vacation picks, have Tuesday and Wednesday as your steady days off, and never be able to get a day off on the weekend—for over eight years?" At a loss for a good answer, I said, "Hmmm..." He says, "By the way, how long are *you* on the job now?" He knew I was on about eight years at the time. Very ill-tempered, these dinosaurs.

In 1995, after the merge of the police departments, we changed our uniforms to a new dark-blue shirt, just like the old one they used to wear before the lay-offs. Maybe they switch uniforms to distract us from trauma. Anyway, the new uniform has brought the seniority issue to the forefront since we now wear LAPD-style hash marks on our long sleeves denoting years of service, and on the summer shirt we wear a seniority pin. The first day we had to wear the new uniform, some wiseguy at roll call said, "Hey, Giz, when the stripes hit your elbow that means it's time to go home!" When we changed to summer shirts, everybody starts asking the Giz if he's got any dirty movies. He probably does, but it took him a minute to figure it out—the seniority pins are in Roman numerals. His says, "XXX".

The Giz is not the winner. One of our precinct counterparts in Rockaway has over thirty-five years on the job. Borrowing an old Navy expression, I've told him that *rocks* don't live that long. When we changed to the new uniforms, of course the matter of money entered the picture since we all had to buy new stuff. A bunch of us were talking about this one day and he started to say, "Well, when I came on the job, the uniform allowance was..." Before he could finish, somebody said, "When *you* came on the job, they were wearing animal skins and carrying clubs!"

I sometimes go to the precinct guy for advice, even though I do kid him a lot. One time, while giving me some pointers he used that abuse-triggering expression, "When I came on the job..." I cut him off with, "Hey, pal, let me tell you something—when *you* came on the job, *I* was *walking!*"

Believe it or not, that bold claim could not be made by over ninety-percent of the police officers on the job today. I must be getting old...

Go, Team, Go!

People watch the silliness portrayed as police work on television and have no idea just how precise and demanding a profession it really is. They make it look easy. I can assure you, it's not.

Young Vinny was walking by when the bus full of rowdies passed, most likely behaving in a rude and uncivilized manner. "Oh, yeah? Fuck you, too!" Possibly, airborne saliva was exchanged. I doubt Vinny expected that when the bus came to a stop a block away that twenty or so guys would get off with the express intention of continuing the conversation with him...

They chased him up the block and around the corner, and caught up to him as he was trying to duck into a store. The vicious gang assault was pretty shocking, especially since it was occurring in broad daylight in a busy shopping area a few days before Christmas. Vinny got banged around pretty good until numerous passersby, including a couple of construction workers with pipes and crowbars, interceded to beat the mob away from him. The transit cop up in the nearby elevated subway station also saw the commotion and ran down, but by the time he reached the store everyone was in the wind.

The boys and I were on a robbery stakeout a few blocks away when we heard the cop calling for an ambulance for Vinny. We jumped on a train that was just pulling in and were there in a minute. Aside from some blood and a giant knot on his forehead, Vinny looked like he was going to live. Since we were on foot I put him in the precinct crime car to start canvassing. The description of the mob of assailants was broadcast, vague as it was: "Fifteen to twenty males, number one wearing a black jacket with a red hoodie. Number two through twenty, NFD [no further description]." My team and I then headed south on Cross Bay Boulevard, and a complex chain of events which can be understood only by serious students of the art of professional urban police work was put into motion.

It's December, and there's snow and ice all over the place. Regardless, Kevin, Richie and I hit the ground running. Well, jogging anyway. This wasn't so much a foot pursuit as it was a bloodhound search. We came to the corner of Cross Bay and 107th Avenue, and still-shocked bystanders were directing us as to which way the mob had fled. "Transit lieutenant, central, the perps are headed east on 107 from Cross Bay!" Now we've got the scent and we're picking up speed as we turn right and head down 107th Avenue. We hear the reassuring sound of sirens behind us as we're trotting down the avenue with confidence. Wait, why are they dying out? Aw, shit! "Transit lieutenant, central, that's *west, west* on 107, not east!"

Richie thinks they might've gone south but Kevin and I disagree. He fell a little behind and as he's yelling at us to make a turn off the avenue, Kevin and I are more wisely just trying to breathe. As we're arguing over what's now opening to almost a half block separation between us, some guy pulls up to me and Kevin with a van and yells, "Hey officers, you guys need a lift?" We jumped into his van before it even came to a stop. Richie's running after us screaming, "Wait for me," as we tell the guy to step on it. We were already a block away when Kevin and I simultaneously said, "Shit, where's Richie?"

A precinct cop came on the radio: "Bystanders are saying the perps were headed to the train station at 88th Street!" So were we. "Transit lieutenant, central, I'm right down the block! Have the other units go to 86th and Liberty in case the perps go out the back end of the subway station!"

We jump out of the van at 88th Street and run up the stairs. We explode past the token booth. Like a well-oiled machine, Kevin goes to the left and I go to the right, despite the general rule that plainclothes cops shouldn't split up. We run up the stairs to the separate platforms.

I'm up on the Manhattan-bound platform shouldering people aside. There's a group of guys ahead of me, and there it is—the black jacket with the red hoodie! "Everybody down, down, on the ground!" I'm foaming at the mouth and everyone's looking at me like I was nuts until they noticed the 9mm combat Tupperware® in my hand. "On the fucking ground, now, get down!" *Bam*, the whole crew hits the ground. I'm looking for Kevin, quite pleased with myself, when I realized that all the passengers on the northbound and southbound platforms had also flattened out...

So, I'm holding a bunch of guys face-down at gunpoint and all the cops in the world start showing up. "Transit lieutenant, central, no further units needed. I'm holding one, two, three, four...uh, eight, holding eight. I just need the car with the victim." The precinct crime cops bring Vinny by for a show-up. "That's him, yeah, him too, him,

him, and him..." As we're cuffing up the prisoners, one of the cops said, "Alright! We got 'em!" With a straight face, I said, "What's this *we* shit?"

Froggy

The District 23 office, also known as the Big Two-Three House, is located in the subway station at Beach 116th Street, nestled in amongst the sand-strewn storefronts. District 23 was the smallest district in the Transit Police and is presently the smallest district in the NYPD Transit Bureau. Beach 116th is like the 42nd Street of Rockaway—it's the main drag. It's gotta be five, maybe six hundred yards from Jamaica Bay on one end of the strip to the Atlantic Ocean on the other.

In this veritable small-town, we're more like the sheriff than big-city cops. The buzzword in urban policing today is 'community policing'. Well, we were doing community policing in Rockaway long before it became politically fashionable. In the process we've gotten to know some people very well.

Two unfortunate local fixtures on Beach 116th are Tommy and Percy, our very own mezzanine drunks. Usually, we don't call Percy by his proper name; we call him Frogface, or Froggy for short. I'm not sure why. Over the years we've thrown Tommy and Froggy out so many times we've lost count. We're also had to send Froggy to the hospital several times. Poor bastard would drink so much he'd literally get stiff. He never lost his wits, though. You'd find him unconscious drunk, laying on the concrete floor in the subway. You'd kick him or whatever to revive him, and yell, "Hey, Frogface! Get up! C'mon, get out of here!" He'd come to and say something like, "That's *Mister* Frogface to you..."

This past winter was pretty rough on Froggy. There were a few times when we really didn't think he was going to make it. Tommy always stuck by his side, but there wasn't too much he was able to do for him. One night the cops were throwing them out and Froggy was in bad shape. Tommy came very close to getting smacked as he tried to protect his buddy. I stopped the cops and told Tommy they could stay until Froggy was able to get moving. The cops were pissed at me, but too bad about them.

One day Tommy came into the district and said, "L.T., I gotta talk to you..." He tells me that he thinks Percy is dying. He's boxed, but that's normal for him. He's telling me that he's almost got Percy convinced it's time to go into rehab and dry out, but that they'll never make it—the only place they can go to is the VA hospital in Fort Hamilton. I don't see the problem. I tell him that all they've got to do is take the shuttle train from Beach 116th to Broad Channel, change for the 'A' train, take that to Jay Street in Brooklyn, walk a few blocks to the 'R' train to... Tommy, former Marine and Vietnam vet, is on the verge of tears. He tells me that they can't go that long without their medicine, and that once they start drinking they'll abort the mission regardless of their initial intentions. I know he's not lying. Hmmm... I make a few phone calls and tell him, "You show up here tomorrow morning with Froggy, uh, Percy, as sober as you can be, and I'll get you guys to the hospital, okay?" He thanks me and leaves. I put thirty bucks in an envelope with written instructions to the day tour desk officer to call a cab from across the street, to put Percy and Tommy in for the ride to Fort Hamilton, and that under no circumstance is he to give the money to them, but to the cabbie instead.

The next day, they made the pivotal journey as planned. Turns out there was only one long-term bed open, and Tommy was in even worse shape than Percy. He ended up in the rehab for twenty-eight days. Percy came out in a week. He came to the district to thank me. We almost didn't recognize him. He looked great, not at all like a frog, but very small and tired. I saw him later that night walking down Beach 116th, looking like a lost child. Sadly, I knew what was going to happen.

He was drunk again within a day or two. Tommy came out of rehab a few weeks later and in short order was back on the subway mezzanine with Percy, drunk. Tommy apologized to me.

One day Percy hit me up for loose change. I told him I wasn't giving him any money to drink. He said he wanted it for food. How can I say no? I asked him what he wanted; he said a hamburger. I went into a nearby restaurant and got him his burger. "Froggy, I don't care too much about the drinking," I said as I handed him the bag, "but you better stop fuckin' eating."

Appearances Count

In the early part of 1996 the NYPD Transit Bureau decided to form a new type of anticrime squad in the districts. The program was christened, 'High Enforcement Activity Teams' or 'HEAT' for short. I immediately questioned why they weren't more properly designated as 'high activity enforcement teams' but of course, that would spell HAET...

These transit teams were supposed to work on street conditions near the subways, in close cooperation with the precincts. Sensing that the genie was being released from the bottle, I gladly accepted the nomination as Heat Team Commander of District 23, and then recruited some trained killers who loyally followed me into battle. However, it's never as glamorous as it sounds. I knew I was gonna end up writing reports.

We're out there doing our thing and having fun. About a week after the new program started, the borough commander visited the district and addressed our roll call. As he was finishing up, he turned to me and asked, "You guys got a HEAT team here?" Like a proud daddy, I said, "We sure do, Inspector!" Like an ill-tempered inspector, he said, "Well, what are you doing?" I'm baffled—"Didn't you get my report?" He says, "Yeah, I got it. What the hell are you doing?" He pulls my report out from his briefcase and throws it on the desk in front of me. It said:

"... the following is a recap of all activity, D-23 HEAT Team (first week of operation)

01/17 – Street Narcotics Enforcement Training

01/18 – Street Narcotics Enforcement Training

01/19 – [Presidential security – Clinton visit]

01/20 – nothing to report

01/21 – nothing to report

01/22 – Apprehended one for Robbery / Burglary,
one for Hindering Prosecution
Assisted 101 anticrime with apprehension
for GLA [grand larceny auto]

01/23 – Apprehended one for Sex Abuse," ... et cetera.

Am I glad he's got the report! I guess he just never got the chance to read it. I point out the robbery, burglary and GLA arrests, as well as the sex crime (which, by the way, was a subway caper). Unimpressed, he says, "So what's *this*?" He's pointing to the days where it said, "nothing to report". For a second, I think he's kidding —but he's not. I take a deep breath. "Uh, boss, those are our days off..." He says, "Oh yeah? Well, don't write 'nothing to report'. It doesn't look good."

Goodlittlefellas

Saint 'X' is a group home for boys (read: reform school) out in Rockaway. Many of the kids who live there are rejects from our social welfare system, presently serving out their apprenticeships as junior career criminals. Either that, or they're just misunderstood, I guess.

One February day my partner and I were in plainclothes in the subway station a few blocks from Saint 'X'. We were standing there when this sixteen-year-old kid jumps over the turnstile and walks right past us. Well, our disguises are working anyway... Since we really didn't have anything better to do, we walked up to him, identified ourselves and asked why he didn't pay—an arrestable offense. When he gave me a surly answer, I asked, "What are you, a tough guy?" He replied that he wasn't—and started crying. I noticed that he had a couple of knots on his head.

It seems my young friend was just transferred to Saint 'X'. He's hanging around with a bunch of his new roommates while on a break from some shop class. Everyone is laughing and having fun when he suddenly becomes the focal point of the anger of the ranking thug. Although the dialogue is different, it sounded to me just like the scene from the movie 'Goodfellas' where Joe Pesci unexpectedly goes after one of his dining companions ("I'm funny how? I mean, funny like I'm a clown, I amuse you?"). Next thing you know, he's getting his head banged against the wall. The school counselors intervened before he was seriously hurt and put his assailant into 'time-out', or detention. Unfortunately, after serving his quarter-hour sentence, the unrepentant bully says that the punishment time was going to cost five dollars. Having no money, the kid refused, and was then told he was going to get hurt.

So, it looks like our newcomer is running away from Saint 'X'. I thought about it for a minute, and suggested an alternate plan: he should walk back to Saint 'X' with us following him at a discreet distance. When the other kid confronts him, we step in and make the arrest. That way, I explained, nobody would know that he ratted the guy out – it would appear to be a fortuitous accident. At first, the kid refused. He was really scared of this other kid; he said he was a boxer. I reminded him we had guns.

We walked back to Saint 'X' about a half-block behind him. We told him to simply go by the front of the place. Taking the bait, Joe Pesci comes walking out of the building. We can't hear what they're saying, but then we see the body language of a sudden shift of balance, a feinted punch not thrown. Almost imperceptible, but just as unmistakable as the flinch exhibited by my young friend. We move in.

I tell him to step away so that I might talk to Joe. I ask him what's going on. Of course, he tells me the whole problem is the fault of the new kid, who, according to him, is a troublemaker, a liar, et cetera. I'm starting to think that my plans for the big pinch are going to fall through. My partner watches Joe while I walk back to the kid. Telling him that Joe denied everything, I ask if there are any witnesses. "Yeah," he says, "and they're all his friends." I told him that we could arrest Joe, but without more proof, he'd probably just end up getting released since the whole thing came down to one person's word against another. He was quiet for a minute and then said something surprisingly brave and mature: "I can't live like this. Arrest him."

As I walked back over to Joe, the light bulb went on. "Let me get this straight—how much 'time-out' did you get? Fifteen minutes?" Joe said nothing; I went on. "So, I don't understand the breakdown. You got fifteen minutes, and now he's gotta give you twenty bucks or you're gonna whip his ass?" Joe broke out in a smile and laughed, "*Twenty* bucks? It was only five!" And we were laughing as we slapped the cuffs on him.

As expected, the district attorney wanted some type of corroborating evidence to support our arrest charge of attempted grand larceny by extortion. I gave him the whole conversation with Joe Pesci, verbatim. After he stopped laughing, he asked if I had locked up the dumbest kid in Rockaway.

Who, me?

People say things to us that have unintended consequences: Bob and I are walking down a subway platform one day when we come up on a guy who's fooling around with a small knife, probably manicuring his nails or something. He puts it away when he notices us coming. As we pass by him, Bob says, "You need that for work, right?" [It's illegal to publicly carry a knife in NYC unless you use it for employment.] Of course, he says, "Need what?" We wheel in on him like two buzzards to a dead carcass. "Okay, give it up..." Grudgingly, he surrenders the knife. "Now, let's see some ID, please." He'll be getting a ticket. Out comes a work ID from Kennedy Airport that fails to justify his carrying a knife, and also doesn't have his address on it—only his name. "Mr. Smith, I need something with your address on it." He says, "I gave you that." I tell him, "Not good enough. Show me some ID with your address on it." He says, "What did I do?" I explain, "Look, you're breaking the law by carrying the knife. Show me some ID with your address on it and I'll give you a summons, or else I'm going to arrest you right now." Hey, I'm not being unreasonable. He smirks, "I *gave* you ID." Oh, well... "You're under arrest," and as we each grab an arm, he starts to fight. We folded him up like a chair and took him to jail. His mouth took him from what should've only been a conversation, *past* a ticket and into an arrest, with an additional charge of resisting. Had the entire encounter been videotaped, I believe we would've been able to charge him with public stupidity.

People say things to us that make us laugh: The very next day, Bob and I are sitting in a police car stopped at a traffic light when someone comes up to us and says, "Boy, you got here fast!" We thought this was pretty funny since we had no idea what he was talking about, but we withheld our laughter since compliments don't come easy. "What's the problem?" He says, "This guy, he beat me up and put me in the hospital last week, he's standing right around the corner!" As he's getting in the back of our car he says, "I even got a police report." We turn the corner. "That's him, right over there on the phone." We stop the car and ask our passenger a few last-minute questions about the alleged assault. Satisfied that he's a legitimate complainant, we get out and walk up on the payphone being used by what appears to be a regular Howard Beach wiseguy—well-groomed, jogging suit, lots of gold jewelry. He's busy talking as we come up on either side of him. "You're under arrest." For a second, he thinks it's a joke. Then, he's in handcuffs. "Heyy! Ohhh! Whaddayou guys gotta rough me up for?" We bust out laughing, thinking about the nitwit from yesterday. Rough you up? This arrest was a kiss on the cheek by comparison. "You're kiddin' right? Fuckin' guys..."

The only problem was, after we stopped laughing, we had to explain that we really weren't kidding.

Who, us?

We took the two of them back to the stationhouse in separate cars since we didn't want them going at it again. On the way, we got better acquainted with Roy, our complainant. Roy's in his early fifties but he looks younger. I guess he's what you'd call a knock around guy. According to him, that's exactly what Carmine did—he knocked him around. He says he was sitting on a bunch of empty boxes in front of this store last Friday when Carmine came out of the store and told him to get lost. He says he was getting ready to go, but that he had something in his eye, so he sat there for a minute. Next thing he knows, he's getting smacked by Carmine. Roy seemed perfectly sober as he told me this story but I took a wild guess he might've been drinking at the time.

We get to the police station and I talk to Carmine. I tell him there's been an assault complaint filed against him. He describes Roy and asks if that's who's pressing charges. "Wait a minute, lemme explain..." Last Friday night he was getting ready to close up his shop and Roy's sitting on some crates that he needs to bring inside.

He tells him to get lost, but Roy seemed to be out of it ("Rubbing his face?" "Yeah, how'd you know?"). Carmine wants to go home, so he shoves him off the crates. Roy takes a swing at him. Carmine punches him. Now Roy comes at him with an umbrella, and, "I used to be a Golden Gloves loser, you know what I'm trying to say, baddabing!" Fight's over, Carmine goes home. I ask him if he's ever been arrested before. He says he's done time. I tell him to sit tight while I get to the bottom of it. He says from the cellblock, "Where'm I gonna go?"

Roy tells me his story again. When I ask him how bad he was hurt, he tells me he went to the hospital but they didn't admit him, despite all the pain he was in. Plus, it still hurts. I ask if he had an umbrella the night he got beat up. "How'd you know?" I ask if he tried to hit Carmine with it, and he says, "Well, I probably wasn't acting like a gentleman, if you know what I mean." With utmost diplomacy I ask if he's ever been locked up before and he says, yeah, when he was a kid. I ask for what, he tells me burglary. "When?" Long pause: "Uh, about two years ago…" Big kid, tall for his age.

The more I listened to their stories, the more it became apparent that they were describing exactly the same fistfight, just from slightly different perspectives—Carmine was the winner, Roy was the loser. It appeared that Roy simply beat him to the punch of filing a report. In police jargon, we call this situation 'cross-complaints'.

The reason I asked if either had been arrested before was simple. I explain to Roy that in a cross-complaining incident, when the police don't know what really happened we generally solve the problem by arresting both parties and letting a judge sort it out. In the past, to arrest two guys for cross-complaints of misdemeanor assault would result in both getting released with 'desk appearance tickets' to go to court on some future date. The only problem, I explain, is that due to new and stricter guidelines we can't give DATs to anyone with an arrest record. Roy's eyes open wide. In other words, if I arrest Carmine, I'm also going to arrest Roy, and *everyone* spends the night in jail. "Unless, I don't arrest you guys for assault," I tell him, "but I give you both summonses for harassment instead." Roy's real quiet for a minute, then he says, "Summonses would be good…"

I tell him that the difference between assault and harassment is whether or not the victim is physically injured. Under the law, if you punch someone but don't cause a 'physical injury' as defined by the same law, you have committed a harassment, not an assault—even though the two acts would appear to look identical if you saw them actually occur right in front of you. I'm not sure that Roy followed all my legal mumbo-jumbo so I asked if he understood me. He says, "Oh, yeah! I feel fine!"

I go back into the cell area and tell Carmine, "I got good news and bad news." I explain that, as promised, I got to the bottom of the whole mess and as a result, he wasn't going to be arrested for assault after all. I tell him that the charges were dropped down to cross-complaining harassment, meaning that not only was he going to get a summons instead of being arrested, but that Roy was going to get a summons too. He was real happy with that, and wanted to know what the *bad* news was. I tell him he has an active warrant, and he's going to jail anyway. "Hey! Ohhh…"

Mellow Yellow

It's a beautiful summer day and everyone's returning home from the beach except me because I'm stuck with the desk at the Big Two Three House. Well, there are worse places I could be stuck… Since there's nothing going on at the desk, I'm standing around outside. I wasn't watching all the bathing beauties—after all, I'm on duty, and there's always police work to be done. And it didn't take long.

This guy comes into the subway and I immediately knew something was wrong. Call it skill, call it experience, call it a sixth sense. Or, you could call it a giant reptile. Yup, he's got this big yellow snake wrapped around his neck. When I say big, I mean like well over five feet long. And *bright* yellow. I stopped him and asked, "Excuse me sir, but is that a snake?" Okay, I deserved the look he gave me. "It's a Golden Python, actually."

At my invitation we stepped into the district. I told him it was a violation of law to take any animal into the subway. He said the snake was quite tame, that he had raised it since it was a pup. I didn't dispute the character of his snake (especially since it kept looking at me) but I explained that we didn't even allow more conventional pets on the subway unless they were suitably caged. He conceded that on a crowded subway train his snake could possibly cause other passengers to become, uh, concerned.

He said that he didn't mean to cause a problem, but he didn't have any other way of getting home. Unfortunately, the law is quite clear, so I asked him for his identification. I figured we'd give him a summons for the snake and let him ride the train home anyway. That way, if anyone complained later we'd be able to say that we took action on the condition. More importantly, it was a kind of 'pass' to let other cops know we had already given him our implied permission to get home with his snake.

While Bob was writing the ticket, one of our career restricted-duty officers came out from one of the offices in the back of the district. She walked right by, oblivious to what was going on in front of the desk, not at all surprising for an armed secretary. She was shuffling papers, looking busy and stealing her paycheck when she saw the snake. *"Omigod, what is that?"* We all jumped, even the snake. Four voices in unison replied, "It's a snake." Now she and the snake are eyeballing each other. "Eeeeewww, it's all yellow—that's disgusting!" I couldn't resist: "What are *you* talking about? It's the same color as your hair!" She ran away from the desk as everyone laughed—everyone except the snake, who didn't get it.

The Jack Files

As promised, here are some excerpts from commendation requests culled from Jack B.'s personnel folder. Well, not from his *official* folder...

Jack describes an arrest for robbery:

"On Tuesday, March 1st, Officer John B. was working the common beat that a rugged transit cop is quite used to... he had a bad day and was pretty pissed off... The male the officer was detaining went ballistic, the officer having had a bad day let loose a string of racial slurs while clubbing the now-bad guy with his PR-24... horizontal and vertical chops, power chops, you name it, he did it, the ballistic male was now under his control... Feeling this intense gut feeling surge thru his body he sensed that something was terribly wrong... Officer B. grabbed the man's hand and pulled him back onto the moving train, where he hit him with a massive head-butt... Officer B. decided to end the struggle quickly and efficiently by blinding his opponent with a nearby bucket of graffiti-remover followed by an unhealthy dose of pepper mace... this sent the perp into a crazed, howling spin as he bounced off the third rail... With his last burst of energy he took the flying grasshopper stance and delivered a mind-boggling blow to the perp's solar plexus which would've proved lethal if Officer B. wasn't so battle-worn..."

He describes an arrest for assault:

"With the dexterity of an otter, Officer B. sprang to the area where the cries arose... a quick inspection revealed two males engaged in a knife-fight... The officer used his quick reflexes to disarm the first male by biting a huge chunk out of the man's right arm... he then subdued the second man with a series of sharp, striking blows to the offender's head... With both of them now under his complete control he proceeded to tie the males together with only his belt, a trick he learned in the United States Marines... the officer then rendered first aid by cauterizing their many cuts and abrasions with one their own knives heated white hot with a common butane lighter..."

He describes his kidnapping arrest:

"He heard screams for help... with tiger-like reflexes and time-machine speed, Officer B. was moving... he observed a male with a stocking pulled over his face dragging a female to an isolated stairwell... Officer B. made his move at the speed of light... he was upon the perp before he could cause any harm to the female... with his police training and Marine Corps esprit de corps, Officer B. with minor resistance had managed to handcuff the perpetrator while screaming his Conan victory war cry, 'AAOOOORRAAAHHHH!!!'"

Reader's note: Jack has agreed not to sue me for plagiarism or copyright infringement; in return, I have agreed not to have him court-martialed.

Men of Action

No matter how hard you try to be fair as a police boss, someone's always got a beef. When we created the now world-famous HEAT team in Rockaway, it fell to me to decide who was going to be on it. It started off with my existing plainclothes team, Kevin and Richie. We needed a third wheel, so after a vote, Mike was in. Other cops started bitching because Mike only had so many years on the job, et cetera. Having seen Mikey's work, I offered the dissatisfied officers a simple, technical explanation for my selecting him: "Shut the fuck up."

When Richie got transferred to Narcotics, we needed a replacement. Although Steve had only been with the Rockaway Beach Transit Police for a short time, he worked anticrime in District Four when I was there and I knew he could play cops and robbers, so I used the same explanation previously offered.

When the next vacancy came up, we picked Enrico ('Rick'). People who had been satisfied with the explanations about Mike and Steve felt that there was a definite foul ball here. Little Ricky had neither time nor track record. He did, however, have 'the Eye of the Tiger'. Meaning, he'd do anything at all, without protest.

If you asked Rick to lock up his grandmother, he'd do it. If you asked him to hide in a garbage can on a surveillance, he'd do it. If you took a vote on just about anything, he'd vote 'yes'. Like most good cops, though, just don't ask him for paper.

As exalted leader of the team, I had to suffer through lots of paperwork. One night, I was working on some endless mountain and I asked Rick to help. "Look, I know you'd rather be out there locking people up, but I've got some important administrative stuff I need a hand with." He looks like I put a sharp stick in his eye. "C'mon! Everybody's gonna think I'm a skirt!" Skillfully stroking his ego, I tell him how important the project is, and that if I didn't have complete faith in his abilities I would never ask him to involve himself in such a sensitive matter. Grudgingly, he goes to work.

Several hours later, he staggers into my office with an armload of paper, biceps bulging. "Here you go, boss, here's all the shit you asked for." I looked at the impressive stack of folders and said, "Thanks, honey."

I Knew Him When...

One of the nice things about the Transit Police was that it was, relatively speaking, a small job. People's reputations generally preceded them and you usually knew who you were dealing with. Now, with this merge thing, that's all gone out the window. Not only do we deal much more with precinct cops, but they've even begun to reassign people back and forth. This certainly opens up new opportunities in the field of war storytelling, if nothing else...

We got involved one summer afternoon in a wild melee with many arrests made. At the center of the storm was one of my precinct counterparts. I've run into him quite a few times over the years; I like him, and I found that he's got a reputation in the NYPD as being, uh, a lunatic. My kind of guy.

So, I'm back in the district telling our latest war story to Gerry. He's new to transit, having been just recently assigned upon his promotion to sergeant. I asked him if he knew the precinct lieutenant who was the subject of my story. He gets this funny look on his face, and tells me, yeah, he knows him alright. They worked together in Manhattan. Gerry says, "Now let me tell *you* a story..."

"My wife is a big theater buff, you know? We've got tickets to see *The King and I* on Broadway, with Yul Brynner. She can't wait to see this show, especially since Brynner was pretty sick and nobody knew how long he'd be able to keep on doing the show. This guy's a sergeant then, and I was assigned to be his driver that day. I tell him, 'Hey boss, I got theater tickets tonight, so if we can help it, I don't want to get involved today, okay?' He says, 'Gerry, don't worry, no problem, we'll lay low.'

"The first thing you gotta understand is that when you drove this guy, *he* did the driving. That's the way he liked it. Anyway, the day was pretty quiet. We're about ready to head in when he spots this kid in the rearview mirror up on the sidewalk with a motor bike.

I figure, you know, the kid's taking it somewhere to a building or a shop or something, it's not like he's riding wild or causing a problem or anything.

"Next thing you know, we're flying down the block in reverse, and he's on the radio at the same time calling in a plate check on the bike. How the hell he can even *see* this, I don't know. The kid sees us, he takes off. The plates come back stolen, now we're chasing him, like we're gonna catch a kid on a bike.

"He tells me, 'Get out of the car, I'll go around and cut him off!' So I jump out and start chasing this kid, but I really don't want to catch him. I duck into this alley and there he is. I'm running after him, I hear the car screeching around, and it looks like I'm actually gonna *catch* this stupid kid. I can't believe this! I'm coming up behind him, and I yell, 'Run! Run!' He stops, puts his hands up, and surrenders. I say, 'Oh, what's the *matter* with you?' He says, 'The cops never told me to run before. I thought you were gonna shoot me.'

Reader's note: Gerry and his wife missed what turned out to be Yul Brynner's final performance. Hey, I guess he really does know this guy.

The Box

It seems that every offensive, socially unacceptable form of behavior known to urban man ends up getting acted out in the subway system. Why, nobody knows.

Graffiti is one type of brainless conduct we see all the time in transit. Mostly, it's committed by punky little teenagers who must feel some sense of accomplishment from scrawling their moronic 'tags' all over public and private property, a sense that's most likely missing from their lives otherwise. Well, at least nobody's getting *physically* injured by it.

It's been difficult at times to apprehend these minor criminals, since unlike most other crimes this one is committed when there's nobody else around except the graffiti artists and the property they're defacing. If there's anyone—and I mean anyone—else around, the little shits simply won't do it.

In an effort to gain the upper hand I had our friends at the TA build us a sort of 'duck blind' —basically, a giant box. The idea was that a cop would hide inside the box, and when the kids would be fooled into thinking that nobody was around, they'd do their graffiti. Then the cop would radio the rest of us and we'd be able to catch them. Everyone in the district thought I'd lost my mind. I quickly became a laughingstock over the box, but I knew that as soon as we started making graffiti collars everybody would stop laughing.

It was a bad omen when we almost lost the box before we even set it up. We had taken it (in pieces) to the Aqueduct subway station by train. We had taken everything off the train and then the doors closed and the train pulled out. It's a good thing the conductor saw us running after the train screaming, "Stop! Stop!" Okay, so we *thought* we had everything off...

Although it seemed like it was a great idea at first, it was one bit of bad luck after another with this box. While we were assembling it, who walks by but a couple of local kids who knew we were cops. Now we've got to stay away from it until they feel safe again. After we figured enough time had elapsed, we tried to use it. Now it was too damn hot inside the box from the sun beating down on it. We tried to use it at night and found you couldn't see anything outside the box in darkness. We tried it again when the weather got cooler, only to discover that passengers had been using the side of it as a urinal. Later, we decided to move the box to another location and give it a thorough cleaning, but we couldn't even do that because some TA employee had unknowingly used our box to store a week's worth of trash.

Rick and I went to Aqueduct one day, and believe it or not, we *finally* made a couple of arrests for graffiti. We came back to the district like conquering heroes. Somebody said, "Hey, you guys actually caught somebody with that stupid thing?" With mixed emotion I had to answer, "Well, sort of... they tagged the box."

Truth Hurts

A few years back, Shawn got shot in Brooklyn in an unfortunate incident of attempted fratricide. Unlike other recent 'friendly fire' incidents where minority officers had been hurt, Shawn's harrowing episode attracted little or no attention from the politically-correct news media. Could it be because Shawn was just your everyday, run-of-the-mill Cherokee Indian? Mike would know, because he was with him.

Our commanding officer was known as 'Uncle Joe'. He was a good boss, and he had the best interests of the troops at heart, but he also had very little tolerance for bullshit. Sometimes, if you were starting to annoy him, he'd write down 'June 15th, 1965' on a scrap of paper and silently hold it up while you were babbling away. It was his date of appointment to the department, and your cue to shut up.

Joe rolled out the red carpet for Shawn when he was transferred to District 23. I never gave it much thought; I knew him from Brooklyn and I liked him too. One day, I came in to work and Joe was red-hot. "He's finished, you hear me?" I haven't got a clue what he's pissed off about. "I thought he got shot, well—I didn't know it was another cop! I've been treating him like a hero! That lyin' little bastard!" Uh-oh... Shawn had never misrepresented himself; nobody had ever *asked* him what happened. Not being one to miss an opportunity to fib, though, I said nonchalantly, "Oh, yeah—that. I knew all about it." Joe's jaw dropped: "You knew?" Laughing, I said, "Yeah, sure I knew. Mikey popped him. What do you think I put him on the HEAT team for?"

Everybody Pays

The Transit Authority came up with a new idea to charge people for riding the subway: The Metrocard. Basically a credit card, you swipe it through a specially-designed turnstile and it automatically charges your Metrocard account.

As cops, we really couldn't care less since we don't pay to ride the subway anyway. Then, the department decided that all Transit Bureau cops would be issued a Metrocard. This caused a bit of a stir, because now the cops felt that they were being held accountable for another unwanted piece of department-issued equipment—in other words, if they lost the stupid thing, they'd get in trouble. Why should they, as Transit Bureau cops, be encumbered with an additional responsibility not shared by their precinct counterparts? It didn't really seem like such a big deal to me, but the cops tried to make it a labor-relations issue.

I knew we could count on Jack to put the matter into perspective. He says, "I don't need a Metrocard. I've got a token tattooed on my cock." Huh? Maybe I missed something. "When I go home, I can beat the fare!"

Transit Highway Patrol

Steve and I were driving back to the district one night after having made an arrest for, of all things, leaving the scene of an accident. Not a standard job for transit cops, but shit happens. We're driving down Cross Bay Boulevard, the main drag through Howard Beach, when we stop for a red light. When the light turns green, some jerk in a car in front of us decides to prove the theory about young men using cars as extensions of their penises by flooring it and spinning his tires for about fifty yards. He only realized who belonged to the headlights behind him when we turned on the rest of our lights. I mention in passing that our police cars are pretty cool. They've got all kinds of gadgets and really big engines, like we're state troopers or something. Anyway, the guy turns off the boulevard and pulls over on a quiet residential side street. As we normally do when we stop cars, I tell him over the loudspeaker to remain in his vehicle.

We get out of the police car and walk up. Steve does the talking: "Sir, do you know why we're stopping you?" I'm on the passenger side of his car but I hear the driver's response through the open window, "Oh yeah, no, see I just bought this car, officer, and, like when I stepped down, see, you know like this thing got caught on the wire with the, uh, over here, right, and the clutch popped out with the thing, right..." We both started laughing and Steve says, "Do me a favor, just give me your driver's license and proof of insurance, okay?" He does. We walk back to the police car.

We're sitting in the car getting ready to issue the guy a summons, still chuckling over his dopey attempt at an explanation when Steve says, "Oh my God, this geek, he even looks like a fucking loser!" He shows me the driver's license, and I've got to admit, he's right. The photo displayed a pimply teenager with a bad haircut and coke-bottle glasses in the most unflattering light. "Check out his name!" His name was something like, 'Fiorello DelGuido Astispumante'. Now we're both howling. Steve's last name ends with a vowel but this is just too much, even for us.

So, we're sitting there getting the traffic ticket ready, laughing and talking (mostly laughing), and the people in the neighborhood are starting to come out of their houses to see what's going on. They do that a lot in quiet residential neighborhoods. I guess it's exciting to see a real police car with all the flashing lights and stuff. We're having a good time doing our police work when this off-duty cop who used to work with us walks up to the car; apparently, he lives in the neighborhood. "Hey, what's up? How ya doin?" Handshakes, et cetera, and he says, "Great, uh, you're on the mike." He's a good guy and we used to have a lot of laughs. "Yeah, yeah, so anyway, how's every..." Wait a minute—What? I look down and see I'm sitting on the loudspeaker microphone. I've *been* sitting on it. Everything we've been discussing has been going out over the loudspeaker. The same loudspeaker I used to tell the guy to stay in his car. In the nice, quiet residential neighborhood.

Well, it got nice and quiet in the police car for a minute. "Steve, what do you say we give this guy a break this time?" He said, "Well, maybe just this once..."

Remember, always wear your seatbelts.

Deputy Patel

One night Steve and I were out on patrol, poaching on precinct territory. We respond to a radio call of a man robbed. The call wasn't for us, but that's the way it goes—we got there first. We find this gentleman waiting for us on the corner. He's a well-dressed Indian about forty, forty-five years old. I ask him what happened, and he says that as he was walking to his car these three guys rushed him, one pinned his arms, the second took his wallet and cash while the third one acted as a lookout. I ask him how long ago did it happen. I should've realized what we were getting into when he said, "It happened at 7:28 PM." Not fifteen minutes ago, not about seven-thirty. Seven twenty-eight, PM.

We ask Mr. Patel to take a ride with us to see if we can spot the guys who robbed him. He does. He gives us very detailed descriptions of all three. We drive around for a while, no luck. I ask him if he'd like to come to the precinct and look at photos. He says, "Do you mean mug shots? Oh, yes, certainly!"

No luck at the precinct, either. He can't pick out a face. I know it's hard to look at photos. I tell him that he was in a traumatic situation and that it's very understandable that he might not be able to identify his assailants. He tells me that he will never, ever forget their faces. Hmmm... I feel a scheme coming on. I ask Mr. Patel if he'd be willing to come out with us again in the future to go looking for the guys who robbed him. "Oh, absolutely!" It's tough to make a living in anticrime.

We picked him up at his house the following Tuesday and began what would be the first of several canvasses. Two of my cops and I drove around the neighborhood for a couple of hours with Mr. Patel. He immediately wanted to know why there were three of us, and I explained to him that since we were anticipating multiple felony arrests we brought along an extra officer for safety reasons. "Oh, very prudent!" We didn't catch anyone that night but we learned quite a bit about Mr. Patel. He was from England, he was an accountant, and apparently, also a police buff. He told us all about the English police and how they handled emergencies. According to him, they were very organized, very precise and very businesslike. He related a story (one of many) about how, when faced with some violent situation, they quickly cordoned off a section of his town, brought in some reinforcements, communications equipment, et cetera, and patiently negotiated a peaceful outcome. American police were a bunch of cowboys by comparison. No offense intended; none taken. Mr. Patel was a likeable guy.

We started to wonder just how productive our relationship with him was going to be after the third canvas. He was very happy to come out with us and we always enjoyed his company, but let's face it—we weren't taking him out with us for the company. We wanted to make some robbery collars. We would ride around the neighborhood with Mr. Patel, telling war stories and having fun, but he would never see the guys who robbed him.

Steve, Kevin and I were on our way to pick Mr. Patel up again one night when Kevin says, "What a waste of time! This guy's full of shit, he just wants to ride around in a police car!" At this point I'm inclined to agree, but since we didn't have anything better to do at the moment we picked him up anyway. We're driving around the neighborhood, swapping stories and wasting time. There was a call on the radio about some guy in a car who threatened to shoot some other guys. It wasn't too far away from where we were. Some other cops answered the call and it turned out to be for real. They had a good description of the guy armed with the gun and even had the make, model and license plate of his car, which they broadcast on the radio. I told Mr. Patel in the most dramatic tone of voice I could manage: if we spotted this bad guy, we would pull our car over, tell him to get out, and that for his own safety he should immediately get as far away from us as he could. He loved it...

It's starting to rain, it's late, and we're all starting to get pissed off. Mr. Patel is having a ball. I'm continually spotting people and asking him to take a look at them, and he's continually saying, "Oh no, definitely not," and continuing the pleasant conversation. I don't know how long we can remain polite. He's dismissing people as possible suspects in his robbery from two blocks away with statements like, "No, I can tell from his gait that he is not the man." Gait? I can't count how many *legs* the guy has at that distance!

Kevin and Steve are giving me some real dirty looks. I've pretty much decided that this is going to be the last canvas with Mr. Patel when, in the middle of one of his stories, he says, "By the way, the car you are looking for just passed us." Triple whiplash as the three of us spin our fat heads around: "Holy shit, he's right!" Kevin slams on the brakes, and the three of us yell in unison, *"Get out!!!"* We left Mr. Patel standing in the rain as we smoked our tires in a U-turn.

"Transit lieutenant, central—priority—we're following the gray Lincoln from the earlier gun run, westbound on Liberty at 106... crossing 105..." The gray Lincoln gets stuck in traffic at a light. "We're gonna take him at 104 and Lib!" Kevin floors it, swerves into the oncoming lane and skids to a stop alongside the Lincoln, whose startled driver finds himself looking down a three-Glock broadside. He didn't have time to shit in his pants before we had yanked him out of his car. Cop cars are flying up from all directions. Click, click, one under. While we were searching the car, I see Mr. Patel in the gathering crowd. The precinct is just a few blocks away; I tell him to meet us there and we'll give him a lift home.

Later, while driving a slightly soggy Mr. Patel back to his house, he tells us that he saw the whole incident from where we dropped him off. We apologized to him for putting him out in the rain. Annoyed, he said, "You'd never make it as cops in England."

Collar Thieves

No matter how much I tried to avoid it, every so often I'd still get stuck with the desk. Today, the four-to-twelve sergeant banged in sick, leaving me as the only supervisor working the tour, and the desk has to be covered. No big deal, since I've got 'inside' plans anyway – Mr. Smith is coming in to the district to give me the dirt on Dan, a local thug who we'd locked up a few times already. But first, I've got to turn out the troops.

While I'm holding roll call, Mrs. Jones walks in the front door, hysterical. The outgoing platoon goes on a coffee break. In my office, she calms down and gives me her tale of woe: she had a fight with her husband, who then slapped the shit out of her and threw her out of their apartment. She's not physically hurt. I ask if they've got any kids, and she tells me yes, a five year-old and an infant. "Where are they?" She doesn't know. She *thinks* they're in the apartment. "Well, your husband can take care of them, right?" Wrong. He doesn't take care of them, ever, according to her.

As I'm telling Shawn and his partner to take a ride over to Mrs. Jones' apartment, in walks Gerry, who's about to go off-duty from the day tour. Not so fast! "Hey Gerry, do me a favor, okay? See what's going on with this. I'd feel better if a boss goes over there." No problem, he'll take care of it. I throw the rest of the goldbricks out, and sit back to wait for Mr. Smith.

A few minutes later Mr. Smith came in as planned. We're in my office, and he's giving up Dan's next collar, when the phone rings. It's Gerry. "Hey, boss, we got a little problem over here..."

Always the professional, on the ride over Gerry had asked Mrs. Jones a few questions, including, "Does your husband have a gun in the house?" She said yes. Upon arrival Gerry asked Mr. Jones the same question. He, too, said yes. Gerry then asked him to surrender the weapon, and Mr. Jones told him to fuck off. "So, Gerry, what do you got over there, a stand-off, or what?" He says, "No, boss, I'm inside the apartment now. He's out in the hallway with the guys." Hmmm... I don't want to know. "I'll be right over."

I make my apologies to Mr. Smith and tell Bob, "Grab the keys to a car, we gotta go make a gun collar." He thought I was kidding until he saw me throw on a vest. "I'll explain on the way, let's go!" Coffee's in the trash, and we're out the door. Somebody'll watch the desk until I get back...

Sure enough, Mr. Jones is in the hallway of the apartment building with the two cops, and Gerry's inside with Mrs. Jones and the kids. It seems that the sergeant wasn't too sure just how far he could go without a search warrant. "Don't worry about it, Gerry, that's why *I* make the big bucks." In the hallway, I introduce myself to Mr. Jones with a handshake. "Listen, is it true you've got a gun in the house?" He says yes. "You got a permit for it?" He says no. "You don't wanna give the gun to the sergeant?" He says, "You guys ain't got no warrant." With a smile, I say, "You're under arrest." Click, click. *"For what?"* he says, in disbelief. "For endangering your children. Now, tell me where the gun is, because if you don't, I'm gonna tear your fucking place apart until I find it." He told me where it was. He kept the loaded .38 revolver in the kitchen, in a cabinet—right behind the Cocoa Puffs cereal.

Out in the hallway, Bob has got Shawn's partner all revved up. As I'm leaving the apartment, I hear him saying, "Hey, he *is* the lieutenant, he can do whatever he wants..." Shawn's partner blocks my way, fists clenched, and says, "You ain't stealing our collar, Lou!" Laughing, I say, "Down, piss boy! How's this *your* collar? You got this job from *me*, those are *my* cuffs on him, and *I* got the gun!" Unmoved, he growls, "Oh yeah? Well, I know how you HEAT guys operate!"

Reader's note: Desk officers don't take collars, so I gave this one away—to Shawn.

Dragnet

We ended up taking Dan for a past burglary. Unfortunately, he was out on the street in a week. It was only a few more days before he was once again up to no good.

Before long, we're looking to pick him up on a misdemeanor complaint of menacing. We ran into the precinct anticrime guys and it turns out they were looking to pick him up on a different misdemeanor complaint of larceny. "But it might end up being a robbery!" Robbery's a felony. Guess what? Our menacing complaint might turn out to be 'intimidating a witness'—also a felony. So, I made a deal with the precinct: whichever team finds him calls the other team, and whoever can build a felony case gets the collar, since the object of the game is to *end* this guy's game. Agreed.

We got a line on where this mutt was staying. We swung by the precinct to grab some help. Their crime team was out, so we asked a couple of precinct detectives if they wanted to come along for the ride. They're in. Everyone wants this collar.

We pull up at the location, an old three-story rooming house. One cop out behind, one cop out in front, and the rest of us go in. The house is a maze of single rooms. We stream into the place in silence and people get out of our way, leave or go back to their rooms without a sound. There's no mistaking the seriousness of our purpose and everybody seems to know just who we're looking for. Could the precinct crime guys already have been here?

We get to his floor, and there aren't any names or numbers on the door. A woman in a bathrobe is shocked by the four armed men who suddenly appeared in her hallway. I gestured, 'shhh!' She's frozen. I whisper, "Where's Dan's room?" She looks around to see if anybody can see her, then shows us. I tell her to go. She's gone. We set up outside his door. We can hear a radio or a television on low inside. We knock. Nothing. We knock again. Again, nothing. Kevin's giving me a raise of the eyebrow. The door *is* pretty flimsy. Yeah, we could boom the door, but... I'm thinking it over. All we've got, really, are misdemeanor charges. Oh, and there's that other thing, uh, the Fourth Amendment or something like that. I shake my head, we pack up and leave. We spent the rest of the night searching between the bay and the ocean for Dan, but no luck.

The next night, I figured before we committed the whole tour to looking for this guy, let me check to see if he's been locked up by our competition. I call the precinct, and they tell me he was arrested. Well, that's good news, I guess. "When?" They tell me Sunday night. "When?" We hit his house Monday, the night *after* he had been arrested. He got locked up by two uniformed cops from the sector car on the midnight tour, about twelve hours before. Dan was sitting in jail while we were standing outside his door.

We didn't feel too stupid, since unlike the precinct crime guys, *we* had professional sleuths in that hallway with us.

Rendezvous

I had to take a leak, and as is my habit, I entered the toilet stall and attended to my business. Then I hear Mike come in, and while I'm still in the stall, he begins to use one of the urinals. We're just tinkling away when he says, "So, how come you don't stand out here and pee like a man?" It's pretty tough to trade lines with Mike but I quickly think up a clever comeback—from inside the stall, I reply, "Listen, I know all about you. I'm afraid if you *see* me, you're gonna *want* me." Mike laughs, "What for? I already *got* two thumbs."

The Price Of Justice

When I got into court, I couldn't be-lieve my eyes
The judge was a fishin' buddy that I reco-nize
So I say, Judge, ol' buddy, ol' pal.
I give you that hundred I owe you
If you get me outta this spot!

Well, he gave my friends a little time to pay,
Then he turn around to me and say,
Ninety days, Jerry
When you hot, you hot!

Jerry Reed 1971

We were just coming over the Cross Bay Bridge into Rockaway when the call came over of a dispute with a firearm at (XXX) Beach 110th Street. Steve gives me this innocent look which at this point in our partnership is basically the grownup equivalent of a dare. "Yeah, central, transit lieutenant's gonna pick up the gun run, just give me the address again please..."

We pull onto the block and find the 911 caller. "My next-door neighbors's gone nuts, man, he's threatenin' everybody!" He points out where the guy lives—another typical Rockaway Beach rooming house. We don't see or hear anything going on, so we cautiously enter the house with *our* guns out, easing (well, creaking) up the stairs. As I get to the top of the landing, I see the name on the door: James Good. I almost crashed into Steve as I turned to go back down the stairs. "Central, have Emergency Service respond to Beach 110, no lights, no sirens. The perp's inside his apartment." The dispatcher asked if it was a confirmed barricaded suspect. "No, central, but we've locked him up before, and, uh, he's gonna give us a hard time."

Several days earlier, James had stormed into the district after having been ejected from a bar across the street. He had the new desk sergeant flummoxed with his paranoid demands and complaints, so I stepped in. "Sir, do you remember me?" He said no. "I threw you outta here the *last* time you came in causing trouble." He got very indignant, insisting he'd never seen me before. "State your business, sir!" He started rambling again. "Well, at least we don't have to worry about *deja vu*. Get out!" Now, he's making incoherent threats. Steve, Jack and I physically escorted him onto the subway mezzanine, and as we're about to put him out on Beach 116th Street, he took a swing at me. "You jerk, *now* you're under arrest!"

So, tonight, Steve and I are outside his house waiting for ESU. Neither one of us wanted to end up shooting a drunken boob in his own apartment. The neighborhood crowd quietly gathered.

Many months later, I happened across the report on the incident. It sounded really dramatic. Hmmm... I'm thinking about 'writing it up'. Might as well make it look good, so I called a friend downtown who has access to a computer that tracks court cases. "Yeah, James Good, arrested for Criminal Possession of a Weapon and Menacing." She puts me on hold for a few minutes. "PGSI, four to five." Wow! Now *that's* impressive police work. Pled Guilty, Sentence Imposed, Four to Five Years. "Can you fax me a copy of that?"

The fax was not exactly what I expected. It seems I'm not up to speed on my acronyms. PGSI stands for 'Pled Guilty, *Surcharge* Imposed.' James didn't get four to five years in jail, he got a *forty-five* dollar fine! I mention in passing that a parking ticket in NYC is usually $55.

Reader's note: I had another pending commendation report in my pile; a midnight cop grabbed a guy for shooting up a train in a drunken rampage. My friend checked that case, too—*one hundred and forty five bucks*. Apparently, losing control and actually letting rounds go will cost you a C-note in the Big Apple.

The Great Impostor

The radio call was for a 'TA employee holding someone with stolen property' at Broad Channel. Citizen's arrest? Hmmm...

"My name's Smith, Car & Equipment supervisor," our caller says, pointing to the station cleaner, "and he is *not* a TA employee." I look at the cleaner, who's busy scraping some chewing gum off the concrete floor in front of the token booth. "Hey, guy, you work here?" He thinks it over for a second, then says, "Huh?" I'm reminded of the scene in 'The Untouchables' when Officer Malone first meets Eliot Ness. I look back at our Mr. Smith. "You got some ID on you?" He starts sputtering, "Hey, I'm the one who *called* you!" Giving him my best Sean Connery impression, I replied, "Who would claim to be that, who is not?"

To my surprise, Mr. Smith had proper company identification, but our cleaner didn't. He starts to doubletalk. Then, the computer burped when we fed it the employee ID numbers he gave us. Click, click...

We get back to the precinct, and find that this 'cleaner' has an impressive amount of gear. He's wearing a complete TA uniform and he's got a full equipment belt, including some keys even we don't have. All NYCTA issue—and all apparently stolen. Turns out he's been locked up for Criminal Impersonation several times before.

We needed the local TA superintendent to come down to the police station to sign the paperwork as our complainant for the stolen property. I get him on the phone in the arrest processing area. He'll come down, but he needs a lift. "Steve, have the 'King' car go pick up the station manager at his office at Howard Beach, okay?" The prisoner innocently asks, "What's a 'King' car?" I turn to him and say, "Oh, uh, that's just the radio designation we use for the— *Ow!*" Steve had kicked me under the table. We look at our prisoner, the human brain-sponge, blissfully soaking up information. "Don't you worry about what a 'King' car is, okay?"

The TA superintendent comes in. He, too, was amazed at all the stuff this guy had. "Wow. You mind if I take a look at him?" No problem. One of the cops took him back to the cell. He came out a second later with a funny look on his face. I ask, "What's the matter?" He looks around uncomfortably, then whispers to me, "I offered him overtime last week."

Close But Cigar

Steve and I worked together for a few years. We're normally in sync as a team, but sometimes I wonder if maybe we've been together a little too long.

One night there was a report of a robbery at 115th Avenue and Lefferts Boulevard. We were listening to the description on the radio. "Two male blacks, one with a red jacket, one with a blue jacket, both on bikes. Believed to have fled east toward the 113th precinct; one is armed with a gun." Steve and I are coming from the other direction. We're headed east on Rockaway Boulevard, which runs sort of on a diagonal. We're arguing about where Rockaway Boulevard crosses Lefferts, above or below 115th Avenue, when we almost run over these two kids on bikes coming in the opposite direction on Rock. I get a quick view of one of them and he's got that 'deer in the headlights' look on his face—and a red shirt! "That's them!" Steve slams on the brakes as they fly by us. He starts to make a U-turn, then stops and says, "No, it's not!" That kid wasn't black, he's Spanish!" We're both twisting around in our seats, "Yeah, it's them, the other one's got a blue jacket, go, go!" I hit the lights, he starts his turn but abruptly stops again. "They're headed towards Brooklyn, not the 113!" We're bickering like an old married couple, and the way our car is lurching and swerving, it looks like the driver is having an epileptic seizure. "Fuck it, they're in the wind now, anyway." I kill the lights. Just then the first unit from the 106th precinct arrives at the scene of the robbery and comes over the radio, "Six sergeant, central, update on the perps—one male black with a blue jacket, one male Hispanic in red." I slowly turned to Steve and growled, "Elwood..."

Bystanders watching have got no clue what's wrong with our police car, which is once again lit up and squealing into a power huey. "Ah, transit lieutenant, central, those perps just passed us at 96 and Rock—they're headed west on Rock Boulevard toward Brooklyn." Some wiseass on the radio says, "So, *stop*'em!" I give Steve a dirty look as I lamely answer, "Yeah, we're pinned in traffic." You could hear our engine screaming and we were already two or three blocks west of where we failed to stop them, but I had to say something.

We're well into the 102nd precinct trying to catch up to these kids. As we're approaching a red light, we see what looks like an unmarked police car in front of us blowing the light. "Who the fuck are *these* guys?" We blow the light too, and then another voice comes over the radio, "Queens Robbery, central, we got two possibles in sight, 92 and Rock!" *We're* at 92 and Rock. "There's a marked unit coming up behind us, central, we're gonna make the stop at 91 and

Rock!" I see two kids riding bikes at 91st Street and they're not the two we were after. As the detectives were jumping out of their car with guns drawn on the first kid, I'm saying on the radio, "Fellas, it's not them! It's not them! Wrong guys!" They didn't hear me.

So, it looks like we're committed. We screech up behind them, right on the second kid. Steve and I took him at gunpoint too, but not before he dropped something as he was coming to a stop. Then, one of the detectives yells, "Gun!" Whoa! Both kids are face-down, on the ground, and cuffed up in a flash. The first kid had a fake gun in his waistband. It was only plastic, but any cop in the world would've blasted him had he had it in his hand. We go to retrieve what our kid dropped, turns out it was a face mask. Halloween's not for a few months—go figure. Now Steve and I are confused. These two are definitely *not* the kids who passed us at 96th Street and Rockaway Boulevard, but they also fit the description. Did we just blunder into a great collar? We're scratching our heads, but we couldn't care less how we got the collar. All we know is we got it. Well, *they* got it.

"Transit lieutenant, central, I'm with Queens Robbery, we're holding two at 91 and Rock. Can the six sergeant bring the complainant over for a show-up?" No problem, he's on the way. About five minutes later the sergeant pulls up. We're all ready to do some high fives when the sergeant says, "It ain't them." Damn! Anyway, if the kids Steve and I saw on 96th Street really *were* the perps, then they're already home in bed in Brooklyn by now. Crestfallen, the detectives ask if we want the imitation pistol collar. They only want robberies—possession of an imitation pistol is just a misdemeanor. It's not much, but it's better than nothing, so we agree to take it. I then made a cryptic radio announcement, considering that only the cops on the scene knew anything about the gun and the mask: "Transit lieutenant, central, that's a negative on the show-up. Like I said, it's not them. But, uh, we're taking them anyway. Two under..."

Give it to Mikey...

We were a little annoyed when they scheduled us for a three-day 'plainclothes' training course at the Police Academy. Most of these courses are really a waste of time and prove the saying, "If you can, do... if you can't, teach." We figured, at least we were going together, Kevin, Mike and me. Call us the anticrime squad, the HEAT team, whatever—the three of us have worked together off and on for years to the distress of many a local mongrel. So we sleep through three days of bullshit, no big deal.

We're there the first day and the class is a mixed bag of Transit crime and Manhattan North narcotics cops, mostly teams or partners who work together on a steady basis, all experienced cops. Everybody looked about as interested as we were. The instructors come in and tell us that this was going to be a tough course but if we put forth the effort we'd be rewarded. Yeah, yeah. They say that before every course. Then they tell us how concerned they are for our safety, they don't want us to get hurt. Yawn. This is a course being given by a department that threw out their physical test when too many fat and lazy recruits couldn't pass it. They explain that the curriculum was developed on the old courses given by Transit in the mid-eighties. Huh? Then they invoked the name of Dennis, formerly head of the Transit Police Defensive Tactics Unit, and we are wide-awake.

Transit cops historically worked alone with a nearly useless radio system on some of the most dangerous territory in the city. It was not without reason that we often referred to ourselves as the Marines of the police departments. After we graduated the NYPD recruit school at the Police Academy, we then underwent an additional three weeks of classes which included some notoriously brutal self-defense training at the hands of Dennis and his associates. Despite my status as a hardened military veteran, I bled and bruised like everyone else. I suffered my first line-of-duty injury when I was struck in the leg with a nightstick while fighting. Dennis had to order me off the floor, which really pissed me off since I wanted to finish the fight and kick the other guy's ass. I was younger then.

So, here we are again, a dozen years later. Kevin and I came on the job about the same time; we're both old married men with children and gray hair. Mike is the baby, he's in his twenties. He's about as old as Kevin and I were when we went through the Transit tactics training. We began what would be about the best three days of training I've been to since 1985. The first day was really cool. I love the idea of getting paid to have a great workout in a gym.

The second day was equally excellent. We're beating the crap out of each other. The instructors are great—the only problem is you can't learn enough and you know you aren't coming back next week.

I worked at the Police Academy for a year and a half, so I know a lot of people in the building. I run into an old friend in the hallway. He takes one look at me, sees I'm soaking wet and all lumped up, and asks if I'm in the 'plainclothes' course. When I tell him yes, he asks, "They take anyone out yet?" He says they have yet to finish a cycle without removing someone on a stretcher. Thanks for the tip, pal!

Unlike the original Transit curriculum, quite a few of the techniques taught in this course were team-oriented: they took into consideration that plainclothes anticrime cops normally work in teams of two or three officers. One particularly nasty technique for subduing a violent subject involved one officer distracting him from the front while the second officer would sneak up behind and put the person down, very unpleasantly. The instant the person was face-down, the second officer would then lay across the subject's legs, holding on for dear life—remember, this is for a violent subject. As the subject would reflexively go to the push-up position to try to regain his footing and stand, the first officer would then engage the subject and basically make him into a human pretzel while handcuffing him. The instructors cautioned us for the umpteeth time that if the technique was done improperly or too severely that the subject would suffer a dislocated shoulder and other assorted indignities. Then they tell us to break up into groups of threes, and we begin.

The first order of business was to decide who would do what. Kevin and Mike outvoted me, two to one, and I was the violent subject. So, I'm eating the rubber mat. Mike's got me by the legs and Kevin's on me like a ton of bricks, putting my arm into an evil hammerlock. I'm not proud; I'm screaming, "EEEYAAAAAHHH!!!" One of the floor instructors runs over, yelling, "Get off him," and literally knocks Kevin off me. I'm still screaming. It wasn't Kevin—Mike is *biting* me.

The instructor says, "You guys work together?" I tell him, "Not by choice... you can't get good help anymore." He says, "Holy shit, you're a sergeant?" Mike cuts in, laughing, "Nah, he's the fucking lieutenant!" The instructor didn't believe us. Then again, he wasn't Transit.

One last reader's note: This story isn't completely true. Mike didn't really bite me—it just makes the title of the story work better. He did do something else that made me scream. Actually, I bit Kevin.

Epilogue

In early 1997, we had a change of command. The new boss and I didn't see eye-to-eye (to put it mildly), so after a year-long successful run, the HEAT team closed up shop and headed back to the subway for good. Nothing lasts forever.

After doing some time in narcotics, Kevin also came back to Rockaway. I had some old business to take care of with him, but after searching my bottomless pit of a desk, I came up empty-handed. "Ah, never mind, it'll turn up sooner or later…" I was looking for a copy of the paperwork awarding him an 'Excellent Police Duty' citation, signed and approved by Joe, our former captain, that I had only received after Kevin had already been transferred. I knew he'd get a kick out of it when he saw it.

To set this one up, we have to go back to Jack. Right around the time that Jack collared the guy with the shotgun at Broad Channel (a repeat customer, if you recall) the Transit Bureau was hot and heavy on an informal program called 'Cop-of-the-Month'. I thought taking a loaded shotgun off a guy on a subway train was pretty neat, so I nominated Jack. Joe gave it the nod, and Jack became king for a day. Well, for a month, anyway.

The trouble started when I submitted the paperwork for a more permanent attaboy—official department recognition. Cop of the month was okay, but it didn't give the cop the little 'buff-bar' to wear over his shield. Naturally, I also wrote up Jack's partner, as well as the two cops in the other RMP who had backed them up.

When Joe got the commendation paperwork for the four cops, he said, "Time out. First you tell me it was Jack, *now* you tell me it was Jack and three other guys." I said, "Hey, Captain, the program's called cop of the month, not *cops* of the month. Of course there were other guys on the scene, it was a gun run!" Sensing that someone (me) was trying to pull the wool over his eyes, he threw me out of his office and disapproved the paperwork for the three back-up cops.

Not too long after this, Kevin was on a payphone on the corner of 88th Street and Liberty Avenue, while his partner (Mike) was upstairs in the subway. A guy comes flying out of the subway and runs down the block. Seconds later, Mike yells down, "Some woman just got her chain snatched up on the platform!" Kevin put two and two together, and they were off to the races. They ran for blocks looking for the guy Kevin had seen, and correctly guessed that he might try to go back to the subway to escape. The next station was 80th Street, and that's where they caught him. Mike was 'up' and he took the collar.

I was off that day but I heard all about it. The next day, back at work, I was giving Kevin a hard time. "Good thing Mikey was there, you fat bastard. If you had to *walk* eight blocks, you'd bang in sick!" Everybody was howling, except Kevin. And Joe.

Although I was gleefully torturing Kevin, I had every intention of doing the right thing by him, since it really was a good collar. As soon as I had all the documents together, I submitted the paperwork for department recognition. As soon as Joe got it, he kicked it back. "Don't bullshit me, Tre, what really happened?" I have no idea what he's talking about, and I tell him so. He says, "I heard that Kevin didn't make the run, that Mike caught the guy by himself." I'm dumbfounded. "Cap, you heard that from *me!* I was only kidding!" He says, "Don't try to pull that same shit on me like you did about Jack," as he shows me the door. Oh, no…

Even though I wasn't there when it happened, I had worked with Kevin too long to think that the story was anything but exactly what he told me. We had even made a similar trot together when we collared the gang at 88th Street, back around Christmas of '95. I got the paperwork back from Joe with a nasty note attached: 'I want to know what really happened, otherwise forget the whole thing.' A couple of the guys tried to talk to him, but he wouldn't budge. Me and my big mouth.

Unfortunately, Joe retired suddenly some time later. Nobody wanted to see him go. Despite his sometimes gruff demeanor he was extremely popular. He decided to leave on a Tuesday, and by Friday, he was gone. The district was like a funeral home that week. I thought of the commendation paperwork for Kevin and Mike which had been a dead issue (no pun intended), and I walked into the captain's office as he was boxing up his personal effects. "Listen, this thing with Kevin, I swear on a stack of pancakes that this is just how it happened..."

Back to the present—it turns out, the night Kevin came back to Rockaway, I'm working with Jack. Of all people, he could most appreciate the whole winding yarn, especially since it indirectly involved him. We're standing on the platform of the Broad Channel subway station for about twenty minutes as I'm telling it to him from the very beginning, starting with his shotgun collar. Just as I'm finishing, a train pulls in, and Jack gets this really funny look on his face—"Nah, *couldn't* be..." Who steps off the train, but the guy Jack had locked up for the shotgun!

We spent the next few minutes talking to him and found out he had just gotten out of jail, and no, he didn't have another gun on him (we checked). We were laughing so hard, he left half-insulted, thinking that we were laughing at him. Hey, screw him if he can't take a joke.

Even if you *could* make this stuff up, what would be the point? Unless, of course, you just like telling war stories...

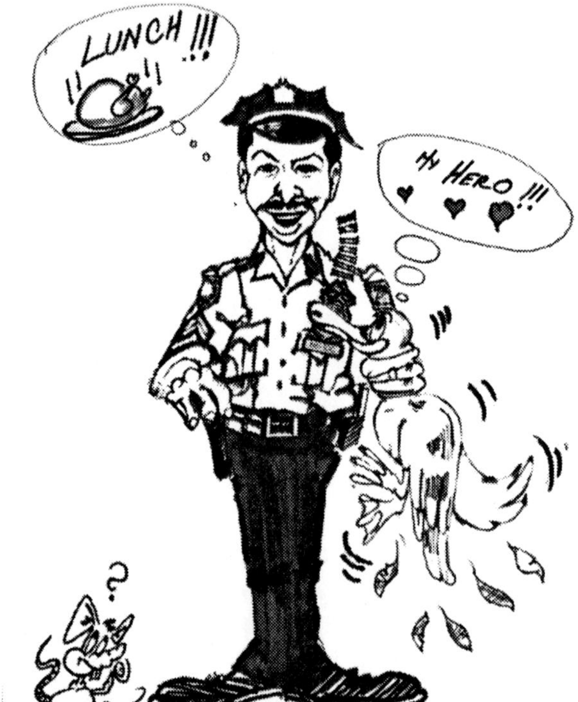
LUNCH !!!
My HERO !!!

About the Author

A Bicentennial graduate of Far Rockaway High School, Trebor Nehoc lives in Queens with his wife and kids. Upon his promotion to captain in 1997, he was transferred from the Transit Bureau to Manhattan.

About the Illustrator

Ronnie Morales retired from the NYC Transit Police in 1993, and has since forsaken the Big Apple for the wide-open space of the Lone Star State. Ride 'em, cowboy.

Glossary of Terms

Anticrime – Patrol officers (not investigators) assigned to work in plainclothes for the sole purpose of apprehending violent felons immediately before, during, or after their crimes. This is not to imply that other officers are pro-crime.

Apocrypha – "Writings of questionable authenticity" *(Britannica-Webster)*

Bodega – Spanish word for grocery store or general store.

BMT – "Brooklyn Manhattan Transit" system, merged with Interboro Rapid Transit (IRT) and Independent Transit (IND) systems to form the New York City Transit Authority (NYCTA) subway system.

Boss – A police supervisor.

Collar – Arrest (used as either a noun or a verb)

Collar brass – The metal insignia worn on the shirt collar that indicates what command the officer is from.

Command – A specific police unit. The Transit Police command covering a given geographic area is called a district, the similar

NYPD command is called a precinct, and the Housing Police command is called a police service area (PSA). The three do not necessarily cover the same geographic areas.

Counting Tiles – A method of passing time in the subway during periods of excruciating boredom (self explanatory).

DAT – "Desk Appearance Ticket" A summons to appear in court at a later date, given in the police station under certain circumstances after someone has already been arrested and fingerprinted. *See also: Disappearance Ticket*

Desk Officer – A supervisory officer (sergeant or lieutenant) who is in overall charge of a district, a precinct or a PSA for a given tour of duty.

Dog-pile – Advanced police technique for subduing violent subjects. Requires precise timing, teamwork and coordination, and is only to be undertaken by trained professionals.

EDP – "Emotionally-Disturbed Person" (Everything is relative)

Farebeat – A person who enters the subway without paying the fare, and without permission. This can be done by walking in through an open exit gate, by going over or under the turnstile, by manipulating the turnstile, or by showing fake ID. Farebeats are summonsed or arrested. *See also: Beat*

Gypsy cab – An unlicensed taxi or livery cab.

Hoop-de-Scoop – Complete, utter bullshit. *See also: Hoopty-Scoop* Origins unknown.

Job – 1. "A job" - any police assignment, sometimes assigned by radio, usually finalized by some type of paperwork.
    2. "The job" – the police department.

Locked up – Arrested.

Merge – A euphemism for the hostile takeover of the Transit Police by the NYPD.

Mezzanine – The floor level in a subway station where the token-booth is located.

Mutt – A citizen of questionable character. Some mutts are perps.

Nightstick — Wooden baton formerly carried by patrol officers in New York City throughout most of the twentieth century as a symbolic "badge of office." *See also: Wood Shampoo*

Perp – Short for 'Perpetrator'. All perps are mutts.

Post – An officer's assigned area of patrol.

Probie – Probationary Police Officer. Newly-hired cops are on 'probation' for a year or so, meaning they can be easily fired during that time. *See also: Rookie*

RMP – An acronym for "Radio Motor Patrol," which must have meant something back when foot cops didn't carry radios. All it means now is 'police car'. RMPs are referred to as marked (blue and white) or unmarked (civilian autos).

Road – as in, "on the road" – patrol.

Roll Call – The start of a tour, where attendance is taken, posts are assigned, with orders and information given to the officers.

Roscoe – Gun.

Shield – A police officer's metal ('tin') badge, worn on the uniform.

Skell – 1. (Transit Police usage) Homeless person, undomiciled. *See also: Outdoorsman*
　　　　2. (NYPD usage) Mutt.

Steel dust – Mysterious black substance found on every surface in all transit districts, inside all cops' lockers, on their handkerchiefs, et cetera. Long-range health effects on humans unknown; medical studies inconclusive. Believed to cause hearing impairment.

Summons – A ticket issued for a minor violation of law, given in lieu of arrest.

Sweep – Mass arrests, usually of farebeats.

TA – The New York City Transit Authority. The parent organization of the TA is the New York State Metropolitan Transportation Authority (MTA).

Tour – Work shift. The three standard patrol tours are 8AM to 4PM ("day tours"), 4PM to midnight ("four to twelves") and midnight to 8AM ("midnites").

TPF – "Tactical Patrol Force"—Late-night train patrol unit; over 400 officers assigned to ride trains, alone, from 8PM to 4AM. The second-largest single command in the Transit Police Department, after the Restricted Duty Unit (injured officers and officers in trouble).

Train run – A TPF officer's post, usually given as a schedule.

Turban – Cotton gauze formerly used to identify transit prisoners at central booking.

Wind—*meteorological* – as in, "he's in the wind"—Where perps go when cops are looking for them.

Printed in the United States
25401LVS00005B/142-195